KRISTIN McCLOY was born in San Francisco and spent her child-
hood in Spain, India, and Japan. A graduate of Duke University, she
currently lives in Los Angeles, and is the author of the highly
acclaimed novel *Velocity*.

KRISTIN McCLOY

some girls

A PLUME BOOK

PLUME
Published by the Penguin Group
Penguin Books USA Inc., 375 Hudson Street, New York, New York 10014, U.S.A.
Penguin Books Ltd, 27 Wrights Lane, London W8 5TZ, England
Penguin Books Australia Ltd, Ringwood, Victoria, Australia
Penguin Books Canada Ltd, 10 Alcorn Avenue, Toronto, Ontario, Canada M4V 3B2
Penguin Books (N.Z.) Ltd, 182–190 Wairau Road, Auckland 10, New Zealand

Penguin Books Ltd, Registered Offices: Harmondsworth, Middlesex, England

Published by Plume, an imprint of Dutton Signet,
a division of Penguin Books USA Inc.
Previously published in a Dutton edition.

First Plume Printing, August, 1995
10 9 8 7 6 5 4 3 2 1

 REGISTERED TRADEMARK—MARCA REGISTRADA

The Library of Congress has catalogued the Dutton edition as follows:

McCloy, Kristin,
Some girls / Kristin McCloy.
p.   cm.
ISBN 0-525-93837-0 (hc.)
ISBN 0-452-27273-4 (pbk.)
1. Young women—New York (N.Y.)—Fiction.   2. Man-woman
relationships—New York (N.Y.)—Fiction.   3. Friendship—New York
(N.Y.)—Fiction.   I. Title.
PS3563.C3417S66   1994
813'.54—dc20   93–42404
                                                     CIP

Printed in the United States of America
Original hardcover design by Steven N. Stathakis

for Deb, and for Gayle —

In this world
Love has no color —
yet how deeply
my body
is stained by yours.
                    — Izumi Shikibu

SHE REMEMBERED LEAVING HOME AS IF IT HAD HAPPENED to someone else, how she had wanted to stretch in the front seat while Paula drove her to the airport, wanted to fling her arms out and behind the seat, back arched, but she hadn't because her sister would see. Would see and maybe guess what she was thinking — that she was better than this. That life was bigger than Alamogordo, than El Paso, than New Mexico, even bigger than Texas.

It had seemed inevitable then, all of it — her one-way ticket to New York, the apartment waiting in the city, and eventually, vague but beckoning, success. She was aware of her spine, the strength of her pelvic bones, the arches of her feet. It was all she needed to support her. She had everything, and five hundred dollars cash. It is me, she'd thought. I have chosen.

And then she arrived in New York, the airport like an airport in a third world country, chaotic, dirty, crowded. People yelled at each other in harsh, urban voices, obscenities. In the corner, a parrot screeched through its plastic carry-on case. Whose parrot, a man kept asking. Whose parrot!

She waited for her suitcase, thinking, It will be better in the city, it will be different, and then her suitcase lurched down the conveyor belt, corners newly dented, abused, the suitcase of an immigrant, absurdly hopeful.

She clutched the handle and rode into the city, the taxi meter clicking and clicking, and she knew already; the city was a terror, glossy buildings rising out of a slum, a place of anarchy, crooked and lawless, impenetrable.

She was an orphan the moment the taxi pulled away, her fortunes depleted, leaving her in the tall darkness of the neighborhood: White Street off Broadway. A rickety wooden structure walled off the southeast corner, and through the cracks a crane loomed silent over the wound it had dug in the ground, crude, raw, that dark earth an incongruous abyss among so much concrete, and she felt it tugging at her as she walked by, a burial place for out-of-towners, people like her with illusions thinking they would be welcome, they would be noticed — she could tumble over and in the morning no one would know she was missing, the city would roll over her like an ocean with its huge, impersonal tides.

The building was like a warehouse, plaster walls cracking, and she had to drag her suitcase up three flights of wooden stairs, each one long and steep, her breath harsh in the narrow passageway. The hall had its own smell, aged, fusty, like old books and stale air-conditioning and something else, something subtle and foreign, what she imagined another country, another culture might smell like. The apartment was at the end of the third floor, next to last, and just as she finally put her suitcase down, that last door opened, and in the dim light she saw her neighbor, a woman moving with the brisk efficiency of one who is just rising, whose day lies ahead — Claire stopped, the keys in her hand, and her heart rose, because the woman was young, she could see that, it was in the way she bent to lock her door, agile and fluid. Her hair was dark, falling just below her shoulders, and when she straightened, her face was a pale oval, eyes so deep you could not see their color. She smiled when she saw Claire, but she seemed unsurprised by Claire's presence, her eyes distant, fixed on a point on some other horizon.

Moving in? — she already moving past, so lightly, and all Claire could think was how little she wore, thin sleeveless shirt that showed her collarbone, black tights that stopped at her knees, and on her feet only the slight straps of wafer-soled sandals. She had nothing else, no purse, no wallet, nothing but a gold bracelet twisted around the slimness of her upper arm. How could she go out like that, down and into the streets, into that darkness, so blithe and careless, alone.

Welcome to New York, she said as she reached the top of the stairs, smiling again, and the rest was just her footsteps, a quick light rhythm leaving. Claire heard the bottom door swing shut — her neighbor was a woman of the city, it was obvious, breaker of men's hearts, a woman who would move swiftly

2

through airport terminals, traveling light, unconcerned with what she left behind, sure of her destination.

The last lock was the hardest, as if the apartment itself begrudged her entrance, and it wasn't till she slammed her knee against it, cursing, sweat stinging the corners of her eyes, clinging like tears, that it gave.

2

SWEAT TILL YOU CRY, THAT WAS NEW YORK THE FIRST TWO weeks for her. On the streets she had nothing but the speed with which she walked and her sunglasses to protect her. Everything had a kind of rawness, a wild volatility; it wasn't humanity as she knew it, as she had grown up with it. Everything seemed to touch everything else — pedestrians grazed the bumpers of moving cars, they ran into each other, seemed somehow more tangible, more dangerous, than the people of Alamogordo, who were always insulated by their cars, their traffic lights, their well-established codes of behavior. Sometimes the GIs would come out drunk at night, yelling, making their tires squeal, but even that was predictable, had its place. People shouted out to strangers here, their voices were hoarse with it. They talked to her, men, they passed by deliberately close, murmuring words — gorgeous, they said, and much worse, things she didn't want to hear, muttered like promises. She wanted to forbid them to look at her but their eyes were penetrating and insolent, they saw her, raw behind the eye makeup, behind the clothes. They confirmed it at the same time as they repulsed her, made her flare with a silent and murderous violence. She was electrified, she could not eat, her stomach was too constricted, she could hardly sleep. The noise of the city astonished her, it came through the window a soft roar, the hum of traffic, machinery, construction and motion, a hum that kept nudging her awake again and again to think, I'm here, I'm in New York City, a shock each time.

She joined the throb of people on the streets in the morn-

3

ing as if she were one of them, a citizen, head up. She memorized her phone number, signed up at an employment agency, Perfect Temps. The women who worked there were all of a type, they had city accents, ashtrays that overflowed, and a fraudulent warm manner that she clung to, her only human contact.

Some days they called her in the morning, she already dressed and waiting by the phone, a subway map clutched in her hand, and gave her addresses —

Fifteen Fifteen Broadway, got that? It's up at Forty-fifth, you can catch the R going uptown, okay?

The rush in their voices infected her, she'd spread her map out, say, Wait, wait —

Okay, hon, write that down. No hurry. Their patience was elaborately false.

The assignments were brief, half mornings and afternoons filling in for someone who'd called in sick, answering the phone at some ad agency, a publishing company, law firms; when she left their offices at the end of the day, nobody knew her name.

Other days there was nothing, but they told her to come in and wait, in case someone called later that morning. She sat in the waiting room with a handful of other women, all of them attempting the corporate uniform, some more successfully than others. There was one girl, not much older than Claire, who came in at eleven, dark circles under her eyes, always wearing the same thing — an unironed white shirt and black jeans. Sorry I'm late, she'd say, and the agents would exchange looks — can you believe it.

Is there anything for me?

There never was, but the girl would prop herself up in a corner with a magazine to wait, and then she'd doze, head slumped to one side, magazine falling from her hands.

After a couple of hours, they would tell everyone to call again tomorrow, and then Claire had nowhere to go but home.

She bought her groceries between her subway station and the apartment building, did not venture out after dark. She went to bed early, refused to look at the clock — and still, helplessly,

4

she calculated. It would only be dinnertime at home, and the huge weight of desert silence just beginning to press against the roofs of her town, sinking through, making people yawn, making their limbs heavy. How big night was there, and she hadn't even noticed. Here, it was never truly dark. The sky seemed to hold the lights of the city like a fog, shimmering and low, never lifting. There were no stars.

3

SATURDAY DAWNED, THE FIRST WEEKEND. SHE DEVISED CULtural excursions for herself, the Museum of Modern Art, the Public Library. The museum was crowded, the cafeteria prices were high. Standing before a wall of Picassos, all she felt was the eyes of the guards who stood at the door, lecherous and bored.

The library was better. She liked the hugeness of it, the massive, beatific stone lions carved in semi-alert repose, the wide expanse of steps, and the cathedral-like hush on the inside, but when she'd gathered an armful of books, she found she was not allowed to check them out. It was a research library only, the librarian said, she would have to go to the Fifty-first Street branch.

You can get a card, the librarian said, if you have proof of residency. A piece of mail would do.

She had not received any, Claire said. It seemed a terrible admission, the admission of an orphan, a spinster, the admission of one unloved. The librarian, a woman with large breasts and thinning hair, raised her hands, palms up. I'm sorry, she said. She was not unkind.

Claire left empty-handed, swollen with homesickness. She had not known what a legitimate illness it was, how it persisted, undermining everything, refusing to be named.

She was at the deli on the corner, looking for something to eat for dinner, when a woman came in, an apparition in a long black evening dress so tight it made her body the slimmest of silhouettes, bared her back all the way down to the beginning of that last brief curve, exposed the long ridge of backbone and her skin, the palest shade of olive. Claire didn't recognize her till she moved, bent over suddenly to scoop up the store's cat, her waist pliant and her hands reaching so swift the animal could not escape. When she pressed her nose against the cat's face, Claire saw her eyes close, and in that instant she was light-years away, there was a fatigue in her pose that seemed eons old. His paws stretched and it wasn't till he dug his claws lightly into her shoulders that she returned.

You love me, don't you, Taker, she murmured, voice lower than Claire would have imagined from such a small face.

His name Tiger! the deli man said. No Taker, Tay-gur!

He was from Lebanon, and he stood behind the counter and called out to his customers with a brusqueness that Claire found alarming, made her stutter, spill her change, but her neighbor paid no attention, she smiled, and in the light Claire could see the fine angles of her face, how her smile made everything, the corners of her eyes, her lips, curve up.

Don't correct me, she told him now. I've had a white night.

What this, white night? You talk some guy? Some boyfriend, yes?

No boyfriend, she said. No sleep.

What! You no boyfriend? This I not believe!

Say you love me, Taker, she said, and when she bent to let go, the cat leapt from her arms to her left shoulder and kept a fine balance there.

He has one thousand girlfriend! You no special! the man said now, grinning, hands on his white-aproned hips.

I know, she answered, as if she had taken his statement to heart. She lifted one arm to stroke the cat and Claire saw her hands, different from the rest of her, strong-knuckled, blue veins delicate ridges, and though she was utterly cosmopolitan, her pose, the slight sway of her hips, the cat's raccoon-striped tail dangling down her bare back, evoked another era. Arabian nights, Claire thought, the image in sharp contrast to the store with its crooked shelves and fluorescent lighting, and yet no one paid attention, people glanced at her and moved past, reaching for what they needed, the most ordinary staples of life, quarts of milk, toilet paper, bread.

Okay, maybe he love you more, the deli man said, his voice softer. Maybe he marry you.

Her neighbor smiled again, but her eyes, indigo, smoky as her scent, remained untouched. The deli man's voice rose again, as if to lift her spirits.

What you want today! Everything good here, everything fresh! What you want — I make, me, myself!

She looked through the glass counter, wound the cat's tail around her neck, watched while he pulled out different containers, sun-dried tomatoes in olive oil, smoked salmon, green peppers and feta cheese and black olives, and she pointed, told him stop when he scooped, and then he scooped in a little more — This for you present, he said, to make you fat! You need bigger health, more good food, yes!

They had a dialogue, she and Taker and the deli man, it was obvious, and Claire wanted to know, how long had she lived here, how long before she had learned to talk that way, to walk into a crowded deli to buy exotic salads for breakfast in the evening, if it was something you could learn, something that came with living in the city, or something you had to be born knowing.

She lives next door to me, Claire thought; the proximity was unfathomable.

She walked back across the street when her neighbor did, trailing her just a few feet. The woman gave no indication that she had seen Claire, neither in the deli nor outside, but when she unlocked the front door she turned unexpectedly and held it open.

Thanks, Claire said, moving quickly to get it.

You're welcome, she said. Her smile was brief, and there was something hard in her eyes, an intense directness that took Claire off-guard, she could not match it. The woman walked up the stairs ahead of her, she did not turn around again.

4

MONDAY CAME AS A RELIEF, AND SHE WAS ALREADY
dressed and ready when the agency called at eight-thirty and said
they had a ten-day assignment for her.

It was at an accounting firm on Wall Street, in a soaring
building made of blue glass that overlooked the water, and Claire
had to take two elevators just to get to her floor. The firm was
huge, one hundred and twenty employees, and she was just the
temp replacing a secretary on summer vacation. The other secretaries on her floor showed her where things were, supplies,
the fax, the Ladies' Room key, but they had their own society.

We take our lunch from one to two, the receptionist informed her, but someone has to stay and pick up the phones.

So she went out by herself each day at noon, bought an apple from the fruit cart on the corner, pretended not to be excited by the people, streams of them, converging impatient on
street corners, pushing out into the traffic, their faces closed,
purposeful. Single men in sunglasses and ties, young secretaries
with teased hair and bronze eye shadow, talking loud, lighting up
as soon as they were out those revolving doors.

She drank murky coffee through the afternoon, left at five
o'clock sharp and took the subway home. You'll get used to it,
Jocelyn had said, but she found herself holding her breath each
time she descended those stairs — some of the stations were
clean and tiled, modern transit centers, but the train was a dinosaur; it came with a heavy shriek of metal, lurching and rattling, a carnival ride from hell.

On Thursday night, it started to rain, the sound drifting to her
through her sleep, soothing but insistent; she was amazed to
wake up and find it was still coming down, amazed at the sheer
vastness of the quantity, its unendingness.

It rained all day Friday, and she stayed inside during lunch,
stood by the window of her supervisor's office when he went
out. The river was dark, it churned. Wind blew the rain in

8

gusts, in sheets, against the glass. She was on an island, it came to her for the first time — it was island weather.

In New Mexico, the sense was always of land, stretching as far away as you could think. In New Mexico, this kind of rain would be unimaginable, an act of God, mythic. She was overcome with the desire to show them, her mother, her sister — Look how far I've come, she wanted to say, and fantasized that they would hardly recognize her.

She would write her mother a letter.

Dear Mom. It's been raining all day. She stopped, crumpled it up. You wouldn't believe, she wrote, how much it can rain.

She read the words over; they communicated nothing. Dear Mom, she wrote again, and then she sat there, pen poised over paper, unmoving. She had never written her mother a letter before; she had never been far enough from home. It made Ginny seem a stranger, made the words come out without inflection, flat and polite. She picked up the phone, punched the 505 area code quickly. They made a thousand long-distance phone calls from here every day; no one would know.

It was eleven o'clock in Alamogordo, Ginny had already been at the shop two hours.

Chic Boutique, she said, and in those professional tones Claire could hear her mother's whole day, see her squinting in the morning sun to unlock the door, flipping the sign to Open, unlocking the register. Everything was there, the dark closet in the back, the radio that played Light Oldies all day long, and the two ancient mannequins in the window, years of dust making their eyes blank, even their forms outdated with their pointed breasts, their voluptuous hips.

Mom, it's Claire.

Claire? Where are you?

I'm in New York, on the thirtieth floor of a building, she said. I'm at work.

Oh! For a second I thought something was wrong, hearing your voice like that in the middle of the day . . .

I can't talk long, Claire said. I just wanted to say hi.

9

Is everything all right?

Everything's great, she said, her voice like the voice of a newscaster, cheerful and false. I've got this assignment, it lasts for another week —

Another week? And then will they offer you a job?

There's no job, I'm just replacing a secretary who's on —

Yes but I'm sure if you do a good job — are you sure you should be making this call?

It's all right, Mom, she said, she couldn't keep the irritation from her voice. Everyone's at lunch now anyway.

But what will they say when they get the bill? They might make you pay for it, Claire, and it's the middle of the day, you really —

It doesn't matter, Mother, I can afford it — they're paying me a lot here, fifteen dollars an hour —

Fifteen . . . !

— Before taxes.

My God, Claire, you're making more than I am!

But everything's more expensive here — a cantaloupe costs two dollars — but you can get salad in all the delis, they have everything —

Don't tell me that's all you're eating — cantaloupe and salad.

They have egg rolls and noodles and sushi —

Sushi? What, raw fish? Please don't eat that, Claire, you don't know where it's come from, and it can make you very, very sick.

Okay, Mom, Claire said, she spoke sharply to cut her mother off. I heard you.

Just a minute. Claire heard a Bobby Vinton song playing faintly in the background, and then her mother's professional voice again, pitched slightly higher, saying, I'll be with you in a moment.

I'll let you go, Mother, Claire said. I was just wondering if Paula went to that interview on base yet.

Oh, that. No, the appointment's for later this week, she said — I don't know how she thinks I'm supposed to manage this place all by myself. I've had to stay late four days this week alone, just doing the damn inventory —

Well, I think it's great, that she found something —

She hasn't got it yet, Ginny said, her voice sharp now too. And anyway, it's certainly not going to be great for *me* — I can't, I simply can*not,* run this shop by myself.

Claire imagined her mother's face, how it looked after a bad night. Pale and tight, extra-help makeup thick under her eyes. She wore sobriety like punishment, never saying a word, pouring coffee with hands that shook, painting over the chips in her nail polish before work.

Have you spoken to your sister?

Claire knew from her mother's tone that she already knew the answer to that. She expelled her breath.

No, she said. I thought maybe she would call me, when —

Well, you know, she's angry.

Yes, Claire said, she could not help her sarcasm. I gathered.

She heard a faint click, the sound of her mother's lighter, and then she heard Ginny exhale.

Okay, listen, Claire said after a moment's silence, I really have to go.

The city's filthy, and dangerous, Ginny said in a sudden burst, I wish you would just come home.

Oh, Mom.

Claire had a vivid picture of her mother standing there behind the counter, alone all day, speaking in those bright tones to the occasional woman who came through to finger through the sales rack, then locking up again at five, bending in her heels to fit the padlock, and she was crushed with sadness, she had no words for it.

I've got to go, she said. I'll write you.

5

IT WAS PAST THREE IN THE MORNING WHEN SHE WOKE UP, and for a moment she thought she was at home, in her own room, her mother just down the hall, but she could not make sense of the angles of the walls, or the streetlight that made shadows on the ceiling . . . and then it came to her, she was here, she was alone, the knowledge penetrating as ice water, inescapable, and she felt her own presence like a ghost's, floating out beyond the perimeter of the room to permeate the city itself, a spy seeking to defect.

The phone rang, and she came back to herself in a rush, grabbing the receiver before the bell could shatter the silence again.

Hello?

That was quick, Tommy said, his voice as instantly familiar to her as her own, that slow deep timbre unchanged by the high miles of wire that connected them.

I was awake.

Oh yeah? You just get home or somethin?

Tommy, it's three o'clock in the morning.

Yeah, he said, Saturday night in the big city, right?

Yeah, she said, she sat up. Right.

They were both quiet for a moment, listening to each other breathe.

Saturday night. If she were home, she would be in Cloudcroft right now, Tommy would have made dinner. Steak fajitas with hot green chili, tortillas warming in the oven, the beer ice-cold. Sometimes they ate sitting on the kitchen steps, watching the last pastel light fade to blue, and then the dense blackness spreading out and out and out, hiding the Sacramento Mountains in the distance, pierced only by the light that shone through the open kitchen door.

So you got a job, huh? You a career girl now?

News travels fast.

12

Saw your mother comin out of the gas station this afternoon.

I'm a temp secretary, she said. It's no career.

She said you had some view.

I was thirty floors up, I could see everything.

Like what? Traffic and smog? People killin each other?

Like the skyline — the Empire State Building, the World
Trade Towers. They go up a quarter of a mile, she said. That's
as high as an airplane.

Yeah? Someone taken you up there?

Someone like who?

I don't know, he said. Some stockbroker millionaire.

She laughed. I don't know any stockbroker millionaires.

Huh.

Really, she said. I don't know anyone.

Sounds pretty lonesome.

It's okay, she said, she hardened herself against his sympathy. I'm fine.

He didn't say anything and in the small snag of silence she
felt his retreat, heard the bed creak as he changed positions, and
she was filled with a momentary panic, that he would cut her
off, hang up, that he would never call again.

Tell me everything that's happened, she said, since the day
I left.

Nothin's happened, he said, and even in those brief words
she heard his loyalty, she read his life without her, everything the
same, a space where she used to be. The bed empty.

Nothing at all?

Truck broke down.

What this time? she asked. As if she were right there, the
curves and bumps of his life lay claim on her, snaking out unbid-
den to pull her back.

It was a gas pump leak, they fixed it. Took me for it, too.

When're you going to learn to fix it yourself?

Got no time to lay under a truck, he said, both of them
taking pleasure in this familiar exchange.

How're the horses? she asked.

13

Horses're great.

Do they miss me?

Nah, they forgot you already.

Not Cody. Bet Cody's pining away.

Cody's got a girlfriend.

Really? Did you rent him out?

Yeah, some guy from Socorro came out to see him, said what a stud.

He *is* a stud, he's the best.

He's got a rep.

He deserves it.

He made a sound, as if to say, I know, and she thought of how often they had lain together, saying nothing, her cheek pressed against the broad muscles of his back.

Talked to some travel agent today, he said then.

Oh, yeah?

Said if I buy 'em now, I could get tickets to New York pretty cheap.

. . . You're coming to New York?

Only if I got a place to stay.

When?

I don't know. Whenever.

But what about . . .

What?

Who's going to take care of the ranch while you're gone?

Don't worry about it, he said. It's just a fuckin weekend, I think I can handle it.

I was just asking —

Yeah, he said, maybe I should just forget the whole thing.

Tommy . . .

He didn't answer, and she thought of the last night she had been in Alamogordo, how he'd come to get her in his pickup truck; from here, its high, dusty interior seemed a haven of safety, well-loved. She remembered looking out the window, thinking, This is the last time I'll see the desert at night. This is the last time I'll ride this road.

It had made her feel extraordinarily lucid, made every-thing, even the dark, low desert scrub, look sharp.

They'd gone to White Sands with a bottle of wine, climbed over the part of the fence that sagged and through the soft, shift-ing sand before they found the right dune, tucked out of sight. The sand was cool, slid like silk through her fingers. It was chilly and Tommy took his denim jacket off and wrapped it around her. She stared up at the stars over his shoulder, their lights half-blotted by the light of the half-moon.

I'm leaving, she'd thought, again and again, and each time it had come as a revelation, startled her anew. It heightened ev-erything, made the ordinary — the frayed cuffs of Tommy's jacket, the rip at the knee of her jeans — seem poignant and rare.

They made love and afterwards he ran his hands over her body, petting her as if she were an animal, one of his horses, un-til her limbs felt like butter. His hands knew Claire by heart, the curve of flank when she lay on her side, the freckled slope of shoulder, the length of her neck.

I could pick you out of a lineup with my thumbs alone, he'd said, his only words, and she'd turned to press her face against him.

In the light of imminent departure, his body seemed pre-cious, almost fragile, despite its breadth, the wide strength of his legs. He had held her face, searched her eyes in the dark. There was nothing she could promise, and nothing she could ask for. They loved each other then. It would have to be enough.

It had been nearly dawn when he'd finally dropped her off, and she'd stood on the sidewalk outside and watched his red tail-lights disappear from sight.

What, he said at last.

Just let me think about it, okay? I'll call you.

6

SHE HUNG UP AND COULD NOT GO BACK TO SLEEP. SOUNDS floated through the window, and she went to stand next to it, pressing herself close to look out.

Garbage trucks rumbled down the street, starting and stopping, men hefting cans the way she'd seen Tommy do with bales of alfalfa. They called out to each other, their voices strong. She watched them disappear around the corner.

She was about to turn away when she heard another voice, a man's voice, wretched.

Angel, he called. Angel, wait . . . wait for me . . . wait . . . !

He was nowhere, his voice carried up from around the corner, disembodied and full of entreaty. Then there were rapid footsteps, the sound of someone running, and a woman appeared, slight in a pair of cutoffs and T-shirt, keys glinting in one hand, and this time, Claire recognized her instantly.

I'm not your angel! she shouted. Leave me alone!

A man emerged in the shadowed glare of the streetlight, his voice rising unintelligibly. She had almost reached the building when he swung out with drunken volatility and caught her arm.

You're my goddamn angel, he said. I put all my fucking money on *you* —

Please, Claire heard her say, her voice gone quiet with fear. You're mistaking me for somebody else.

Claire pushed her window up hard, it rattled in its hinges, and the girl looked up. Their eyes met. Help me, she said, her mouth shaping the words, not making a sound, and Claire ran to press the buzzer that unlocked the front door.

She materialized on the landing seconds later, her face so white it seemed to glow, as if the bones beneath were burning, her indigo eyes all pupil in the hall's dim light. Steps pounded right behind her, and Claire pulled her in just in time, threw the locks, and both girls pressed their backs flat against the wall, breath held.

He hammered on all the doors, his voice the voice of a monster now, hoarse, bloodthirsty. Bitch! he shouted, tripping and swearing. Fuckin whore!

On the next landing up, a man came out, his voice raw with sleep, angry. Get out of here, he said, before I call the police!

And just then, outside, sirens. There were always sirens in New York, at every hour. Always someone in trouble.

He left, shouting still; they heard the hitch and shuffle of a drunk on the stairs, the weighted heft of his body slamming along the hall. It wasn't till then that his prey let her breath go, a long sibilant sound of relief.

Thank you, she said, she turned to Claire. I'm Jade, I live in number nine, next door.

Claire.

They looked at each other in the dark, curious, pulses still racing. The sky outside not so much lightening as dimming, from soot to the deep blue of earliest dawn, the moon a pale crescent, paling.

They sat at the kitchen table, Claire put water on for tea. Jade illumined up close for the first time, those high, burnished cheekbones, chin a cat's chin coming to a sweet, sharp point, eyebrows as dark as her hair and thick, forehead smooth as a child's. She ravaged her purse single-handedly until she found a pack of cigarettes, half-crushed.

Can I smoke, she asked, then opened the window with a quick, violent gesture. When she cupped the match to her face, there were deep shadows in the hollows of her cheeks, the valley of her throat. She sucked the smoke in like a drowning person coming up for air, and Claire sensed her inner agitation as a constant — it was in the absolute slimness of her arms, her wrists, the way her pupils contracted when she spoke, her voice a low current, hushed, confessing.

He was at this bar where I work, she said. He sat there all night, gave me the most enormous tips . . . kept buying me drinks . . . I didn't think he'd follow me, usually that type — I thought he was too fucked up, you know?

Why didn't you take a cab, Claire wanted to ask, why did you go out on the street with him after you —

But she felt forbidden, by the curve of Jade's neck as she looked away, the distress in her hands as she ran them through her hair, obsessively pushing it back, away from the small shape of her face.

He was so lonely, Jade said unexpectedly. It's not as if I don't know how it feels.

You're obviously not from New York, she said before Claire could respond, her smile quick, cynical. The way you let me in like that.

I knew who you were, Claire said, and Jade raised an eyebrow as if to say, Really, her sudden cool unnerving, making Claire rush her words.

I saw you the day I moved in, and then in the deli — we were both in the deli, and after you held the door for me, remember?

Jade exhaled smoke, she seemed to have regained her poise absolutely.

Yeah, she said, I remember.

She glanced around then, at the kitchen, at the apartment, as if she were seeing it for the first time.

I've never been in here before, she said. I used to see the woman that lived here coming home from work — she played country music all the time, I never saw her go out.

She looked at Claire appraisingly. You're nothing like her.

Her words pushed at something in Claire, made her smile, flush with pleasure; the crushing sense of anonymity that had dogged her ever since she had arrived suddenly turned to reveal its other face — here where she was not yet known, she was free, for the first time in her life, of her past. She did not say she knew Jocelyn. They came from the same town, Jocelyn had signed the lease over to her; it was the only thing they had in common.

She got up to pour Jade another cup of tea, but her guest refused it, she stood abruptly.

I can't, she said. The caffeine . . .

She saw Claire's bed, the covers rumpled, thrown back, and turned around. I didn't wake you up, did I? I'm not keeping you —

I wasn't sleeping, Claire said.

No, Jade said. I guess you weren't.

She looked out the window. It's almost morning, she said softly, in the tone of one who has been waiting, of one who has spent years waiting, for the sun to rise again. The city seemed hushed for the first time, as if everything had stopped for a few seconds, gathering its strength for the onslaught of day. They both looked out, caught in the brief respite of silence.

I wish I was tired, Jade said. She leaned her head against the window, closed her eyes for a moment, and Claire saw the dark fringe of her lashes against the curve of her cheek — the brief pose so like peace it could almost fool you, until she spoke.

God, she said. He came too close . . . he came far too close.

Claire wished she had something to offer, something magical and rare, something that would chase the hunted look from her guest's voice, wished it so violently it surprised her.

Are you hungry? she asked. We could have something to eat . . .

Jade looked up, she smiled. Have you ever had breakfast in Chinatown?

7

THEY WALKED OUTSIDE, THE CITY QUIET ON A DAWNING SUN-day, walked down side streets, down narrow alleyways cob-webbed with jungles of brittle iron fire escapes that hung precariously from the backs of buildings, calling forth a different era, immigrant children swinging from the rusted ladders, young women combing their wet hair in the sun, stringing up lines for their laundry to dry. Toward the south, the World Trade Towers rose up like the future, two glorious straight and clean lines, a thin strip of sky between them. Down another block, temples of a different country, a Chinese pagoda, three stories high, scarlet red and deep green, its curving tips painted gold.

This way, Jade said, she moved quickly, indifferent to the surge of traffic, focus trained ahead, and Claire thought she had already forgotten about her near-assault — she was fearless by nature, Claire thought, it seemed perfectly clear.

Chinatown just past dawn, and everyone was awake, everyone was Chinese. They spilled off the curbs, the cars nudged around them. Their talk was high and choppy, they shouted to each other, everybody selling something, nobody speaking English. It was as if they'd left America behind at Canal and Broadway, crossed a national line. Young men wove their bicycles through the traffic. The old women had beautiful, wrinkled faces, impassive stares. They looked through Claire as if she were invisible, and she was seized with an energy she had not known she had; it was the energy of the city, human, sleepless, constant.

They walked past an open fish market, the smell strong and clean, the fish gleaming silver in the sun, eyes blank circles flat against their heads, and moved past store windows full of dark spices, ground roots hanging in nets, stores that sold bright toys, lacquered umbrellas, cheap portable radios.

Here, Jade said, and they turned into a small restaurant, its windows splashed with black calligraphic characters, the smell sweet and pungent. The far wall was mirrored in an attempt to make the place look larger.

They sat at a table with paper placemats and yellowed chopsticks, bottles of dried spice in the middle. They were the only white people there.

How old are you? Jade asked abruptly, she threw the question at Claire as if it were a challenge.

Twenty-three.

Jade shook her head, she sat back, looked at Claire in the

mirror. You shouldn't be hanging out with me, she said, I'm way too old for you.

How old are you? Claire asked, she could not have guessed — Jade's face was so smooth, but her eyes were ringed with darkness.

Ancient, Jade said, I'm a vampire, I'm a bad influence. This whole city's a bad influence — what's an innocent like you doing here, anyway?

Claire's reflection glinted back at her, face still tanned from the desert sun, freckled, lips a rusted red, gray eyes dark, her hair still wild from sleep, copper-colored, uncombed, and she thought how plain, how obvious it all was — the blue jeans, the boots, the white shirt. She should be selling tractors in an ad, smiling wide, unthreatening, beneath a broad-brimmed hat.

She turned away from herself, she shrugged.

I'm just temping, she said.

Just temping, Jade said, her smile faint, that hard look in her eyes the flash and spurn of a rebel, defiant, ironic.

I haven't decided yet, Claire said.

Yeah, Jade said. Neither have I.

Jade! A woman emerged from the back, she was older, a small, compact dynamo. You up early!

No, Lien, Jade said, she stood to kiss the woman on both cheeks. I'm up late.

Lien laughed, she lifted a finger. When you going to stop this crazy bar life and get married, huh? I know very nice man, good job, he ready for wife, what you say!

Who is he?

What you care, who is he! He keep you very nice house, give you children, Lien said, she winked at Claire. He even like girl baby!

I don't know, Jade said, I'd have to see if I loved him first.

Love! Lien said, she threw her hands up. My son Chang all the time telling same thing to me, has to be love — all this love talk, what it got to do with marriage?

Her voice rose, such incredulity it made both the girls laugh.

21

In China, we have saying, Lien said. Put cold pot in oven, it warm up — put hot pot outside, it get cold!

And what does Chang think of that theory?

Pah! Chang never listen — he say don't talk fortune cookie to him, he American, not Chinese, Lien said. Sometime I worry, who will take care of poor Lien when she get old?

Don't you worry about that, Jade said, I will.

Lien put an arm around her, she beamed.

I wish you my daughter, Jade, she said. Such good girl you are, always coming to see Lien! You sit, I bring you kitchen best dish!

It was unlike any other Chinese food Claire had ever eaten. The noodles were paper-thin, delicate, and there were spicy scallops, lightly charred shrimp, bananas fried hot with sweet sesame sauce.

Jade used her chopsticks as deftly as the other customers there, she ate like an anarchist, ate directly from the serving plates, mixed banana with shrimp, ordered a beer.

I'll sleep if I'm full, she said, she tilted her head back to accommodate a long bite of noodles. This is my favorite breakfast in the whole world.

Do you always go to bed in the morning?

I told you, I'm a vampire. Don't say I didn't warn you.

She pushed her plate away finally, lit a cigarette.

I quit smoking last week, she said. Lasted five days, and I was such a bitch the whole time . . . but it made me euphoric in a weird way — at the thought that I was changing, you know what I mean? That I *could* change.

Yes, Claire said, she felt an excitement stealing over her — the possibility that she, too, could become something other than who she knew herself to be.

And then last night I just slid quarters into this machine, I didn't think about it. Jade shrugged. It was worth quitting, actually, that first cigarette tasted so good. But after that it's just habit again.

She took another drag, then put it out. Claire watched the ash turn black, neither one of them spoke. They both looked up

22

at the same time, and something passed between them, elemental, intimate.

You saved me, Jade said then. Thank you.

You don't have to thank me. I did what anybody would have done.

Jade laughed, she pushed her hair back from her face, held it there. Where do you *come* from?

New Mexico.

The land of enchantment, Jade said, her grin contagious, I should have known.

Have you been there?

I've driven through. I remember it as nothing but horizon. Earth and sky.

Yeah. There's a lot of that.

Jade laughed again, her laugh like her voice, unexpectedly low.

Lien came up to take their plates away, asking, How everything? You like it?

Don't you throw any of that away, Jade said, I'm taking it home.

She started to put money on the table but Lien pushed it back at her, saying, How many times I have to say, this your house!

We have this argument every time, Jade said to Claire. She turned back to Lien and spoke in a rapid, fluent burst of what Claire realized must be Chinese. Lien laughed, she fired something back, and Jade shook her head as if in resignation.

O.K., I pack this to go! Lien said then, smiling at Claire. You come back see me soon!

The shock of broad daylight when they emerged, Jade saying, Let's go home, walking into the street to flag a cab.

You speak Chinese, Claire said, fatigue coming over her now like the beginning of a dream.

My father was a diplomat, Jade said. I grew up overseas.

She lifted her hand just then, swift and decisive, as if to dismiss the topic, and a cab stopped. Jade gave the driver their address, then sat back and lit another cigarette, ignoring the No

23

Smoking sign, window rolled down, letting the wind whip her hair, letting it tangle against her face. Silence seemed her natural state now, and though Claire wanted nothing more just then but to hear her speak, to unravel herself, story by story, asking, somehow, was unthinkable.

8

IN THE SAME WAY, IT WAS UNDERSTOOD THAT JADE WOULD come back to Claire's apartment with her, that they would not go their separate ways. They were conspirators in the dislocation of time, still bound by the possibility of menace, ducking home when other people were rising, everything heightened by lack of sleep.

I'm grimy, Jade said. Every day in this city is another adventure in filth.

That's what my mother says about New York, Claire said. That it's filthy and dangerous.

She got that right, Jade said, her grin irrepressible. Do you mind if I run a bath?

Minutes later Claire heard her sigh deeply, as if the weight of the world had just slipped from her shoulders. It's better than anything, she said, her voice floating out. Better than sex.

Claire walked over when she heard Jade speak, found the door open. She had left the light off, so the room was ghostly, twilit. The steam made the short hair around Jade's face, at the back of her neck, curl in small, tight tendrils, and she looked like an ivory sculpture, her limbs sleek, elegant, submerged, her eyes deep in shadow.

Claire immediately averted her gaze, she was suffused with embarrassment to be caught standing in the doorway, looking, she could not move.

Jade's eyes opened as if from a dream, she was as casual naked as she had been clothed, she didn't even seem to notice Claire's rigidity.

The water's perfect.

Claire turned her face out of view. It's so late, she said, and thought even as she said it that it wasn't, that it was, in fact, very early, the freshest part of the day. I should go to bed . . .

Jade put her hands on the rim of the tub at that, pulled herself forward with some effort, as if she were pulling an enormous weight.

Please don't, she said. Not just yet. Sit and talk to me for another minute . . .

Asking like a child, defenseless, her shoulders a pale gleam in the dim light, her breasts showing, and Claire felt her own awkwardness falling away. She sat on the toilet lid, pulled her knees up close.

Water such a quiet sound, and the city had receded, there was no one in the world but them, nothing but this room, the tub's enamel turned copper blue where the water had dripped, the pale morning light filling the room with false depths.

Just the thought of getting up and going home exhausts me, Jade said, her head bent forward so Claire couldn't see her eyes. I think I've been alive too long.

You don't have to go home, Claire said. You can stay with me.

Jade raised her head, she looked at Claire, her eyes illegible.

I remember the first time I saw you, standing in the hallway . . . you had all that wild hair, those huge eyes, and I knew you had just arrived, I knew it was all just beginning for you — I couldn't even stop to speak to you, you had this glow, I thought, I had that once, but I lost it, and I'll never have it again . . .

The information stunned Claire, she wanted to answer but she had no words, she just sat very still, listening.

I didn't want to know you, Jade said, and then she smiled, a smile like sugar making her lips turn up. Isn't it funny how things turn out.

They slept together in Claire's bed, Claire in one of Tommy's T-shirts, turning her back to change, while Jade slid between the sheets, carelessly naked, her wet hair streaking the pillow.

I can't remember the last time I slept in the same bed as somebody, Jade said, pulling the sheet tight around herself. God, I can't even remember the last time I had sex.

Claire had an instant vision of herself with Tommy, the desert huge around them, soaring space, white sand shining beneath a crescent moon, his hands around her waist, goose bumps rising along her arms, sand between her toes and his face rough against her cheek, his fingers closing on her wrists so tight they still bore the faint prints when she got home, fingers like a vise, wanting to hold her, to keep her with him.

It's hard to believe, she said now, and it was — the sight of Jade immediately conjured up the idea of lovers. Claire imagined a whole arsenal of them, mysterious New York men falling to their knees before her, taking her down with them.

Actually I can, Jade said, she closed her eyes. I just don't want to. Loveless sex. I can't do it anymore. I'm getting so hard to please in my old age.

You couldn't stay up all night if you were old, Claire said. You wouldn't want to.

Jade smiled faintly, she didn't open her eyes.

I'm so tired, she murmured. She reached for Claire's hand under the covers, held it, did not let it go. It was the cling of a child, yet confident, sure that Claire would want to hold it, the touch of a woman who knows her own powers. She sank into unconsciousness soundlessly, still as a corpse. Claire lay with her eyes half open until Jade's fingers had relaxed, and then she gave up custody and fell asleep too.

9

WHEN CLAIRE WOKE UP, JADE WAS GONE. IT WAS UNNERV-ing, how little trace she left. Claire watched out the window, listened for music, knocked on her door, but there was nothing. Like a cat, Claire thought, and wondered where else Jade went, what doors opened for her in this town, who stood behind them.

And still, though she was alone once again, everything seemed different — it's me, Claire thought, but it was as if the city itself had undergone a subtle transformation, had finally opened to accept her. She caught people smiling at her in the streets, and she saw how you could live here, how you could find your place amid the great crowd.

She walked into the office and said good morning, her voice strong, cheerful, was amazed when the receptionist greeted her by name. When they ran into each other later in the bathroom, Claire turned to her impulsively, asked her if she wanted to have lunch.

Sure, the receptionist, whose name was Iris, answered. If you don't mind taking a walk.

They met in the lobby at noon, walked down narrow streets shadowed by buildings that flung themselves up toward the sky, heedless of gravity, shutting out the sun, zigzagging across cobblestoned alleyways, Fulton, Gold, Wall, ending finally at Battery Park, the blue expanse of New York Harbor a miracle after the dense chaos of the streets. Behind them, old women sat on benches and fed the pigeons, unruly, scrawny, squabbling flocks of them. Next to her, an ancient black man turned an ancient tape recorder on and tapped a dance to "Yankee Doodle Dandy." People tossed coins, they glittered silver at his feet.

They leaned against the railing that overlooked the water and ate their lunch, Iris talking nonstop while Claire watched bright, white boats moving, pulling free of the city, away. In the distance, the Statue of Liberty looked small, an island unto herself, proud.

I'm going to get a pretzel, Iris said, just as a man came walking up to them, whistling a song from *Fiddler on the Roof*. She had turned to go when he burst into the lyrics, throwing his arms wide.

Iris rolled her eyes. Claire, she said. Such —

And then she walked away without finishing her sentence. Iris, Claire started but the man's voice drowned her out.

Alarmed, Claire turned her back to him, and he stopped singing abruptly, walked around to her other side and looked at her. He was in his early thirties, had salt-and-pepper hair, a lanky frame.

Claire who? he demanded with the imperious tones of a spoiled prince.

None of your business, she said, surprised into a defensive hauteur, and his eyebrows shot up, smile like a reflex, his teeth crooked.

Hey Iris, he called out. Who is she?

But Iris was just paying the vendor for her pretzel, she didn't look up, and the man stood there, his hands in his pockets, still grinning, watching Claire.

Who are *you*? she asked stiffly, meaning it as a brush-off, but he immediately extended his hand.

Such, he said. Temporary employee of New York City.

It was only then that Claire realized Iris had already introduced them, and she put her hand out, felt the blush in the roots of her hair.

Sorry, she said. I thought —

I know, he said. You thought, such what?

It's a funny name. What's it short for?

My mother's sense of humor. She's from Long Island, he added, as if that were explanation enough.

Really? It's real?

Are you from out of town? he asked, and another heat wave swept her face.

Why? Is that a common name around here?

He burst out laughing, yielding to a sense of mirth larger than what had provoked it, laughter that carried the infectious undercurrent of hysteria, made Claire's mouth tremble into a smile even as she asked, What? What?

Nothing, he said. I just meant, you have color.

He indicated her face.

It was my accent, wasn't it, she said, each word deliberate with the weight of self-consciousness.

28

Why is it, he asked, grinning again, that everything I say insults you?

It doesn't, she said quickly, and looked down so her hair fell like a wild curtain on either side of her face, hiding her. When she glanced at him through it, he was slouched casually against the railing, studying her.

I'm from New Mexico, she said. Alamogordo.

Now there's a musical name for you, Such answered. Alamogordo.

Claire! Iris was waving at her. Come on, we're gonna be late!

Such straightened. Very nice to have met you, he said, and shook her hand again. His were beautiful, she noticed, large and finely made, the fingers slender. Artist's hands.

Who is he? she asked Iris as they walked back.

Iris shrugged. Some temp from the fourth floor — I think he's a singer or something in real life.

Real life, Claire thought. I wonder what I am in real life.

She kept an eye out for him the rest of the day, but it wasn't until five o'clock, when she stepped into the elevator going down, that she ran into him again.

So what's there to do in Alamogordo on a regular night?

He was standing in the back, his tie pulled down loose, smiling his crooked smile.

Nothing, she said, but in her smile was the rush of affection one feels for a brother, for an old friend.

Oh come on, he said, as they got off, and something in his tone egged her on, made her reach for the outrageous.

Well, you can always hang out at the Roadrunner and pick up GIs if you're a slut, she said, unmindful of her accent now, which was not so much a twang as a certain flatness that stretched her words out like the land she'd grown up in, stark and full of space. Such grinned wider, pointing at himself, but before he could say anything, two women walked between them, cutting them off.

I never asked about it because I figured I didn't want to

know, right? one of them was saying, and lifting an eyebrow, Such motioned her into step behind them.

I mean if he told me something I didn't want to hear, then I'd have to, you know, I'd have to break it off, because I can't have him thinking he can treat me that way. There's no way we're gonna last if he thinks he can treat me that way.

Three to one, Such said to Claire under his breath. Ratio of women to men in New York — straight men, that is.

They went through the revolving door and out, then stood just outside the building, people hurrying past them on either side, a human stream.

What's there to do in New York on a regular night? Claire asked.

Well, let's see . . . there's always Circus Maximum.

I don't know . . . maybe I should start with minimum first.

Don't let the name fool you, Such said. It's just a little club where they happen to have one or two fabulous musicians.

Really? Does it cost a lot to go?

Not if you know the pianist, Such said, checking the shine on his nails.

That wouldn't be you, would it?

It might, Such said airily, looking away.

Well, Claire said. Maybe I'll go, then.

First Avenue between First and Second, Such said as they parted. Just tell them you're my wife!

10

SHE WALKED PAST HER SUBWAY STOP, MOVING AMID THE citizens of the city like one who has just joined its ranks; she kept her head up, her eyes forward. There was a tremendous sense of energy, of a forward-moving flow, and she moved as if in flight, swiftly, unencumbered by doubt, anonymous, glancing at a thousand strangers' faces, her future skittering just ahead, just past the next block.

She kept thinking she would get on the subway at the next

opportunity, but she passed that one too, and the one after that, she just kept walking, walked past the Brooklyn Bridge, curving away from the city, supremely elegant, cables sweeping gracefully down from brick towers, holding firm over water.

She headed north, went down Centre Street and saw the city's buildings, stately, pillared, grand — the Municipal Building, the Criminal Courts, the Federal Courts Building — huge and thick and stained with soot that made long, dark tear-like gashes down its sides. Claire imagined high-ceilinged courtrooms, how the judge's voice would echo, the bloodshot eyes of manacled men, life sentences. A woman with prematurely gray hair sat on the steps, feeding a small child a piece of bread. When she looked around, her eyes were hollow. People coursed all around them as if they were inanimate objects.

There were no more subway stops in sight, but Claire knew she wasn't far from home; all she had to do was head west. She stood at an intersection waiting to cross. A cab swerved through a red light and a man carrying a huge garbage bag full of cans stood in the middle of the street, screaming and ranting, shouting obscenities, his eyes rolling wildly in a face scabbed with dirt, stopping traffic. People walked past him, jostled him forward. She veered off to the left, glancing desperately at every street sign until she saw it, the legend, Broadway, its big buildings with windows like eyes, blank and surprised.

She knew where she was now, that knowledge like triumph, and she thought for the first time how she knew every street in Alamogordo, every alley, where you could stop on the side of the highway to get a match lit, all the dirt roads.

She moved with the river of people that poured down to Canal, separating from the crowd to turn on White Street and past the crane, that hole still gouged behind the makeshift wall, waiting, she thought, for some other unsuspecting tourist. Not me, she thought. I live here.

Exhilarated, she buzzed number nine, but there was no answer. Waiting outside the door, Claire felt herself beginning to deflate. She saw the evening stretching out before her, nothing to do but fix dinner and go to bed, waiting for another day of

31

work. She turned around abruptly then, and, without thinking twice, she was back on the street and headed uptown.

She veered off Broadway at Eighth Street, everybody around her was young. On St. Marks Place, people spilled off the sidewalks, small-time street vendors standing behind their wares, antique magazines, coffee-table art books, extinct comic books. Little restaurants lined the street, they were swollen with people, restaurants of every kind, Thai, Afghan, Japanese, and through the windows you could see narrow tables jammed right up against each other so that no conversation was ever truly private. New York was crowded with such places, it existed to house them. City people with small apartments, they lived their lives in public, stepping off the street to duck into bars with yellow light, bottles stacked and gleaming welcome through the windows. Pockets of people, open till four in the morning, open till dawn, defiantly nocturnal, unapologetic. How everybody talked in this city, Claire thought, as if they'd been issued a deadline after which they would never be allowed to speak again.

On the corner teenagers slammed against pinball machines, a man in a tattered beard asked for change, his eyes gummy, his pants tied below his belly with a piece of twine.

Hey, he said, lurching toward her. Pretty girl — you got something for me?

She had reached the curb, had to wait there for the light to change, and he moved so close she could smell him, dank urine and worse.

I don't have anything, she said, backing away.

Rich cunt — fucking lying bitch —

His hand flew out, the reach sudden and volatile, his fingers snagged her hair, and she screamed, snapped her head back, jumping backward —

Watch out! Someone caught her from behind and she felt the thick rush of wind of the car that went blaring a quarter of an inch past her, driver still leaning on the horn. The homeless man let out a bark of laughter and wheeled back, ready to accost the next.

You okay? Gentle hands at her elbows turned her around.

She was facing a young man in a black leather jacket, hair caught in a ponytail at the back. He kept his eyes on her, his grin the wide smile that comes after sudden fear.

She smiled back, her vocal chords closed tight in her throat. He held her by one elbow still, as if he were not yet sure that she wouldn't walk back into the traffic, and she was unspeakably grateful for that grip, the only thing that held her to the world.

Yeah, he said. You're okay.

The light changed; he let go.

Okay, he repeated. Take it easy.

Wait. Without knowing what she was saying, she stepped forward with him, his body like a shield against which she crossed the street. He looked at her, he seemed amused.

Hey, he said. You're not a tourist, are you?

No, she said, I live here.

She seized his arm, did not know herself. Let me buy you a drink, she said. You saved my life.

She saw something in his eyes then — the swift pinprick of curiosity, interest, but more than that, she thought it was something like respect.

They went to a bar at First Avenue and Seventh Street, it had no name, just a big neon clock hung in the back, glowing pink and green. Claire ordered a glass of wine.

Name's Rich, by the way, he said, Rich Pepper. Kinda sounds like James Bond, don't you think?

I'm Claire, she said. They shook hands, the introduction making them both formal, making them both smile.

I'm not keeping you from anything, am I?

I have to meet some people later, he said. But it's just to check out a gig.

He wore black jeans, cowboy boots, a loose V-necked sweater. His skin was smooth in the V, hairless. He had two earrings in one ear, a diamond stud and a small ring; it made him more masculine somehow, gave him the dashing air of a pirate.

He was a musician, he said, played bass in a band called

Geronimo. It sounds like heavy metal, he said, but it's not. Want to play the juke?

He put money in and made her choose every other song, his fingers rapping a beat out against the glass, restless and professional. When she hesitated he said, Go ahead, I won't laugh — you want to hear the Bangles? Hey, I'm way into the all-girl thing, I'm serious.

He touched her arm, he grinned, he was charming; he had an air of irresponsibility, as if regular work were not part of his schedule. He didn't ask her what she did.

Claire ordered another glass of wine, already lightheaded from the first. More people were crowding in now, it was getting late; she was comforted by their proximity, the way they leaned over her to ask for a drink. She felt welcome among them, part of the human race. New York no longer seemed impenetrable, a city of walls — it was public property, open to infiltration by small-town immigrants, yielding.

This gig you're going to, she asked, can anyone go?

When he didn't answer immediately she flushed, she said, I almost died today, I can't go home . . . not yet.

No, he said, I'm glad you asked.

He was on the verge of saying something else but then he didn't, and their eyes met. Claire held his gaze without blinking, felt the tremor all the way down to her crotch. He smiled, he stood up.

I'm hungry, he said. Let's get something to eat.

They walked up Second Avenue and everybody else was young too — strolling indolently along, loud groups, men with John Lennon glasses and dreadlocks, and teenage girls with crew cuts, their noses pierced with thin gold hoops, wearing filmy white blouses and heavy black boots, glancing at them carelessly.

Just past Eighth Street, there were black men hustling unlikely items, their merchandise spread thin across the sidewalk — broken clocks, ragged sweaters, used pornography, half-empty bottles of hairspray, old records. People stooped to finger things shamelessly, connoisseurs of stolen goods, and a woman wrapped in newspapers spoke in a rapid murmur, unintelligible save when her voice rose — It's mine! she said, and when people looked she shouted, louder, Mine! Mine!

He took her to a restaurant that advertised Yemenite cuisine, because Claire had never heard of it. He ordered for both of them, hot mint tea in glass mugs, babaganoush, tabouli with pita, a piece of baklava for dessert. Eating that honeyed pastry, Claire was overcome with a sense of triumph, of utter happiness. When she looked up, he was watching her. He smiled. They didn't speak.

Out on the street again, he took her arm. I have to watch out for you, he said.

The gig was at CBGB's on the Bowery. Its scarred-up, graffiti-vandalized exterior seemed to denote a different world to Claire, an insider's New York, half-ghetto, half-exclusive club; now she was walking in the back door. The club was full of people, surprisingly unassuming inside. There were wooden tables and chairs, machines that sold peanut M&M's.

Rich approached a group standing at the bar, he didn't introduce her. People, he said. Buy me a beer.

Claire hung back, grateful for the anonymity.

Rich, man — where've you been?

I miss the show?

Where's Yvonne?

Where's my beer?

Who's your date?

Rich turned around. This is Claire, he said. A friend of mine.

Claire had to turn then too; she smiled. They seemed to have multiplied since she'd turned her back; they were all looking at her.

Trellis. A young man stepped forward, his hair dyed jet black, silver bracelets jangling on his wrist. He gestured at the rest of them, naming each one. Aviva, Ralph, Andrew, Debra, Bobby.

She nodded, forgetting each name instantly. All around them, to her immense relief, the lights went down.

The band was a trio of women, outrageous-looking, a

blonde and a redhead, sisters, both with wild curly hair, and a beautiful tall black girl who wore a short spandex skirt, turquoise sneakers and a bass strung over one shoulder.

Hello, they said. We're Betty!

All around Claire the crowd roared back. Hello Betty!

The music began.

Claire stared, rapt; they were mesmerizing. The redhead wore a short top and low-waisted jeans; she had the eyes of a seer and the navel of a belly dancer — she kept breaking from a hypnotic stillness into a crazed Dionysian dance, her smile a thousand volts of radiance. Their energy bounced off the walls, insane, controlled, hilarious. The blonde, self-proclaimed diva, her hair pinned high atop her head, pulled out a cello. The crowd's response was palpable, a wave of adoration, contagious, intoxicating.

More! They stamped their feet. Again!

Claire turned to Rich while they waited for the encore. Do you know them?

Oh sure, he said with exaggerated nonchalance. Known them for years. Want to go backstage and meet them?

She looked at him, could not think of what she would say to such women, how she could possibly impress them.

Come on, he said. Don't be shy.

Shouldn't we wait . . . ?

But he was already weaving his way through the crowd toward the stage; Claire glanced back and saw his friends watching, she saw one of the women turn and whisper to another.

Rich —

He turned, his hands out, as if waiting to catch her again, but his face was vulnerable, open, his eyes on hers seemed unsure, full of desire, and she had a sudden sense of her own power, startling and swift. She put her hands in his, smiling, and he bent forward and kissed her lips.

The encore was over.

This way, Rich said.

They waited a few minutes before knocking on the stage door. Rich opened it. It's me, he said.

Hey, hey, Dr. Pep-per!

They were putting their instruments away, all three of them smoking cigarettes.

Good set, Rich said. You guys gonna remember me when you're rich and famous and have major label connections?

Hell, no. The redhead stood with one hip cocked out, squinting against her own smoke.

She laughed, she caught Claire's eye. Hi, she said. I'm sure Rich would introduce us if he knew how — I'm Bitzi, and this is Amy, and Alyson.

You were great, Claire said, and wished she could control the blush that swept up her neck, wished she could think of something less banal to say.

Thanks. Bitzi smiled again, they all did.

You two come alone? Alyson asked.

No, the whole crew's back there, Rich said. Ralph wants you to autograph his neck — he's buying shots, Cuervo gold.

Did Yvonne come?

No, Rich said, I don't think she could make it.

Bitzi burst out laughing again, a laugh, Claire thought, that should have been illegal. Rich, you perv, she said, and Rich fixed her with a look but it only made her laugh harder.

Okay, he said. I should have known better than to try to come back here and compliment you —

Yeah, Bitzi said. Get the fuck out of here, will you?

Wait, Amy said, she was still looking at them in the mirror. Aren't you going to stay and tell me how great we sounded, song by song? She swiveled in her chair, her cigarette still burning, addressed him directly. Obviously you don't want to talk about your personal life, which is fine with us, and yet not — but what about how great my voice was? Can you tell I'm going to quit smoking? Can you believe my lung power?

Gotta go, Rich said, I'll catch you all later.

11

THE AIR OUTSIDE WAS WONDERFULLY CHILLY AFTER THE overheated club, fresh against Claire's face. It was just past midnight, the night was full of yellow cabs. Rich grabbed her hand, he grinned at her.

I got a view of the Empire from my place, he said. You wouldn't believe how tall.

Who's Yvonne? she asked him then, the question abrupt between them. He blinked.

No one, he said. A friend.

Before she could respond, someone shouted out behind them. Rich!

It was Trellis, coming out in his shirtsleeves. Hey, he said, he looked at Claire. You leaving?

Yeah, I think I'm going to hit it, Rich said casually.

Trellis stood there, Claire could see the gooseflesh on his arms. Come on, he said. We're going to the Lismar in a bit, see if The Funktones are playing.

Report to me in the morning, Rich said. He waved for a cab.

Rich, man, don't be an asshole.

Don't worry about it, Trey, Rich said. His tone of voice never changed. He held the cab door open for Claire.

Nice meeting you, she said.

Rich — !

Whatever else Trellis was going to say was lost as the cab drove off.

Twenty-fourth between Sixth and Seventh, Rich said, and then he leaned back and scooped Claire close to him, all his uncertainty gone.

Wild thing, he said, his voice an instrument in her ear, You make my heart sing.

It was true about the view, the Empire State Building loomed up through his living room windows, lit orange and blue, close. His apartment was a loft, with only the bedroom closed off. There was a stack of equipment in one corner, monumental speakers, but otherwise, it was surprisingly cozy, with a small gold velour couch, a funky old lamp, an antique mirror hanging on the wall.

Claire stood by the window, thinking how she would never have imagined it, this place, from the outside — wondering how many apartments like this the city housed, a thousand personal little nooks, idiosyncratic crannies, and what others, what hidden splendors, palatial apartments with halls wide as buildings, living rooms like ballrooms, chandeliers hung up high, fireplaces big enough to walk into . . .

Take your shoes off, Rich invited. He was taking an open bottle of wine from the fridge. Make yourself at home.

She walked the perimeter of his place, looked at the authors on the bookshelf. She traced the spines, could not help thinking what it would be like to wake up here in the morning, how the light would look slanting in, northern exposure, different from her own place — she imagined a small party, herself the hostess, a black velvet dress cut low, fitted tight, Rich's hand on her waist.

She reached the bedroom door, started turning the knob. Can I —

No, don't. His voice sharp. She looked up, surprised. It's a mess, he said. I haven't done my laundry in weeks.

Come over here, he said, he patted the couch. Come and drink some wine with me.

She accepted the glass, knelt on a cushion on the floor, aware of his eyes on her, how he held his wine without drinking it.

Your friend, she said, Trellis — he seemed upset when we left.

Oh, Rich said, waving his hand in dismissal, he was just jealous.

Of what?

He plays keyboards, Rich said, as if this were explanation enough, and she had to smile. He leaned toward her, his hand came warm around the back of her neck, intimate beneath her hair.

You're gorgeous, he said, voice so low it cracked. His skin was very clear, she could see faint smile lines around his eyes.

You make my mouth water, he said, even lower now, and her eyes closed as he kissed her, his tongue shocking in her mouth, and it came to her only then that this was the first man she'd kissed since Tommy, it had been years now — she held his wrists, as if to hold him back, but his mouth was on her neck, his hands already sliding under her arms, pulling her on top of him. She was awkward, clothed. Her shirt was twisted around and his hands were underneath it, fumbling with her bra snap.

Wait, she said, wait —

When she sat up to undo it herself, he took his T-shirt off. His body was beautiful and young, sinewy, smooth. She watched him looking at her, watched his eyes as she let her shirt fall off, heard him groan all the way down in his throat, and he pressed her back against the couch, hot mouth on her breasts. She gasped at the contact, could not respond, but he didn't seem to notice; now it had begun, he couldn't go fast enough. He pulled at her zipper, one hand tugging at his own. The phone rang.

Ignore it, he said harshly, as if she might be thinking of picking up. He had a small square package in one hand, he was tearing at it with his teeth. Claire was awed at his passion, she tried to help, her own excitement like confusion inside her, but the phone kept ringing, insistent, until finally a machine came on. Over Rich's rapid breathing, Claire heard two voices on the tape, a duet, male and female, harmonizing. The beep that followed was loud. It seemed to be calling a halt, and Claire held his shoulders, fingers pressing into that smooth skin.

Wait, she said again, but he didn't answer, he pressed on, pushing against her, and she understood that he couldn't wait, that he was beyond it. She tried to succumb, tried to catch up, and then he entered her; it was like a shock of cold water, it made her eyes fly open, sharpened all of her senses, like waking from some deep dream, and all she could hear was the voice speaking into the machine now, female and low.

40

. . . guess you're still out . . . I'll probably be home before you are . . . I'll see you later, baby.

Please come, Rich was saying. Please come, please come, please . . .

His release was violent, shuddering. She was left breathless, sprawled. He fell on her and she felt the sweat of his face against her neck. In the silence that followed, they both heard the sound of the machine rewinding, the last small click.

He tugged his jeans back up, wouldn't look at her. It was shameful to struggle up from the couch cushions to find her blouse, shameful to cover herself while he stood to pick up his T-shirt; even after she was dressed, she felt exposed, raw, desperate for a sign of tenderness.

Rich crossed the room and turned the machine off.

She's your girlfriend, isn't she, Claire said. Her voice sounded young and childish in her own ears. He didn't answer.

Yvonne, Claire said. She lives here, doesn't she.

She looked around, could not believe she hadn't seen it before, the evidence of a woman's presence in this place — it fairly vibrated now, her life here, their lives together.

She did not know who she had been this evening, who she had been five minutes ago, eyes wide under this man's wracked body, knowing nothing about him save what she'd wanted to know, which was a lie. He stood by the window now, rubbing his eyes, and he looked entirely different to her, thinner, his profile strange; his life had been revealed finally, it was complicated, intricately bound up with another, and she had been his blunder, his crude trespass against himself; it was so clear on his face she wanted to slap him. She wanted to punish him but she could think of nothing to say; the orgasm was over, she meant nothing to him. She felt herself a flat, two-dimensional figure, a young girl willing to take a ride . . . and what willingness! They were both frauds.

There were no goodbyes. Alone on the street, buildings large as warehouses and utterly dark on either side, she hated him. She could still feel his dampness on her thighs. She walked quickly, afraid of the silent, windblown streets, but there were no cabs. She kept walking, because standing in one place invited crime. Claire's teeth chattered against each other. This, she thought. This happened to me.

It would never have happened to Jade, she knew that. It was unimaginable.

12

SITTING BENEATH THE STERILE OFFICE LIGHTING THE NEXT day, last night's hangover pushing at the back of her eyes, she kept flashing on herself sprawled on that couch, gasping like a fish out of water, and each time it was an assault that left her flushed and breathless, she could not meet anybody's eye.

She thought it would be better at home, but the minute she shut the door behind her she knew she could not stand the solitude, she didn't have the strength. She picked up the phone before she'd even taken her jacket off. It rang twelve times before he answered it.

Where were you?

Who is this?

Claire bit her lip at that, silent.

. . . Claire?

Who else did you think it was?

I don't know. Some other babe.

What other babe? Her voice sharp, she had no cool to lose.

He laughed, she could hear the surprise in it. Who wants to know?

Forget it, I don't care.

What's up, you got PMS?

I had a bad day.

They not treatin you right up in that skyscraper?

I don't know anybody.

Thought you weren't worried about it.

I'm not worried, okay? Lying on her back on the floor, tears slid into her ears, warm and nasty.

You cryin?

42

No.

He was quiet for a moment, and she felt him shifting gears, listening.

How's Cody?

Fine. You want me to put him on?

Yes.

She heard a creak, and then the screen door hinge.

I'm outside now, he said, and she could hear his footsteps crunching dry earth. She closed her eyes and imagined the exact angle of light, slanting down hot past noon, a rush of white gold.

Almost there, Tommy said, his voice crackling with distance, and she strained to hear the wide wood barn door open, the warm thump and snuffle of the horses looking up.

Here she is, she heard Tommy say, and then, distinctly, Cody's snort, such absolute self-assertion she laughed out loud.

Hi, Cody, she shouted. Remember me?

In the background she could hear Tommy talking to him, the words unintelligible but the smooth, soothing river of his voice like balm, endlessly comforting.

Tommy . . . !

There was a pause, and the next time he spoke she could tell he was moving closer to the house, the static fading.

That travel agent called me up today. Said if I want to get the low fares, I have to decide now.

He loves me, Claire thought, and the sense she had of being essential to his life brought inexpressible relief, overwhelming.

I'll show you the city, she said, I'll show you everything.

She would be his guide, she thought when she hung up, he would see it all through her eyes; by the time he got here, she thought, she would possess this town. It would be hers.

She changed her clothes and went out, crossed Broadway and headed down Church, the heels of her boots loud on the pavement, wanting only the solace of motion, but the slight chill of the air against her face made her remember last night, made her shove her hands deep into her pockets.

A door opened from a building on the corner and music spilled out, smoky bar smell. Men stood in front of it, waiting for a cab. Talking sports. Goes the distance, Claire heard one say, and the others nodded, solemn as judges. They looked at her walking up, she had no place to put her eyes. They know, she thought. They can tell, I'm alone, I have no place to go —

She lifted her chin, full of false purpose, and saw the surprise on their faces when she turned into the bar.

There were drapes, faded dark green, and another man, his eyebrows lifting. Hello, he said. She brushed past him.

It was another world inside, another atmosphere, everything red-lit, blue cigarette smoke converging overhead, the music all rhythm, and around her, nothing but men. Men crowded at small tables, beer bottles sweating in their hands, all of them staring at the stage where two women were dancing, their bare breasts shocking.

Claire stood where she'd walked in, riveted as the rest of them. The one closest to Claire was tall, she had brassy blond hair and strong thighs, an athletic smile. She danced with her hands held high over her head, her hips undulating, her seemingly hairless crotch covered only by the smallest triangle of satin. She smiled at the men who pressed their money forward, fingers grazing at her G-string, she threw her shoulders back and made her breasts shake, laughing, her pelvis insinuation itself.

Can I help you? The barmaid was young, boyish. She had short cropped hair, freckles across her nose.

Claire ordered a beer, she could not move; a curious shame kept her from leaving. When she finally looked around, no one was looking at her. It was a low-key clientele, the bar itself small. There were no lights, and nothing flashy save the women themselves, their nakedness gleaming. The one on the far stage was younger, she had the face of innocence itself, small breasts, a perfect body. Her hair curled down to her waist, and like a serpent in the garden of Eden, the tattoo of a snake was draped across her collarbone, dark and sinewy. Her eyes glanced across Claire's with an indifferent, businesslike friendliness. She could be anyone, Claire thought. She could be me.

She left a dollar on the counter for the barmaid, and her beer, untouched. *Ciao,* said the man near the drapes.

Outside, it wasn't quite yet dark. She stood on the corner, so disoriented she couldn't remember which way she'd come.

A car swerved past, someone honked. She started walking. Halfway down the block, she looked behind her, and it wasn't till then that she saw the broken neon sign. *Go Go Girls,* it said, the letters dusty, unlit, sad-looking somehow, like a child's broken toy.

She stopped at the Lebanese deli man's and asked for coffee, but it was the cat she wanted, she wanted to press the warm weight of him against her cheek, that unquestioning animal love. She prowled the aisles, found him curled on a shelf in the back, behind the spaghetti. Psst psst psst, she said, crouched low, and saw his eyes half open from a warm daze of sleep. She reached in and pulled him out, held the animal's soft body against her own, speaking the universal language of gibberish.

Coffee, one regular! To go! The deli man peered at her over the counter. Ah. Tay-gur like you, I see!

He has a thousand girlfriends, Claire said, and the deli man grinned at her, delighted.

Yes! he said. Dam cat get all the girls — what his secret, I ask him, you think he tell me? No way! No way, Jo-sé!

Claire smiled at him, she dug in her pocket for change.

Here, you take, the deli man said. For you, free! For such a smile, this free!

Crossing the street to go home, Claire jaywalked the way she'd seen other New Yorkers do, stepping so close to the cars they had to tilt their hips back to keep from grazing the door handles, the look on their faces professional as bullfighters.

13

SHE DREAMT OF FLOODS, HOUSES DESTROYED, INUNDATED, in such a state of chaos she knew the damage was irrevocable, the wood swollen, distorted beyond repair, and everything in it, furniture, armchairs, floating out to sea in a stream of ruin.

She kept waking just long enough to realize it was a dream, only to sink back into the same place, thinking, no, this is life, this is what's real.

She thought she was dreaming still when she heard the knock, but it kept intruding, insistent, and she moved toward it without thinking, opened the door as if she'd been waiting, as if she'd been expecting just this.

Hi. Jade stood in the hallway in a pair of baggy Levi's and a man's jacket, a bag slung over her shoulder. I know it's late, but I keep knocking on my way to work and you're never here — I figured if I didn't bother you now, I might never see you again.

What time is it? Claire asked, she shut the door behind her.

Late, Jade said, she stood just inside. Listen, just tell me if you want to go back to bed — I hate to be woken up, I know what it's like —

No, I've been trying to wake up all night, Claire said, she took Jade's bag and put it down. I was having the same dream, over and over, it was a nightmare . . .

It's hot out tonight, Jade said. Maybe that's why.

Maybe, Claire said. Do you want anything? Something to drink?

I'll get it, Jade said. You go back to bed.

She stepped out of her shoes and padded over to the kitchen in her bare feet without turning any lights on, moving in the dark as if it were her natural milieu.

There's one beer left, she called. Want to split it?

Sure.

She came back and lay on the bed fully clothed, the jacket bunched high around her shoulders.

Aren't you hot in that? Claire asked, she lifted the hair from the back of her own neck, felt the skin damp there.

I've been covering up ever since that guy, Jade said, I don't want anyone on the street to see me.

But when she sat up, the jacket opened and Claire saw the

top she wore underneath, the fabric a dark, shimmering gold, brief as a bra.

That's pretty, she said. Did you go somewhere after work?

Jade looked down at herself, as if she didn't know what Claire was talking about.

Oh, I just wore this, you know, she said, she looked away. I thought maybe I'd end up someplace . . .

Well, she said, she smiled at Claire. I guess I did.

I ended up someplace last night, Claire said, she focused intently on a small tear in the bedspread, picked the thread loose with her fingernail.

What do you mean?

I didn't want to go home, so I just kept walking, and I ran into this guy.

Someone you knew?

I thought I knew him, Claire said. But it turned out he knew me better.

What happened?

I got taken for a ride, Claire said, trying to be dismissive, but she could not control the brief shudder that traveled through her. Oh, I wish I could forget those dreams . . . She pressed her eyes shut tight. I wish I could forget — whole nights.

The important thing isn't forgetting, Jade said. It's forgiving yourself.

Looking into Jade's dark, liquid eyes, Claire had the feeling there was nothing she could say to shock her, and it dawned on her for the first time that last night's incident would, in time, become trivial.

What are you doing tomorrow? Jade asked, rolling over to put the bottle on the floor.

I don't know, Claire said. Working, I guess, if they call me.

Maybe they won't call you, Jade said, she pulled a pillow under her head and turned her back to the window, tucked her knees up close. The sun's not up yet, is it?

Not yet.

Oh God, Jade said, she closed her eyes. Please let me fall asleep before the sun comes up.

47

Is that the vampire's prayer? Claire said, and slid down to lie on her side, too, so that their profiles were facing.

I just want to disappear, Jade said, she didn't open her eyes, and Claire heard the exhaustion in her voice, the volume gone. Here, with you.

She didn't say another word, and her body assumed an instantaneous stillness that was almost eerie, corpse-like; it made Claire aware of every one of her own small movements, and how loud the sheets sounded grazing against each other.

She thought Jade was asleep when in the darkness she spoke, her voice faint, as if it were coming from the inside of a deep well.

Don't let me dream, she said.

Claire had no answer.

14

THREE HOURS LATER, THE PHONE RANG.

Claire? Eileen, Perfect Temps. I got an assignment for you, you ready to go?

I, um . . . She sat up, tried to clear the sleep from her throat.

I wake you up? Listen, I'll call them, tell them you'll be a little late — from now on, though, you gotta be ready to hit the streets by nine o'clock, okay, hon? We gotta be able to rely on you, okay, Claire?

She looked at Jade, curled into herself like a child, eyes closed, lashes a dark fringe against the curve of her cheek, and the sight of her there was like a holiday, unexpected, hard to believe.

Okay, listen, Eileen was saying, don't worry about it, happens to everyone — can you be out the door in ten? You got a pen? The address is Fifty Gold, between —

Eileen —

What? In that one word, Claire could hear the woman's voice tensing, becoming hostile.

I don't . . . I don't feel that good . . . I'm — I think I'm coming down with something . . .

A brief pause, more full of disbelief than any words could have been. All right, Claire, she said then, her voice sarcastic with false sympathy, you call us when you're feeling better.

She hung up before Claire could answer.

. . . Claire? Jade was up when Claire came out of the bathroom, her jacket rumpled, her eyes still dark with sleep. Are you going to work?

I called in sick, Claire said.

Jade's smile slow-breaking, the first smile of the day. She knelt on the bed, opened the windows wide. It was hot as summer outside, the sky August blue, white clouds skimming high overhead. Looking out, Claire had a soaring sense of freedom, it would not be contained. Below, the yellow crane lumbered forward, big as a dinosaur.

Hey, desert girl, Jade said, she shrugged her jacket off. Have you ever seen the Atlantic?

They went to the beach in a car Jade said was part hers — I split it with a girl at work, she said, two hundred bucks apiece.

It was parked at the pier, green beat-up Buick, all its hubcaps missing.

I don't know who she bribes, Jade said, but it's never been towed — and I can start it with any key on my ring.

The engine caught on the fourth try.

My chariot! she cried, and they drove away from the river and into the streets, skimming yellow lights, confident amid the narrow, one-way roads. Jade drove, she manhandled the car, strong fingers spread wide over the gearshift, capable, and she pushed forward in bursts of speed, braked hard, blasted the horn, drove barefoot.

The key to driving here is to watch what's in front of you, she said, and don't worry about the back.

The front seat was big as a boat, they slid around on it, laughing, they were girls on holiday, two bottles of champagne and a bunch of grapes in a brown paper bag between them. They went to Jones Beach, Jade knew the way. They parked in one of a series of big lots, paved black, tar soft under their toes as they walked across barefoot, their shoes tossed in the trunk, car open, empty, so no one would break in.

The beach was long, it wasn't crowded, they walked past people who'd set down just near their cars, a group of black women, all of them fat, leaning back in small chairs, laughing, kids playing in the sand by the radio, making castles with discarded Styrofoam cups.

They walked through thick soft sand to the water's edge where there was no one, the horizon hazy in the distance, sun a blurred disk up high, the air much cooler. The waves broke over their feet, the water was cold but Jade was already pitching the bag behind her, stepping out of her shorts. Her bottoms were the same gold as her top, the back of them nothing but a thin strip of fabric that left her flanks bare. She stood shivering, laughing, saying, Come on, Claire, come in with me, but Claire was afraid of the undertow, how it sucked at her ankles, insidious, pulling her out.

Wait, she said. Maybe if I get hot first —

But Jade couldn't wait, she dove in, she was fearless, she swam out past the breakers, then turned and waved, beckoning.

Claire waved back, but she retreated up to dry ground and lay on her back, arms flat along her sides, eyes open, and imagined a bank of light filling up behind them, a store of light she could call on later, bricks of light, square and solid, blazing white.

Jade flung herself down next to Claire, her body wet, gleaming, her eyes luminous, sand like sugar where it clung to her hips, to the smooth concave curve of her abdomen.

Oh my God, she said, it's the greatest thing — it's like baptism.

She reached behind herself and undid her strap with one deft tug and then she was topless, she did not even look around to see if anyone was watching, just let her head drop back, putting her face up to the sun as if to be kissed.

I wouldn't care, either, Claire thought, if I looked like that —

But even as she thought it, she knew that Jade's unself-consciousness went deeper than her physical attributes, that it was a spiritual quality, something unquenchable at the core of her being.

The sun feels so good, Jade said, it's hard to believe it's bad for you.

She covered herself with sunscreen, its smell lush, tropical, held the bottle out to Claire. Want some?

No, Claire said. I'm a lizard. I've spent my whole life in the sun.

Where? Jade asked. Not just in one place . . .

No, Claire said, she shaded her eyes to look at Jade. How did you know?

I can just tell, Jade said, stretching out on her side, and Claire could see her hip bone pushing the fabric of her suit out, small round shape like a shell. It's how quick you take things in . . . like you know how to adapt — like you've done it before.

We moved a lot when I was a kid — not overseas or anything, just from base to base — San Diego and Phoenix and Albuquerque . . .

Jade watched her through dark sunglasses, her face just inches away.

I was fourteen when we moved to Alamogordo, Claire went on. We were only supposed to be there nine months . . . but then my parents split up. My father got transferred and my mother moved into town. She shrugged. And that's where we stayed.

She could see the sun now, a round circle of fire, and she knew she should close her eyes, but it was such a perfect thing, hung high, the edges shimmering. When she shut her eyes the darkness was tinged with red, like a piece of coal being heated up, like the flat desert of Alamogordo at noon, with only that one road running through it, no other choice.

But still, you must have felt so safe, knowing everyone, and everyone knowing you, Jade said, and Claire bit the true words

51

back — how nothing had been safe after her father was gone, nowhere — torn between wanting to tell Jade everything, to spill her life into Jade's lap, and wanting to offer only the best, the most precious, the essential.

They must miss you, Jade said, the people you left behind.

Claire thought of Tommy then, probed the thought of him the way one probes the gap in one's mouth where a tooth is missing, and found there was no pain.

I don't know, she said, I haven't been gone that long.

She leaned up on her elbows, gazed at the ocean. She could not get over the expanse of it, gray-green, unfurling white along the beach. She tried to imagine the ocean floor, what lived there, tried to imagine the desert as an ocean, how the water would cover everything save the low hills.

Next to her, Jade sat up to light a cigarette. Her hair shone wet still, a dark cap, and her skin looked poreless, pale and golden beneath the sun. She was possessed of a careless, innate glamour, it informed everything she did, she looked like a movie star, traveling incognito.

What about you? Where does your family live? Claire asked, suddenly craving something real, a fact, something solid to hold Jade up against, to define her in indisputable terms.

I grew up in the Far East mostly, but they moved back to the States two years ago, to D.C. It's just my dad and my step-mother, I don't have any brothers or sisters.

So your parents are divorced, too, Claire said, immediately ashamed of the surge of pleasure it gave her, the thought that they were alike, she and Jade, that they had sustained the same injuries, survived the same pain.

A long time ago, Jade said. My mother left when I was born.

Oh, Claire said, I'm sorry . . .

It doesn't matter, Jade said, she shrugged, her eyes completely obscured behind her dark glasses, and Claire had the sudden impression of a vault, locked, impenetrable. I never knew her.

Oh, Claire said again, nodding as if she understood, although each piece of information seemed more heartbreaking than the last.

How old were you when your father remarried? she asked.

Six, Jade said. We'd just moved to Hong Kong . . . Evelyn was the British consul's daughter.

Oh, so she was really more like your mother —

Never, Jade said. She was never my mother.

Her words came out harsh as reproach, but before Claire could apologize, Jade was smiling again.

It's okay, she said, I'm a big girl now.

I'm a free agent, she said. And that's the way I like it.

Me too.

Jade smiled, she dropped her glasses on the sheet.

I think it's time, she said, to drink champagne.

The cork flew out with such force the birds around them scattered, then swept low and bickered over it, thinking it was something to eat.

They drank it straight from the bottle and peeled grapes, throwing the small bitter strips of skin to the gulls, who stalked close, their yellow eyes unblinking.

They turned around when they heard music, a heavy bass beat that carried, an incongruous urban sound, and saw a group of boys walking up along the water's edge, lanky black teenagers in baseball caps, shirtless, their jeans hanging low, their boom box big as a suitcase. They started clowning around when they saw the girls, throwing themselves skyward, throwing themselves down, their moves liquid as water, shouting with laughter.

Look at them, Jade said. Aren't they gorgeous!

She gazed after them until they were long gone, their music still a faint pulse along the horizon.

Sometimes when I see people like that, she said, boys, strangers I pass on the street — something about them . . . the way they dress, or how they need a haircut — it's like hope. I imagine the possibility of wanting someone like that, I imagine a future, different futures . . .

The possibility, Claire echoed. You make it sound so far away.

It seems far away, Jade said, she watched the sand run through her fingers. It's my own fault — it's the way I live here, the things I do . . .

She hugged her knees, pressed her chest flat. I have to change.

It's waiting on people, Claire said, serving them — I bet you can get really sick of it. I don't think I would last very long.

No, Jade said, she kept her eyes on the horizon. I don't think you would.

It was clouding over, getting cooler. Seagulls swooped near them, their cries melancholy. In the distance, the black women were leaving with their children, bright towels draped over their arms, the sound of their radios drifting away.

I just can't imagine it, Claire said. You, a waitress.

Jade turned, she fixed her gaze on Claire, the same unnerving stare. Why do you say that?

Because, Claire said. I can't even picture you in a uniform. You seem more like . . .

Like what?

Like an actress, or an artist, I don't know — you could do anything, Claire said. You could be famous.

Jade shook her head, she said, You're crazy — but she was smiling now, smiling again, and her look was thrilling, electric.

The first time a boy kissed me, she said, I was eight years old, and we had sneaked away at recess. We met in this dusty little shed, it was crowded with gym equipment, and dark, there was no place to stand . . . my heart was pounding so hard it was all I could hear. He held my arms and kissed me, just pressed his lips against mine, like this —

And then she kissed Claire, her mouth open, lips salty, a hard kiss, a surging forward, taking something that hadn't been offered, taking Claire's lower lip between the edges of her teeth before letting go, her eyes opening.

I thought my heart would burst, she said, she put two fingers against the pulse in Claire's neck, pressed Claire's fingers against her own, and they both felt the quick thump, rapid as a drumbeat. Jade laughed, sound making the moment dissipate like the bubbles of champagne, she jumped up.

I don't miss anyone, she said, I don't miss any place, or any thing!

This time when she ran toward the water Claire followed, both of them shrieking, their hands laced together, running until the ocean tripped them, until tides of gray water covered them, salty and cold, swelling with mysterious currents, connecting them to the unknown continents that lay on the other side, hidden and vast.

15

THE HORIZON WAS GRAY WHEN THEY LEFT, THEY COULD NOT tell where the sea ended and the sky began, and their car was the only one left in the lot.

They rolled their windows down for the last of the sea air, turned the radio on loud, but they had only just turned onto the road when the right rear tire blew. The car skidded, lame, and Jade wrenched the wheel, braked hard. They squealed to a stop, the road was empty.

This car has nothing, Jade said. No tire, no jack.

She got out. The breeze lifted the hair from her face and she looked like a figure on a ship's prow, neck a graceful curve. The light was turning blue.

Well, you know what they say, she said. It happens to the best families in America.

Behind them, they heard an engine. Jade jumped into the road and stuck her thumb out. When the driver saw her, he screeched to a halt.

It was three young Puerto Ricans riding high in the front seat of a jacked-up Chevy. When they opened the door, Claire smelled the burnt sweetness of marijuana, saw their eyes, rimmed red. They grinned foolishly at the sight of the two young women, looked at each other.

Thanks for stopping, Jade said. She was smiling, face lit. We left home without a spare.

You don't got another tire? The driver, he looked eighteen tops, walked up to the car, squatted on his heels and checked out the damage. He wore jeans, a short-sleeved T-shirt. He was short, had a powerful-looking body, a broad chest, strong thighs.

No problem, man. He whistled for his friends, who kept on grinning. You girls take it easy, we'll take care this, okay?

His name was Mannie, and he was clearly the leader. In a brief burst of Spanish so slangy Claire couldn't catch a word, he set his friends about the task while he parked the Chevy behind them, keeping both the headlights and the radio on, salsa music tinny in the open air. Jade walked up to the car before he got out, climbed in. Claire followed and stood by the door, not knowing what to do with herself.

In the car, a pale green plastic Virgin hung from the rearview mirror, empty beer cans rolled on the floor. Jade looked as out of place as rare porcelain, her skin startling. She asked Mannie if he had any brothers or sisters while he rolled a joint, sat with her legs crossed as if she were sitting in a fancy bar, as if they were having dinner on a white tablecloth, waiters in tuxedos hovering nearby. She had an air of formality, it contradicted her behavior, her loose hair, the quick laugh; it made Mannie taller. He turned shy but he was filled with pride, Claire could see him glancing at his friends, knowing they were watching even as the car rose from the road, punctured tire suspended high.

My cousin grows it, he said, handing Jade the joint. She held it like a cigarette, casual, ladylike. She bent her head toward his cupped palm when he lit it. A look of reverence crossed his face.

Where you from? he asked, voice as husky and tender as if they'd just made love. Jade exhaled, passed the joint down to Claire.

New York City, Jade said.

What're you doin all the way out here for? Wasn't no sun at the beach today!

56

I like it that way, Jade said. Keeps me pale.

She peered through the windshield. The other two were removing bolts, kneeling on the ground.

Wouldn't they like some? she asked, meaning the joint. They're doing all the work.

You kiddin? Mannie said quickly. They're already high. They been high since five o'clock. Work's done, man. We been partyin the whole time.

I've got something, Jade said then, and when she jumped out, Mannie followed. She reached into the back seat of the Ford and emerged with the second bottle of champagne. Here, she said, this is for you — our rescuers.

On Mannie's face, a slow grin spread. The night was unfolding, miraculous. He gave Jade the last of the joint and ran to the Chevy, turned the music up.

Ever smoke shotgun? Jade put the lit end in her mouth and slid her hand behind Claire's neck, her palm was warm. She blew the smoke in Claire's mouth, eyes closed. Her face was exquisite, lashes made shadows by the headlights and the smell of the sea, of coconut oil, came off her skin, sweet and salty. All the boys stood still, their jaws slack. Jade smiled, marijuana gave her the eyes of a seer, all-knowing, distant.

Just so they know, she said, I'm with you.

Baila conmigo! Mannie shouted behind her. He grabbed Jade's wrist and pulled. She turned to him, back against his chest, whirled back out. Mannie was prancing, knees high. He shouted in Spanish and the other two began to clap. A car came by, slowed, finally went on. One of the other boys came running up to Claire.

Dance wit' me, he said. His eyes, his mouth were lecherous. He had bad skin.

She shrank back. No. She shook her head.

Come on, he said, but he kept looking over his shoulder at Jade. He didn't want Claire, he just wanted to be out there next to Jade. She was imitating Mannie, picking her knees up high, and his friends burst out laughing. Mannie stopped.

You don't like the way I dance? His feelings were hurt. His

friends laughed louder, and Jade laughed too. She picked the new tire up and handed it to him.

Your turn to work, she said. Her voice had laughter in it still but it was the voice of authority, undeniable. Mannie held the tire with one hand to make his bicep flex. His friends stood back. They had the champagne and they drank it methodically, passing it back and forth.

From the radio, a sentimental ballad wailed, guitars lamenting in the back while Mannie screwed each bolt back on. He pumped the jack with solemn ceremony till the car was back on the ground. Another car came by and slowed, someone yelled out. Mannie said something in rapid Spanish and one of the other boys went over to the Chevy, turned the lights and the radio off.

Let's go, Jade said.

Wait, Mannie said. He blocked Jade's way and she smiled at him curiously, as if she'd never seen him before. His eyes were imploring.

Where you live, he wanted to know.

She shook her head, she was smiling still but she was distant, she was already gone.

Tomorrow you come and meet my mother, he said. He reached for her hand and Claire half rose, but Jade didn't pull it back. She shook her head again, more gently.

You are very beautiful, he said.

Thank you, Jade said, accepting the compliment with ease.

No, you are beautiful, Mannie insisted. He was fervent, he needed to make her understand. *Como la Madonna,* you are beautiful.

Like a virgin? Jade burst out laughing. She slid her hand out of his and leaned over to kiss his cheek at the same time. He was still standing there, stunned, the bottle of champagne dangling from one hand, when she got in the car.

No, wait, he said. Claire started the engine.

Hasta luego! Jade called back, but the wind whipped her words away.

The car was like a beast, a team of oxen, carrying them toward the city, the streets a current sweeping them forward, and the city was a magnet; in the twilight its aura was red, it pulsed slightly, dense and lit, outrageously vertical. Claire looked at it till her eyes burned, it made her heart pound. She would never sleep tonight. She would never sleep again.

She walked into her apartment that night, her face flushed from the sun, hair streaming wild down her back, and saw the red light of her machine blinking, a message. She played it back, did not recognize Tommy at first, how formal he sounded, his voice stiff as a stranger's, as if he thought the machine itself was its own entity, as if he had no faith in its ability to relay the message to Claire.

Plane gets there eight-thirty Friday night, he said. See you then.

16

CLAIRE WENT UP TO THE AGENCY THE NEXT DAY, BUT THERE was no work for her. She was walking home from the coffee shop that evening when she saw two women coming around the corner, recognized that easy, swinging stride instantly. The other girl was black, young, she wore shorts rolled up as high as they would go, her legs long, perfect, and Claire saw her laughing at something Jade said, their arms looped together.

Claire averted her eyes, she kept walking, acted surprised when she heard Jade call her name.

Oh, she said, she stopped. Hi.

Claire, this is Olivia. Olivia, Claire.

Nice to meet you, the girl said, but she leaned against Jade, did not extend a hand.

Where you coming from? Jade asked.

I got something to eat, Claire said, at LeRoy's.

Ugh, that place, Olivia said. They served me the raunchiest salad once, I am *never* going back there.

I'm sure there was nothing wrong with it, Jade said. You're just a snob.

Lookit who's talking, Little Miss I'm-going-to-Paris-for-dinner!

That's different, Jade said.

You're different, Olivia said, she clutched Jade's arm, subsiding into a fit of giggles. Come on, she said, we're gonna be late —

Where are you going? Claire asked, heard her voice stiff in her own ears.

It's a surprise party, Jade said, for a girl from work.

Wanna come? Olivia asked.

No, Jade said quickly, you wouldn't like it, believe me —

Why not? Olivia asked, straightening up to look at her friend. Dina's a nice girl — just like you!

Shut up, Olivia, Jade said.

Claire stood woodenly, stricken with a terrible sense of foolishness, her face burning.

It's just a stupid party, Jade said now, she was already stepping back. I'll see you later, okay?

It was nice meeting you, Olivia called, and lifted one hand languidly into the air.

Claire walked away fast, she kept her head down. She had a note for Jade in her pocket — Wake me up when you get home — and she crumpled it, threw it in the gutter.

She had almost reached the building when the thought occurred. She ran back into the street and flung her arm out for a cab, surprised as a hitchhiker when one of them stopped.

She told him the address of Circus Maximum, glanced at his name on the license. Khmoud Akbar, it said, and she didn't know which was the first and which was the second. He drove with a crazed speed, jumping the lights, dodging potholes so deep it was as if the streets had been mined, and, flung back against the seat, she felt her anger subsiding, strangely calmed by this third world driver's heedless urgency.

It was on First Avenue, unadvertised, the door recessed; Circus Maximum, read the Roman lettering above it. She walked past the bums who sat on the steps in their tattered jackets as if she weren't afraid of them, as if she did this all the time, and opened the unassuming green door.

The inside was unimaginable from the outside, like walking into a mirage, the decor sparse, Roman, furniture made of thin iron, the cushions all in white, the ceilings high, small candles flickering along the bar.

To the far left there were two steps leading to another level, tables and chairs, booths, the clinking chink of expensive silverware, the low murmur of dining chatter, people who ate dinner after ten, and in the back, the quiet sound of cool jazz.

It was a place where evening reigned supreme — drawn out, poised, inviting, the smooth necks of champagne bottles resting against the icy silver buckets, full of romance. Glasses gleamed richly, music lined the room like silk, and candlelight shadowed the women's eyes, softened their faces. They were New York City women, they could not be classified — women six feet tall, mocha-colored women with Oriental eyes, and pale, pale women with hair so black it shone purple, their shoulders, their navels, their legs, their lower backs bare. The only thing they seemed to have in common was a certain darkness, even the blondes — Claire could not imagine them by day, how they would look first thing in the morning, their makeup smudged.

She stood alone in the angled room, and no one looked at her. What am I doing here, she thought then, I don't even know where I am —

She had her hand on the door when she heard him, that ironic contralto rising just above the mingle of dinner.

Bartender, he called, his voice gleeful with false pomposity. Piano player needs a beer!

She hesitated, her hand still on the door, and then he spotted her, his eyes lit up.

Well, well, well, he said, if it isn't my wife!

Actually, she began, I can't stay —

What! When I'm going to sing! He took her hands, kissed both of her cheeks, his face smooth-shaven and cool against hers.

Give me one good reason, he said, already leading her toward the bar.

I don't think I'm dressed right for this place, Claire said, shrugging the shoulders of her brown suede fringed jacket.

Are you kidding? You look fabulous, Such said, without a hint of sarcasm. That jacket's fabulous. And your boots, too. You're the real thing, Claire.

Yeah, Claire said, a real hick.

There are people in this town who spend thousands cultivating your look, believe me, Such said, he patted a barstool. You just sit yourself down right here, he said, and have a drink on Claude.

He motioned to the willowy young black man standing behind the bar. Claude, meet Claire. Claire, Claude.

The bartender smiled at her. What can I get for you? His voice was smooth as butter, the voice of a courtesan.

She looked at the vast array of bottles before her, nothing stood out, she could not decide.

May I suggest something? Such asked, did not wait for her to answer. Claude, can you make a Cosmopolitan?

Did I go to Andrew's School of Bartending and graduate with honors? He spoke with the soft slyness of a Southern belle, batted Bambi lashes. She watched while he made her drink, mixing it expertly in a silver cocktail shaker, vodka and lime juice and Cointreau with a splash of cranberry.

What would Tommy be doing now, she thought as he poured it into a chilled martini glass. Feeding the horses, feeding the dogs — taking care of all his living things, while outside the sun would still be stripping the land of shadows, making everything depthless.

One Cosmopolitan, Claude said. Straight up.

Thank you. It tasted just the way it looked, pink and perfect.

Now *that,* Such said, is what I call an accessory.

Claire took another small sip, she put it down. I feel like I'm faking it, she said, felt she could admit anything to him.

Sweetheart, Such said, leaning close. This is New York,

reinvention capital of the world. There's no such thing as faking it.

Hey, Such. One of the other musicians came up behind him, he had a round face, steel-rimmed glasses. Come on, let's go.

He turned around without waiting for an answer, and Such gazed after him. I wonder what he wants.

I hate to break the news, Claude said, but you work here.

Listen, bartender, Such said, just make the lady another drink, okay? He waved his hand extravagantly through the air. Put it on my tab!

Claude rolled his eyes, he refilled Claire's glass. I'll be lucky, he told her, if he tips me.

The maitre d' came up behind them. Such, he said.

What.

Don't what me, you know what.

Like I said. Claude leaned in close to Such and smiled. You work here.

Do shut up, Claude, Such said, but he stood. Come on, Claire. Here's your chance to see an artist in action —

Claire sat at a table near the piano and watched Such, how his eyebrows rose when he hit the high notes, his hair falling to one side. There was a nobility about him, the high, smooth forehead, his aquiline features, even those crooked teeth. They all suggested intelligence, inherited, the bloodline of royalty. He caught her eye and segued into another song, Cole Porter, his voice dipping low into the mike. Heeeyyyy . . . You're the Colosseum/You're the top . . .

And that was for the little lady, he said. No one seemed to hear it but her, it made her laugh. The evening took on a levity she would not have thought possible earlier, until soon the dinner crowd was almost gone; people lined up before the coatcheck girl, bowing their shoulders in submission, while through the door a new crowd was drifting in, the late-night set, smokers arranging themselves near the arched windows that looked out over the street, that concrete view hidden by tall potted palms, discreet.

When the musicians broke again, Such took her out for a slice of pizza.

We don't want to eat their slop, he said as they left the restaurant. We want *real* slop —

They stood on the corner of Eighth Street and First Avenue and ate standing up, the pizza so hot it burned the roof of her mouth.

A sideburn grows in Brooklyn, Such marveled. Will you look at that.

Claire followed his gaze, saw the sideburns in question, sported by a young man in a thrift-store overcoat and a backward baseball cap, walking quickly, his eyes raking the crowd.

Italian bad boy from the boroughs, Such said. Comes in on the weekend, breaks a few hearts, then hops the D train home again.

He glanced at her. You're not into sideburns, are you. I didn't think so. It's one of the things that distinguishes the sexes — homos like them, heteros don't.

He sighed. I need a new type.

It seemed to her then that she had known, from the beginning, that Such was gay, but still she was surprised, more by the carelessness of his admission than by the fact of his nature itself. There were men she knew in Alamogordo, boys she had grown up with, who would have slit their wrists before uttering such words in public.

Aren't you afraid? she asked.

Oh, sideburns can't really hurt you, don't be fooled by the name.

You know what I mean, she said. Of AIDS.

Are you kidding? I'm terrified! If I got AIDS, my mother might think I was gay!

You mean she doesn't know?

Well, not officially, but she's stopped asking when's the wedding. Always the bridesmaid, never the groom, that's me. Finish your slice already, would you?

I'm finished. She turned to pitch what was left of her crust in the garbage but he snatched it.

I'm ashamed of you, Claire, he said, stuffing it into his mouth. When there are children with eating disorders on the Upper East Side . . .

He draped his arm around her shoulder. You wanna come cruising with me? You'd be a great foil for my manhunt . . .

Is that a compliment?

Your naivete slays me.

Okay, Claire said. I'm going home.

Oh come on, stick around. I'll take you to Blanche's on Avenue A, we'll check out the bartender's wig, maybe shoot some pool, what do you say?

Don't you have to go back to the restaurant?

Oh sure, Such said. Throw it in my face why don't you.

Such hailed a cab for her, then leaned in and gave the driver five bucks. Take my wife anywhere she wants to go, he told the cabbie. And keep the change.

No, Such, I have money —

Hey, he said. Anything for a fan.

She turned around to watch him cross the street, his hands in his pockets, his step easy, and then she sat back and crossed her legs, pretended she was a New Yorker, watching out the window like there was nothing new under the sun.

17

IT WAS FRIDAY EVENING, AND CLAIRE KEPT GLANCING through the kitchen window at the cabs that stopped, she could not sit still, she kept walking through the apartment but there was nothing left to do; everything was clean, in its place, the table set with candles and flowers, the salad made.

She jumped when she heard the knock on the door, ran to open it, then stopped still when she saw Jade on the landing, hair loose around her face and those burning eyes.

Hi. She wore jeans and a T-shirt, the neck cut off and slipping down to expose a shoulder, no strap.

Hi, Claire said. Come in.

For a second she thought Jade was going to embrace her, but Claire stepped back and the moment passed, it was gone.

Claire, she said, something soft in her voice, how've you been?

Fine, Claire said quickly. How are you?

I've been working like a dog, Jade said, this is my first day off since we went to the beach.

Claire nodded, she stood with one foot up against her leg, her arms crossed, she couldn't hold Jade's gaze.

They were both quiet for a moment, and then Jade took a pack of cigarettes from her back pocket, the gesture quick, nervous.

Do you mind if I smoke?

Claire shrugged.

Jade walked toward the window, stopped when she saw the table.

Oh. She turned back. This is a bad time, isn't it — I should've called first —

You don't have my number, Claire said, it came out harsh, and Jade didn't say anything, but she looked suddenly frail, the ridge of her collarbone showing, her arms thin, the package of cigarettes half-crumpled in her hands.

I was just going to open a bottle of wine, Claire said, moving to cover her remorse. Want some?

It's okay, Jade said. You're expecting someone, I shouldn't —

Just stay, Claire said, she faced Jade. For one glass.

Jade didn't answer, but she sat on the very edge of the windowsill, as if perched for flight, she kept looking at the table. Is it a date?

Not exactly, Claire said. He's my boyfriend.

Your boyfriend, Jade said, the unlit cigarette still in her hand. I didn't know you had a boyfriend.

He lives in New Mexico. He's just coming for the weekend.

Is he thinking of moving?

He would never move. He lives by himself on five hundred

acres, he hates cities. He doesn't understand why I ever wanted to leave.

Five hundred acres, Jade echoed. Why did you?

Claire looked at her as if to say, If you don't know then no one does. No one ever will.

Because it's New York, she said, I had to see it.

I hope it's everything you ever wanted, Jade said, she lit her cigarette.

It's not what I thought it would be — even now that I've been here — every day it's different, the people I see, everything — it's like anything could happen. Anything does.

I remember when New York used to make me feel that way, too. I got here and I thought, This is it, this is what I imagined Rome used to be, or Babylon, Constantinople . . . the capital of the world, the center of the universe . . . I thought I would stay here forever.

Claire heard the current beneath her words, carrying her upstream, out of the city, to places unreachable, places Claire could never follow.

You might, she said, almost defiant. You never know.

I don't know, Jade said, but sometimes I think maybe I don't want to be that centrally located anymore.

Claire fell silent, she followed Jade's gaze, and on the street below, she saw steam rising ghostly from a manhole cover.

On the other hand, Jade said, where else would you find a city that hallucinates for you?

You know what they say, she added, grinning. If you can make it here, you'll fail everywhere else.

She leaned forward, struck a match. May I?

It was dark out now, the air coming through the window sweet, balmy, and they sat at the table together, the lit candles their only light.

So what does he need five hundred acres for?

He's a rancher. He raises horses.

Horses, Jade said, she laughed. Did he teach you how to ride?

Yeah, Claire answered, because it was true. He did.

Jade smiled, the angles of her face soft in the shadowed light. I can't believe, she said, he ever let you out of his sight.

She finished her glass of wine, stood. Listen, I should go . . .

No, Claire said, she could feel the wine, how it loosened her. Have another glass with me, please —

But it's getting late — you don't want me to be here when your lover gets here, do you? Not after you've been waiting so long . . .

I'm not waiting anymore, Claire said, and realized only as she said it that it was true; the nagging sense of expectancy that had dogged her all day had vanished the minute Jade had walked through the door.

It seemed only minutes had passed when suddenly the bottle was empty, and all at once they were both giddy. Jade got up to go to the bathroom, she knocked into the wall.

I'm drunk, she said, her laugh surprised. It's not possible — I'm a pro, I can't be drunk! Claire, you're not drunk, are you?

It's because we didn't eat —

I don't think I had any lunch today, either —

Wait, Claire said, she went into the kitchen, started pulling dishes from the fridge, salad, cheese, bread. Look what I made —

We can't eat this — it's for Tommy, isn't it?

I have to take it out anyway, Claire said; she was already carrying it to the table.

Well, maybe just a little nibble, Jade said.

They ravaged the food, they kept tearing another piece of bread off, slicing at the cheese, stealing tomatoes from the salad, their forks knocking against each other, until they were both laughing too hard to swallow, and Claire had to spit her food out; it rendered Jade totally helpless, she slid to the floor, she could not get up.

It isn't funny, Claire kept repeating, she tried desperately to stop — it was too intimate, this shared act of helplessness, this loss of control. It was like seeing someone come, the thought came to her, and she turned her face away, her ribs aching.

The buzzer sounded, long and hard, making them both jump.

It's him, Jade gasped, the words coming out so high-pitched it set them off all over again, it had a momentum all its own, making everything ruthlessly comic.

Oh God, Claire moaned, I have to straighten up, I can't —

Go get him, Jade said, pushing her. Hurry!

18

SHE MET HIM HALFWAY, WAS STILL GIGGLING WHEN SHE caught sight of him, his face startlingly brown.

Hey, he said, what's so funny —

He reached for her before she could speak and they both fell back against the banister, his arms closing tight around her. He smelled like sheets left to dry in the sun, like years of her life, and she was inundated by more than she could name, instantly sobered. She grabbed his bag.

It's up one more, she said, overly animated, chattering. Did you find a cab? Did you have a hard time getting here?

Took a while. Got some cabdriver couldn't speak English.

A lot of immigrants drive taxis — they're very colorful.

Colorful, he repeated, looking at her, amused.

Well, this is it, she said, they had reached the landing. This is where I live.

Tommy stood in the narrow doorway and squinted up. Looking around, Claire felt for the first time how small the apartment really was, how cramped, despite its high ceilings. Two rooms, only one door, not counting the bathroom. She was aware of the people who lived below, the people above, the noise of the traffic coming up from the street. Tommy said nothing. He stepped into the room, his boots heavy, the blue of his Levi's faded where the cloth creased at his hips.

Come here, he said.

Wait, she said, she looked around for Jade. There's someone —

Come here, he said again, no irritation, just that calm waiting, it was the tone he used with his horses. Claire would stand inside the dark barn listening, how he stroked their necks and soothed the skittery ones, his voice flat and rolling, all the time in the world.

She moved too fast, jerked against him, but he was ready, his arms came around her again, she could feel the smooth muscle of his biceps against her back and then his hands were on her face, the callus of his palms sweet and rough on her cheek, his fingers tracing her lips — he kissed her, and she felt the rush in her groin, his tongue in her mouth . . .

There was a sound, water running, and they both turned. Jade came out of the bathroom, hitching her shirt up. She stopped short when she saw him, as if shocked, somehow — by his breadth, Claire thought, how much room his presence took up — but when she spoke her voice was fluent with courtesy, she extended her hand.

You must be Tommy, she said, I'm Jade.

How d'you do. He stared at her, too surprised to hide it.

I live next door, she said, she looked at Claire, her lips were still quivering with the urge to smile. I was just about to go.

Wait, Claire said. There's dessert —

Jade burst out laughing, she had to turn away. I'm sorry, she kept saying, I'm sorry . . .

Claire started laughing then too, and Tommy looked from one to the other, waiting to be clued in.

Somethin funny? he asked finally.

It's nothing, Jade said, believe me . . .

Is somethin on my face?

No, Jade said, this last straightening her out, it's not you at all —

Come on, Claire said, let's sit down.

She opened Tommy a beer, made a plate of food for him, and he sat at the table to eat it, squinting in the candlelight, finally pulling one of the flames close — So I can see what I'm eatin, he said. He looked bigger than Claire remembered him, the spread of his legs, the size of his boots, how wide he planted his elbows. She had forgotten his silence while he ate, too, it made her painfully self-conscious for him, she could hardly look at Jade.

I have some ice cream, Claire said, she jumped up. Anyone want ice cream?

No, thanks.

I'll wait, Tommy said. Have it for breakfast.

Claire got the ice cream anyway, she came back with bowls, spoons, set them on the table. When she sat down again, Tommy had finished his food, he was watching her, grinning.

What? she said.

What're you sittin all the way over there for?

Tommy, she said, embarrassed.

What?

She looked at Jade. We don't always talk like this, she said. Jade smiled quizzically, she raised one shoulder, as if to say, Like what, and the motion exposed her collarbone again, the hollow at the base of her neck.

You a dancer? Tommy asked.

She stared at him, for a moment she didn't answer. What makes you say that?

The way you tore your shirt — like in *Flashdance*, right?

Oh, that . . . Her fingers traced the edges nervously.

So what line of work you in?

What line, Jade said. There's a good question.

Jade speaks Chinese, Claire said abruptly.

That so?

No, Jade said. Not really.

She's lived everywhere, Claire said. All over the world — Indonesia and Hong Kong and the Philippines — she speaks Spanish, too.

Guess you could get a pretty good job, Tommy said, if you speak all those languages.

I don't know, Jade said, I never tried.

71

She smoked, she looked out the window, and Claire had a sudden flash of the way she had been the first night they'd met, restless, chased.

We went to the beach, Claire said, wanting to draw her back in, and we got a flat — these guys stopped to change the tire and Jade spoke in Spanish to them, they couldn't believe it! What was that guy — Mannie? He wanted to take her home to meet his mother, remember, Jade?

Jade smiled vaguely, she didn't answer.

And they danced, Claire said. It was so funny . . .

Danced with who? The flatness of his accent made Claire wince, she wondered if Jade heard it the same way.

The guys, Claire said. Who helped us change our tire . . .

You danced with them?

It was just to the radio —

Tommy stared at her.

You had to be there, Jade said.

There was a silence, and then Tommy pushed his chair back, it scraped harshly against the floor. Yeah, he said. Too bad I missed it.

He stood up and went to the bathroom without excusing himself, and then Jade stood, too.

I think your rancher wants me to go.

No, he doesn't, Claire said. Believe me, he's not like that — he's not like this, he's just the opposite —

Forget it, Jade said, I shouldn't have been here in the first place.

Tommy came out of the bathroom just as Claire was opening the door.

Bye, Jade said. It was nice meeting you.

Likewise.

Bye, Claire. She leaned over quickly and kissed the corner of Claire's mouth.

Thanks for the wine, she said, her smile fast, wicked. I'll see you later.

The door had not even closed behind her before Tommy said, People in New York all kiss like that?

Like what?

Like this. Tommy took her by the arms, kissed her with exaggerated passion, almost rough.

It wasn't like —

But he wouldn't let her finish, his mouth covered hers, fingers strong on her jaw, holding her there, holding her still, and when she tried to step back, to say something, he just lifted her, the crook of his arm strong under her knees.

I'm through chattin, he said.

19

SHE WAS DREAMING OF WATER, AN OCEAN FRESH AND CALM as a lake, warm, washing over her, water like hands, touching her, and she woke just as Tommy rolled her on top of him, his body a strong boat rolling beneath her, early-morning light pale in the room, her hands gripping his shoulders as he rocked her against him, his rhythm easy as a cowboy's till she let out a low sound, then holding her fast, his hips straining higher and higher, gone selfish with ecstasy, pushing her over the edge.

She lay over him; there were no words, just the strong pulse of his heart, slowing, and they moved into a timeless state somewhere between waking and dreaming, floating above the passage of seconds into minutes, and minutes into hours.

You been hangin out with that girl a lot? Tommy's question pulled her back into the world, made her eyes open.

Some.

You talk funny around her.

What?

You talk different — He spoke in a breathless falsetto. You talk like this —

I do not!

Yeah, just like this, and you laugh, oh, everything is just so funny —

Shut up, Tommy, I mean it!

Okay. Just so long's you don't start dressin like her.

What was wrong with the way she was dressed?

Nothin, if you go for the slutty look —

. . . You must be joking.

Well what do you call it when you rip your clothes up so they're hangin off you?

Claire rose on one elbow, she looked down at him, would not answer. He looked back at her, undaunted.

What's her story, anyway?

What do you mean? We told you last night —

We? You said she spoke a buncha languages — she didn't say shit.

She grew up overseas, her father was a diplomat.

Yeah, yeah, so what, she some kind of little rich girl?

No, she works, Claire said, speaking very clearly. She's a waitress.

Waitress? His eyebrows shot up. She sure don't seem the type.

What's that supposed to mean? Claire asked, although she had said the same thing.

What're you gettin all on your high horse about? I'm just askin —

Because I don't like the way you're asking —

The way I'm askin! Tommy laughed. Well, la di da!

Claire threw the covers back and swung her legs over but he caught her wrist, held her.

Hey, he said. Don't take offense.

She's my friend, Claire said, tugging out of his grasp. She's —

What?

Never mind, Claire said, knew her feeling for Jade was inexplicable, especially to him. She got up, grabbed a shirt. You wouldn't understand.

Aw, now look what I did, Tommy said. What're you gettin dressed for?

It's time to get up.

Why?

Because — you're only here for one weekend —

74

That's what I'm sayin —

— and that's not very much time to see New York.

Didn't come to see New York. Came to see you.

Well, here I am, she said, and walked out of the room.

The kitchen was just the way she'd left it the night before, food still out, uncovered, dirty dishes everywhere, and she started slamming them around, clattering silverware into the sink.

You makin coffee? He came up behind her, tried to put his arms around her but she broke away.

No, she said. We're going out.

I thought we were havin ice cream for breakfast —

Everything's dirty, look at these plates —

We don't need plates.

I don't want ice cream.

Okay, he said after a moment. I'm goin to take a shower.

Outside, the air felt heavy, the sky was gray.

You must have brought the bad weather, Claire said. We have more sunny days here . . .

We? That amused tone again. She would not respond.

As he walked next to her, Tommy's presence ceased to seem a luxury; he was merely there, unmysterious as ever, unchanged by the new context of the city streets, his workboots stained with rain.

We goin to the Empire State Building?

The Empire State Building's for tourists.

You been there?

I'm not a tourist.

Well, I am.

I want you to see the real New York — the way people live here, she said.

They had reached a diner.

We can get a real New York breakfast here, she said. Bagels and lox.

Bacon and eggs, he said.

Don't you ever want to try anything new? she snapped.

75

Yeah, he said. The Empire State Building.

She could not return his gaze, and she could not apologize, and then when they sat down to eat, she could not choose.

Are you ready to order? The waitress was back for the third time, one of her eyelids seemingly permanently drooped with boredom and impatience.

Go ahead, Claire told Tommy, indecision mounting in her like panic.

She'll have banana pancakes, he said. And I'll have bacon and eggs, sunny side up.

The waitress snatched up the menus and left, turning smartly on one heel.

I don't want banana pancakes, Claire said.

Okay, then, have some eggs.

I don't want eggs, either!

Maybe you will when they get here, Tommy said, unperturbed by the fury in her face. He stuck a toothpick in his mouth.

Since when do you make decisions for me?

He looked at her. What's wrong?

She fixed her gaze on the window, couldn't answer.

Want to change the order? he asked finally.

Forget it. Suddenly she was ashamed of her petulance, ashamed of the way she had spoken to him. All he wanted was her love; he had no taste for complications, but he put up with them, tried to assimilate them the way he did coyotes and colic and drought — all things he had no use for, but they came with the territory. Tommy was not a man beset by doubt.

She reached out, wound her fingers through his. You know what, she said, we can walk to the Empire State Building from here.

20

THEY HAD TO WAIT IN LINE TO RIDE THE TWO ELEVATORS UP, the lobby crowded with people despite the bad weather. Walking around the lower deck, it was possible to look down and see the street, a vertiginous distance away, but the clouds obstructed the view of the city almost completely.

Kinda bust, huh, Tommy said.

They were leaning on a railing, staring down.

I kind of like it, Claire said. But it's too bad you can't see all the buildings . . .

He shrugged, he didn't care.

Really, they're amazing, you've never seen anything like it.

You don't have to pump the place up for me. I came, didn't I?

But I want you to like it, I want you to see —

I don't want to see anythin, he said, but you.

Oh, Tommy . . . Her eyes slid away from his, she lifted herself up on the railing. People used to jump from here, she said. Can you imagine?

No. He had his back to the view, he wouldn't turn around. Claire . . .

She looked at him, her heart began to pound. Let's get out of here, she said. Let's go.

She started to move but he grabbed her hand, he held her there.

Listen, he began, and then he stopped, he cleared his throat.

Behind them, a father lifted his child. Look at all the people down there, the little boy said. Are we as little as they are?

Tommy, she said, she couldn't stand it. Please —

Just wait a second, he said, his voice was raw. One second, okay?

There's nothing to see, you said so yourself, she said, she spoke very fast. Besides, aren't you hungry?

She saw his other hand reach into his jacket pocket then, saw that he was holding something there, something small, and her glance skittered off it, she jerked her hand from his like a reflex, already walking, fast, as if the decision to leave had been made, had been mutually agreed upon.

Hurry, she called. Let's catch the elevator — !

77

■   ■   ■

It was drizzling when they left, neither of them spoke. They had no destination but Claire kept walking, she didn't know what else to do, and Tommy walked just behind her, moving with grim purpose, block after block after block, his eyes on the sidewalk ahead.

Tommy, she said finally, she touched his arm. Wait . . .

It was a minute before he stopped.

What.

I think we should talk.

People threaded through them, brushed their backs, the tip of an umbrella snagged Claire's hair.

He looked at her as if she'd said the most ridiculous thing, as if he no longer knew who she was. He glanced around himself, his narrowed eyes the look of someone reconnoitering the totally alien. He pointed up at a movie marquee.

You seen that?

Claire shook her head.

They sat in the dark, the light blue over their heads, the music swelling loud all around them. Claire watched the flickering images, she saw the movie stars opening and closing their mouths, but she could not follow the plot, none of it made any sense. The theater was freezing. She pulled her knees up close and waited for the credits.

It was still drizzling when they walked out, and the silence between them had thickened into something solid, impenetrable. Claire stood in the street and put her hand out for a cab but none of them would stop, it was like a conspiracy.

Maybe we should take the subway, she began to say, just as Tommy stepped past her into the middle of the road and whistled, sharp sound between his teeth. Out of nowhere, a cab appeared. Tommy held the door open for her and she got in, but when she sneaked a glance at him, he was staring out the window.

We don't have to go home, she ventured finally, her voice felt rusted in her throat. We could do something else . . .

When he didn't answer, she sat back, she gave up. They rode the rest of the way in silence.

What will we do, she thought as they got out in front of the apartment building, and the image rose of herself and Tommy squared off in that small space, it was unbearable —

Hey, guys! Jade's voice floated out to her like a breeze, Claire's heart soared. She was just walking out, slim-hipped in a pair of faded Levi's, dressed like a boy.

Did you see anything? she asked Tommy.

Empire State Building, he said briefly.

Oh, she said, she looked at him curiously.

And then we went to the movies, Claire said, coming to stand next to him, as if nothing.

To the movies . . . ?

Yeah, neither of us had seen it, so . . . Claire hooked two fingers through one of Tommy's belt loops and he stiffened, but she didn't look at him and she didn't let go. Where're you going?

I don't know, thought maybe I'd shoot some pool . . . rainy Saturday afternoon, what else is there to do. She smiled, it was so easy for her. Want to come?

She stood before them like the third point of a triangle, glanced at them both; her invitation played no favorites.

Well, Claire began, but Tommy just said yes.

They went to a bar at Third Street and First Avenue, it had brick walls and wooden tables, a jukebox. Jade signed them up on a slate board, she put a quarter down.

I'm not going to play, Claire said.

What about you? Jade asked Tommy.

Sure.

Jade broke, she lined up three shots in a row; it made Claire think of geometry, her body a series of angles and curves as she bent over the table, at once masculine and suggestive, unconscious of anything but the cue, the balls, the solid thunk as they sank into their pockets.

Claire leaned against the far wall, the spectator. Tommy

never looked at her, he didn't smile, but she imagined she could detect the pleasure he derived from the game, the relief of concentration. He and Jade were evenly matched, but she marshaled luck as a force that could be corralled, random forces making the least predictable ball drop from sight. Luck was her partner, Claire thought, she counted on it, and it did not let her down.

When she sank the eight ball and won, Claire slanted a glance Tommy's way, as if this were proof of everything she hadn't been able to say — about Jade, about New York, about why she had left Alamogordo in the first place — but Tommy ignored her, he went to the bar and ordered another beer, didn't ask if she wanted one too.

Jade came to stand next to her, it was the first moment they'd had alone.

What's wrong? she asked, her manner casual, her voice quiet. Did something happen?

Claire shook her head, felt herself paralyzed by stubborn loyalty, could not say anything against him.

Excuse me. A tall young man touched Jade's arm, his manner diffident. You and your friend want to play doubles with us?

Not me, Claire said quickly, she pointed. Ask him.

At the bar, they saw Tommy shrug, look at Jade.

I will if you will, she said.

They were a better team than they had been opponents, they ran the table. Peripherally, Claire was aware of one man who had walked by to check out the scene, then stopped when he saw Jade. He had dark skin, black hair, black eyes. He saw Jade, his jaw slackened. When she bent over and drove another ball in, he grinned, the expression crude on his face, those white teeth lecherous.

All *right,* he said. He made a point of going up to the board and writing his name, all capitals in white chalk: Rico.

Hey, he said, can I get you a drink?

No thanks, Jade said, and though her smile was only politeness, it was all the encouragement he needed.

You play good, he kept saying, shaking his head in a slow caricature of amazement. Real good.

Claire watched him watching Tommy, and saw the exact moment when he put it together that Jade and Tommy were not together, that this was only a temporary duet. His chest puffed out in his pressed white shirt, a silver bolo tie the only thing that seemed to keep the buttons from popping. He turned to look at the board.

Yade, he said, and Jade turned around, surprised. My turn's comin up, he said, but I don't want to play against you, know what I mean?

She'd turned to get a cigarette and before she could turn back he was next to her, very close; he moved like a predator, had calculated the angle, the distance. She looked up, startled, frozen as an animal in the headlights of a car.

I seen you before, he said, and the back of his hand grazed her knuckles. You seen me?

Tommy stepped forward at the same time as Jade stepped back; she lit her cigarette as if nothing, but Claire saw how sharp she flicked her wrist to shake the flame out.

Don't touch me, she said.

Okay, I'll just look, he said, his eyes slid down her body. You like to be looked at, right?

She made a sound, contempt, and reached for her cue stick but he was ready; his hand came around her waist and then it slid up until the back of his hand was against her breast, all in the space of a gasp—

The cue stick went flying as the weight of Tommy's body hit Rico's, the table behind them fell over, somebody screamed. There was the sickening sound of bone hitting flesh, the terrible grunts of animal pain, the two men rolling on the floor, a violent parody of clumsiness —

Stop it — stop it — stop it! Claire's own voice a breathless shriek, she had Tommy's shirt in her hand but it ripped and she stumbled back, nearly fell. Then the bartender was there with two other men, they tore them apart, and everywhere there was a hideous mess of blood, spattered on the floor, and smeared on both their faces so she could not tell whose blood was whose.

Out! The bartender shoved Tommy. Get out!

It's not fair — Claire sobbing now, shaking. It was him — he was —

But the bartender pushed her, too, and Claire saw Tommy turning again; she grabbed his arm, dragged him up the sidewalk, cold air sharp and clear, finishing it.

He sat bent over in the cab, his arm against his nose, the flannel sleeve slowly growing darker. Ah Jesus, he kept saying, his voice thick with blood and pain, Ah God.

It was better at home when they washed it off; his nose wasn't broken. Jade filled a washcloth with ice, made him tip his head back while she held it to his face.

Please tell me there's something I can do, she begged. Please let me get you something —

But Tommy only stood, lurching awkwardly to the bedroom, head still back, water dripping from his face.

Oh God, I'm so sorry, Jade said. Claire, I'm so sorry . . .

It's okay, Claire said, I'll take care of him.

Jade left, and Claire tiptoed cautiously into the bedroom. He was stretched out on his back and the effort of his breathing gave his pain away. She sat on the edge of the bed, started to smooth the hair away from his forehead, but he jerked away.

Don't touch it.

I wasn't going to . . . She put her hand back in her lap, hurt. He didn't say anything after that, he kept his eyes closed.

Are you hungry? she asked. I could scramble some eggs . . .

No.

She was quiet for a long time then, listening to his breathing slow. Tommy, she said at last. This morning . . . at the Empire State Building . . .

I don't want to talk about it. He turned on his side, it took great effort. Just let me sleep, all right?

Okay, she said. All right.

21

IT WAS EARLY EVENING, THAT TIME OF DAY THAT SERVES AS a bridge between real daylight and true night, an uneasy hour, arduously slow in passing, full of misgivings. She watched television with the sound off but the light depressed her, dull blue, painful. She flipped through a magazine without stopping, all of the images in it artificial, taunting, giving rise to brief and false desires.

. . . Tommy? Calling his name so as not to wake him. She listened to him breathe, the distance between each breath a stretch as long and flat as the desert itself; it was the distance she listened for, the distance she took as permission. She tiptoed out.

Jade was home.

Claire, she said, pronouncing her name as if it were an invitation itself. Come in.

In Jade's apartment, it was night. The first thing Claire noticed in that darkened entrance was the scent, Jade's perfume, foreign as incense, and yet she recognized it, she knew what it was. I'm here, she thought, and felt happiness bloom inside her like a hothouse flower.

The place seemed huge at first, because it was nearly bare — the living room had no furniture save a light wicker chair shaped like a throne and a lamp with a faded fringed shade. Otherwise there were just some pillows heaped artlessly on the floor and in one corner, a box of books. The walls were white, left blank, the floors bare, there was an echo. It all conspired to give an impression of transience, the sense that the person who lived here had just moved in, or was about to move out; there was a lightness to it, a sense of motion, as if everything were poised and ready for flight.

It was the antithesis of home, of her mother's house, with its dark, unused sitting room, its furniture the heavy, functional furniture of an Air Force family ready to move, old and ugly, taking up too much space. Pieces a man had moved in, and there they'd stayed, rooted by her father's years and years of absence.

How's Tommy? Jade asked.

He's asleep, Claire whispered, as if afraid of waking him.

Oh, God. I hope he feels better when he wakes up.

She led Claire back to the bedroom, she was wearing nothing but a shirt, pale stockings that stopped at the tops of her thighs, you could see the brief band of elastic when she walked, the shirt unbuttoned save for one.

Her room was like the rest of the apartment, no furniture but the bed, one lamp, and glinting silver in the far corner, a beautiful old mirror. There were no curtains anywhere, just dark tarps tacked over the windows.

I have enough trouble sleeping, Jade said when she saw Claire looking at them, without all that light.

Multicolored candles were lit along the windowsill, wax had dripped and spilled down to the floor, red and yellow and blue. There was music playing, layered voices that echoed as if in a church, the words of the song unintelligible, like words from an ancient language.

Claire had the sense that she was somewhere else entirely now, somewhere even further than New York, some exotic unmapped resort, legendary.

Books lay open on the bed, gorgeous volumes, their open pages shining.

Smell them, Jade said, she held one up as if it were a bouquet, and Claire inhaled that peculiar aroma, clean, rich, the smell of centuries of knowledge, preserved.

Look at this one, Jade said, she stretched out on the bed, and Claire stretched out next to her while she turned the pages — Rousseau, Matisse, Picasso — one lush image followed the next in a wealth of brilliance, of genius, overwhelming.

I'm going back to school, Jade said. I'm going to study art — color, light, history, drawing, I want to learn everything —

She raked her hair back, spoke in a rush of energy.

Everything beautiful, she said, I'm going to see it all, primitive, classic, modern, everything — and then at least when I can't sleep I can close my eyes and picture it, the history of humanity in these amazing paintings —

Behind her, Claire saw a sketchpad lying across her pillow, a piece of charcoal.

Can I see? She reached over but Jade snatched it, she tossed it on the floor.

Wait, she said. Wait until I'm better.

They talked, their voices hushed as the music, their legs long behind them, their hair loose.

Your room, Claire said. It's so romantic.

Now that you're here.

No, it was like this when I came in.

Jade shook her head. It's women, she said. It's only when women get together . . . you can't have this with a man.

Why not? Claire asked, knowing already that it was true.

If you were a man, here, right now . . . Jade was smoking, slow and thoughtful. The room might look the same, but it would feel different. Everything would be . . . louder. It would all have to add up to something.

Like sex.

Exactly. The most obvious thing.

She was lying on her back, her shirt open. The space between her breasts was smooth, the skin there seemed to shimmer.

I keep thinking about that guy, Claire said, she covered her face. The one I went home with — I keep thinking I betrayed Tommy, and for *him* . . . oh God, it makes me sick.

Jade faced her.

You didn't do it to hurt him, she said, I know you didn't. You were just being young, and out in the world — that's what you came here for, isn't it?

I don't know, Claire said, I think if that's what I came here for, it isn't worth it.

But sometimes you have to go with your impulse, Jade answered, even if it turns out to be a mistake later. If you didn't, you'd only be betraying yourself.

You don't know Tommy, Claire said, he's not what you think he is, he's not — this isn't his element. He doesn't say that much but he's so smart, he knows me so well — he's amazing, you have no idea . . . he can tell temperature with his skin — I mean exactly, the exact degree . . .

Jade looked at her, fine blue smoke a wreath coming up from her cigarette, and suddenly she leaned over, her hand closing around Claire's, intense.

I want to know you, she said, I want to talk to you all night, I want to talk to you every day — I want to take you places I know, I want you to fall in love with New York —

She cut herself off, her smile mocking her own urgency, but her eyes didn't change, they never lost their focus.

Forget it, she said, she stood. Dance with me.

She turned the music up so it filled the room; there was no question. Claire got up, she didn't know what to do. She thought of Tommy, asleep down the hall, she started to say something but Jade put her hands on Claire's shoulders.

Like this, she said, leading, an easy, swaying step, she did not let go, until Claire's awkwardness dropped away and they moved with a single instinct, their heads touching, the music falling against them like waves.

They ignored the sound at first — it seemed distant, it seemed not to involve them, but then it grew louder, repeating itself, insistent, intrusive — and then they heard his voice.

Claire? You in there? Claire!

Oh my God, Claire said, frozen, it's Tommy . . .

It was Jade who let go first, Jade who disappeared into the dark hallway, Jade who let him in.

Sorry, she was murmuring. We had the music on.

He stood in the doorway of Jade's bedroom, he did not enter, and for a moment, Claire didn't recognize him; his eyes were rimmed with the beginnings of a dark bruise, his nose was misshapen. It gave him a clownish look, grotesque.

What time is it? Claire asked, searching for the appropriate thing to say, the most expected.

How do you feel? Jade asked. Can I get you something — some aspirin?

Tommy looked at her, he looked back at Claire, he didn't answer. His presence was huge, it shattered the atmosphere.

I'm hungry, he said, as if making the most final of pronouncements, and Jade's expression dissolved into a smile, surprised by the sudden absurdity of it all, that grin subversive, infectious. The corners of Claire's mouth quivered, she could not contain it. Tommy reached for her, his hand rough around her wrist.

Let's go.

Claire turned as he pulled her away, her eyes locked on Jade's; there was nothing to say.

22

TOMMY LET GO OF HER THE MINUTE THEY WERE IN THE HALL-way, he didn't say a word. Claire followed him into the apartment, angry with him now for making such a scene, embarrassed. He went into the bathroom and she heard him running water, splashing it over his face. She stood in the doorway.

Are you going to talk to me now or not?

He rubbed his face dry without touching his nose, his eyes. He put the towel down.

I got nothin to say.

Fine, she said then, you stay here, I'm going back to Jade's —

She turned around but he took her arm, made her face him.

Listen, he said, I didn't come all this way —

Let go of me. Her tone was icy. He released her, his eyes gone hard.

What's wrong with you? she asked, hated the plea she heard beneath her voice. Why are you acting like this?

You're the one *actin*, he said, words like a whip, fast, stinging, and Claire made a sharp sound, annoyance, she started to turn away, but he grabbed her arm again.

Listen to me. You can't trust her.

She looked at him in disbelief. You don't even know her.

Hey, I've known women like her before —

Her laugh harsh, it was too much. Women like Jade? Where — in Cloudcroft?

He looked at her from those darkened eyes and she felt his hatred, a penetrating flash.

You think she's so fuckin unique, he said at last. You're in for a big surprise.

She wrenched her arm away, walked into the bedroom. He didn't follow, and a minute later she heard the front door open and close. Her first instinct was to cry out, to run after him — take me with you, she thought, don't just leave me here —

But this wasn't his turf, came the next thought, he wouldn't know where to go, he would walk around the block and come right back, he wouldn't want to get lost . . .

Then she saw him through the kitchen window, how broadly shaped he was beneath the streetlight, how unhesitatingly he crossed the street, and she was devastated by his ability to project himself into the unknown, single and independent, by his ability to simply walk out without once looking back.

She waited twenty minutes, and when he didn't come back, she went back down the hall.

What happened? Jade asked.

He left.

Claire sat with her back against the wall, a pillow clutched to her middle.

Oh, Claire. I'm so sorry.

It's not your fault.

Maybe not, but if it weren't for me, he never would have gotten in that fight —

You didn't start it.

But then when he woke up, and you weren't there . . .

He didn't want me there.

88

Yes, he did, Jade said gently, she was sitting across from Claire. I know he did.

No, he just wanted to sleep.

But he didn't want you to leave —

I don't care. He doesn't talk to me, he won't talk to me — he says he wants me and then he has me and he thinks that's enough — but it isn't, it's *not enough*!

She wiped her face savagely, turned her head so Jade wouldn't see, but Jade scooted in close, unafraid of the violence of Claire's emotion, she put her arm around Claire's shoulders.

He'll come back, she said, her voice low, soothing. You'll see.

Hours later, Claire woke up to his hands on her hips, pulling her against him, his face in her neck. The room was pitch dark, it was as though her eyes weren't open, she kept blinking, whatever dream she had been having still sucking at her, dream like a swamp, dragging her back down —

Wait, she said, her mouth was thick. She tried to disentangle herself but his need was greater, it was as palpable as a third presence in the room, driving him.

Tommy —

He kissed her and she smelled the alcohol on him then, knew from the heavy forcefulness of his mouth that he was drunk, but still she responded, she could not help it, her arms locking around his back — he rolled on top of her, hands on her thighs declaring his need for her, and all the while he was muttering, words low and guttural in the bottom of his throat.

You're mine, he was saying, you're mine, you're mine, you're mine, you're mine, you're *mine* . . .

23

SUNDAY MORNING, TOMMY'S NOSE WAS SWOLLEN. HE looked like the losing prizefighter, his eyes gone purple, still puffy with sleep. He sat at the kitchen table in his jeans, swallowed three aspirin with his coffee. He moved as if everything hurt, he held his head in his hands, even his breathing was labored. Claire couldn't bear it, counteracted with an excessive cheerfulness — I'll make you breakfast, she said, whatever you want!

He held the aspirin bottle up, put it down, as if it cost too much to speak, and Claire was seized with a wrenching tenderness, she had to go and put her arms around him, lay her head against his back.

Oh, Tommy —

French toast, he said. With bacon.

She was happy to cook for him, she went to great lengths, heated the maple syrup in a pan, put cloth napkins on the table. Tommy touched the edges, he recognized them.

These are your mother's.

Claire remembered how violently she had protested when Ginny had insisted she take them. I don't have room, she'd said, I don't need them —

Yes, you do, Ginny had said, she had ironed them, wrapped them in tissue paper. It's the small things that count, she'd said. They make all the difference in the world.

Claire served Tommy, she brought him butter, orange juice, she sat across from him and watched him eat.

It's your last day in New York, she said. What do you want to do?

He pushed his plate away, he looked at her directly for the first time, and she felt it coming, some declaration, an ultimatum, and instantly she was agitated, leaning over to open the window, saying, It's so hot today, I can't believe it — we should go out, just for a walk or something . . .

She felt his eyes on her the whole while, she couldn't stop talking. We could go to Central Park, she said. It's huge, it goes on and on — that's a good idea, don't you think? We'll get out of the city, you'll like it —

She picked up his plate, she did not meet his gaze. I'll just wash up, she said, and then we can go.

■   ■   ■

There were days, Claire had seen them, when the city turned out its worst. That Sunday was one of them. There wasn't a breath of air, the sky was yellow. Garbage lined the sidewalks, empty coffee cups, newspapers, all the private debris of human life soiling the streets.

This fuckin city's nothin but walls, Tommy said. Even when you go out, you're still inside.

It will be better in the park, Claire thought, but it wasn't, it was worse. The trees looked wilted, the grass was brown. They saw a rat, long and mangy, scurrying along the bottom of a hill, its rubbery tail twitching behind it.

Look, Claire said, desperate to divert Tommy's attention, look at the horse!

It was pulling a carriage full of tourists up a small incline, its head bent low with effort, its eyes half closed behind the blinders. The driver had a whip, he kept using it, but the horse seemed inured to it, incapable of expending any more energy.

Jesus, Tommy said. He turned away. Should be against the law.

They're not all like that, Claire said.

You ridden one?

No, but I've seen —

Don't.

I wasn't going to.

She hated him then, hated the way his face looked, hated the stark animosity with which he regarded this landscape, her landscape, New York, hating him most of all for making her see it the same way — a sprawling ugliness, devoid of natural beauty, full of random cruelty.

They stopped and bought hot dogs with mustard from a vendor, stood side by side and ate them without speaking, without looking at each other, and then Tommy balled his napkin up in his fist.

It's gettin late, he said. I gotta go.

She packed his suitcase while he was in the shower, folding his shirts very carefully, although they were creased already, soiled.

He came out, a towel wrapped low around his hips, his stomach a man's stomach rising above it, flat and powerful, ridged.

First you serve me breakfast, he said, now you're packin my clothes — what're you, my wife?

He was only joking, but the word fell with an unexpected heaviness; she could not laugh. She shut his case briskly, said, There! I saved you these clothes, they were clean, I thought you would want —

Yeah, he said. Thanks.

And I was thinking, maybe we should call a cab, just in case, because sometimes —

Claire.

— they just don't stop, like yesterday, remember? But I guess it was raining, wasn't it, maybe that's why . . .

He let her talk until she trailed off, until she had to face him.

I bought you a ticket, he said then.

What?

He picked up his jacket, reached into the inside pocket, held a plane ticket out. She looked at it as if it were something foreign, something she had never seen before.

Here, he said, take it.

You should've asked me first.

Just take it, he said. You can reserve it whenever you want.

You should've asked me first, she repeated, she wouldn't touch it.

Goddammit . . . ! He threw it on the bed and sat down hard, put his head in his hands. This place ain't got nothin for you, Claire, why the hell —

You might be right, but I don't know that yet —

How long's it gonna take for you to figure it out?

I don't know, she said, her voice shaking. All I know right now is what's there for me if I go back —

He jerked his head up at that, eyes defying her to speak.

Just five hundred acres of desert, and you, thinking you don't even have to talk to me!

He stood, he yanked the towel from himself, dressed in

92

front of her, the act like an affront almost, how he shoved the shirttails into his jeans, how he zipped up.

Tommy, wait . . . I didn't mean it like that —

She tried to touch him but he pulled away.

You can't leave like this . . . Tommy, please . . .

But he just bent for his suitcase, his face so twisted up she couldn't bear it, she started to cry.

Tommy — ! She clutched him, head tight against his chest, would not let him go, until finally his arms came up around her. They stood there like that for a long time, they didn't move.

Okay, he said at last. I gotta go.

She followed him to the door, followed him onto the landing, she was still crying, she couldn't stop.

Tommy . . .

What? He stood on the top stair, his suitcase in his hand.

Wait for me, she thought, please wait for me.

Call me.

Something crossed his face, she couldn't read it. See you, he said, and he turned around, and walked down the stairs.

24

SHE HAD NOT KNOWN HOW HIS ABSENCE WOULD STRIKE her, like a blow to the gut, laying her low. There was a note from Jade under the door, Working nonstop — see you when I get off.

When Eileen called her with a job assignment the next morning, Claire was overcome with gratitude — she wanted nothing more than to move forward and into the world of daylight, of mundane tasks, of coffee and telephones and other people.

At home again, everything was as she'd left it, the cup in the sink, the rumpled quilt on the bed, the toes of her shoes touching in the corner; the stillness of a solitary life seemed to have already descended. She took the pins from her hair, hung her suit up, rinsed her stockings.

Evening fell, long shadows. She could hear the swish and wash of the traffic below, everything moving past; nobody called. This is my life here, she thought, without Jade. What if I'd never met her, she thought; all her known faces would be day faces, job faces. How meticulous everything would be, the order of the lonely. Evening would be her sworn enemy, long distance her salvation. It sprang forth, this vision, vivid as memory. She lit a lamp against the dark, tried to envision herself a pioneer, a political prisoner, someone who must call on the depths of her character to endure.

When she dialed home, her mother answered on the first ring.

Hi, Mom. It's me.

Paula?

Doesn't anybody ever recognize my voice anymore?

Oh, *Claire*. Well, it's not as if I hear it very often.

You could call me, too, you know, it's not like —

I have called *several* times, and all I ever get is that damn machine.

Why don't you ever leave a message?

Because, Ginny said. It makes me nervous.

Mother, it's just a machine. Everybody has one, I can't believe that —

What do I need a machine for? It's not as if I'm ever out — unless, of course, Ginny went on, I'm at the store.

I wasn't saying you should get one, you didn't let me finish my —

Yes well I can certainly think of better things to spend my money on.

There was a silence. In the background, Claire could hear the television, and she knew her mother was in bed, an afghan thrown over her lap, cold cream thick and white beneath her eyes.

Where's Paula? Did she go out?

She had a date.

A date . . . ! Claire said, no one in Alamogordo went out on dates; they just went out. A date with who?

Some man she met on base, I don't know. She hasn't introduced me, Ginny said, her voice was brittle. But she saw Tommy in town the other day, and she said he had two black eyes, he looked terrible, and he told her he got them in a fight in some bar in New York . . . !

It was a misunderstanding, Claire said, she did not try to explain.

My God, Ginny said. Are you sure you're safe up there alone?

I'm fine, Claire said. Besides, it didn't happen in my neighborhood, we were at this —

Well thank God for that, Ginny said. It isn't easy on me, you know, Claire, to be worrying about you all the time.

Then don't, Claire said, and the words came out harsh, a brutal command. In the brief silence that followed, Claire heard a clinking noise, the sound her mother's copper ashtray made against the night table when Ginny crushed her cigarette out.

I thought you were going to quit smoking this year, she said, her throat felt tight.

Ginny didn't answer, she said, You want to save your pennies, you better quit calling and get into the habit of writing instead — God knows it'd be nice to get some mail around here besides the damn bills.

I will, Claire said, I promise.

Lying in bed that night, Claire could not sleep. She kept thinking of the way Tommy's horses smelled in their stalls, warm, fragrant, blowing air through their noses when he came in to feed them. She always liked to go with him, liked to feel the coarse hair of their cheeks, the slow strength of their jaws crunching down when she fed them a carrot. And afterwards, the long walk back to the house, built small and close to the ground, thick white adobe walls cool even in the summer.

She turned over, she pushed the image from her mind, told herself she didn't want the consolation of that isolated place, imagined or otherwise; she had come to New York to wean herself of these things, to learn to need them no longer.

25

JADE CAME BY EARLY WEDNESDAY MORNING; SHE HAD THE look of someone who had not slept, her eyes squinting against the sunlight. They sat at the kitchen table together, Claire made coffee.

What've you been up to? Jade asked, she lit a cigarette.

Not much, Claire said, she could not admit her loneliness, her lack of self-sufficiency. Working, mostly.

Me too. Two girls quit last week and I've been doing nothing but doubles inside a smoky bar. What a nightmare. What a way to spend your days, Jade said, her voice hard, and Claire heard the flash of self-contempt there, something familiar, recurring.

At least you were making money. Maybe now you can take a couple of days off . . .

Yeah. Like the rest of my life, Jade answered, her tone unyielding.

You're going to quit?

Jade looked at her.

You make it sound so simple.

You don't have to stay there. You could do anything you wanted.

I could be famous, Jade said, and though she pronounced it ironically, Claire knew how she cherished those words, how close she held them. She stubbed her cigarette out without warning, leaned over to push the window wide.

The weather changed, she said, can you feel it?

It was the end of October, the sky a blue so sharp it almost hurt to look at it. Winds swept the air clean, lifted the hair from their faces as they walked, island winds, ocean winds, and Claire held on to her youth and told herself, I am young, everything is ahead of me, but it wasn't enough, somehow, and it was too much.

They went uptown, they walked down Fifth Avenue,

walked in a river of people, so much of everything Claire could not speak. I live here now, she told herself, but in her own mind it rang false. This wasn't life, it was spectacle — young black men on bicycles ran red lights in tight shorts with racing stripes, and there were seeing-eye dogs next to blind men rattling cups full of yellow pencils, women carrying Pekingese dogs in their arms, sturdy Greeks selling lamb on skewers from carts on the corner, shouting out. She looked up, followed the swift clear lines of the buildings until her head was tilted all the way back. She wanted only the future.

They walked past Rockefeller Center, Atlas with the world heavy on his shoulders, Saks Fifth Avenue, and then Jade took her elbow and led her into the wide, dim cool of St. Patrick's Cathedral, an oasis in the midst of chaos. Inside, their footsteps echoed up the aisle. Old women with headscarves dotted the pews, their lips moving, knotted fingers murmuring over rosary beads. Jade dipped her fingers in holy water and brushed them along the back of Claire's neck. The water slid down past her shirt collar, shockingly cool.

They sat for a moment on the far side of an empty pew. The afternoon light shone through high arches of stained glass, and the hushed cool settled over them, fell lightly on Claire's head and shoulders. She breathed in deeply. She could smell incense, the perfume of religion in the air, somber and sweet. She thought of Alamogordo, and everything — the shop, her mother, her sister, even Tommy and the ranch, all of Cloudcroft — was contained inside that thought, a closed box. She knew it so well, so well. She knew what she would be doing if she were there right now, what she would be thinking, what she would be feeling. Just remembering it filled her with the agitation of a prisoner who has made a narrow escape, who might never have escaped at all. But she had, she told herself, she had, and here she was now, sitting quiet and wondrous in this cathedral, and she felt mystery had pierced the core of her life like a thin ray, a thread of divinity, and immediately she turned to Jade, wanting to tell her, to present it as a gift, but Jade's eyes were closed and there was a distance in her face, sudden and insurmountable. Claire held her hands between her knees and prayed, incoherent in the back of her mind; she didn't know what she was praying for.

26

BACK DOWNTOWN, ALL THE STORE WINDOWS WERE DECO-rated with orange pumpkin cutouts, cardboard witches dangling from brooms, Freddy Krueger masks.

I'm no good at Halloween, Claire said, they were walking along Second Avenue. I never know what to be.

But it's the one day you can be anything, Jade said, she tugged the ends of Claire's red hair. You could be the devil herself.

The words provoked a vivid memory, of Paula taking her around when she was six, seven, eight, Claire dressed in the same costume three years in a row, red leotard and a rubber band that secured devil horns around her head, and every year it was smaller — by the end her wrists stuck out, they had to put a patch in the crotch to make it fit her new height. She had hated that costume after the first time, but her mother made her wear it anyway — she had sewn it herself, the red velour was expensive. You look so *cute,* she always said, stepping back, one eye squinted against the cigarette in her mouth. The last time, Claire had cried, saying how it pinched, and Ginny had scared her by crying too, her face like a bad mask with black mascara running down.

You don't know what I've done for you, she'd said. I've given up my whole life for you!

She was startled back to herself when someone rapped on a window, a hard-knuckled sound, and they both turned and saw the fortune-teller, a young Hispanic girl in a cotton print dress, her eyes smudged-looking, her mouth wide. She beckoned to them, she rapped on the window again, said, I tell your fortunes, half price, half price, her voice made thin by the glass between them.

They went in. The small salon was separated from the rest of the apartment by a thin curtain, and behind it they could hear the sound of something frying, the smell of garlic strong in the air, and somewhere a radio was on, the announcer's voice a high, controlled frenzy.

They sat on a worn red velvet loveseat while the sorceress hastily lit a stick of pungent incense, thick, cloying. Jade sat across from her, and the young woman shuffled a pack of cards, dealt quickly, talking the whole time, her feet planted wide, her skirt falling between her knees.

Here you got diamonds, lots of diamonds, this mean good luck, mean you got great good fortune, like money, you know what I mean? Like you come into good money soon, you don't work so hard, it come easy, you know what I mean? And only one club here this is good, this means nothing bad in your life, only bad thing like easy, you know what I mean?

What about love? Does it say anything there about love? Jade leaned forward, studying the cards.

I'm just about saying that, how much good love there is, see you got here jack of hearts, jack of hearts mean man in your life who love you, this man do anything for you, know what I mean? He is under your spell nothing will change this —

Suddenly the thin curtains separated and an older woman came out, she seized the young girl's ear, shouted something unintelligible.

Ay! The girl wrenched herself away, the cards spilling on the floor, and fled outside. The woman shouted after her, but she was gone. She threw her hands up in the air, shut the door, faced her customers.

You want your fortunes told, ten dollars each, I do both hands, ri an lef, this is bargain prices.

She was heavyset, her legs thick under her black dress, and the undifferentiated heft of her bosom supported a crucifix displaying Christ's torture in tiny, jeweled detail.

No thanks, Jade said, trying to inch around her.

You come sit, the woman ordered. I do your fortunes ri, I give you good fortunes, cheap but true.

She tried to hustle them back into the seat but they followed the young girl's example and ran for it, their laughter loud in the street.

Watch where you're going, a man shouted, he had to veer to get out of their way. Fucking maniacs!

27

THEY DUCKED INTO A STORE ON THE CORNER OF SECOND AVenue and Seventh Street, a place where ratty antique twenties dresses hung from the rafters, and there were heaps of wigs piled in plastic barrels, a pyramid of rhinestone-studded glasses and racks of dusty shirts and dresses and jackets, each one different from the rest. The woman behind the counter had a shock of dyed black hair and she wore a pretty beaded cardigan with the sleeves cut off. Her arms were very pale and the bracelets on her wrists jangled when she moved. She sat on a high stool smoking and looked around as if she had nothing to do with the store, and even less with the people in it.

But when Jade found a light beaded cap with rows of glass beads hanging down and another fringe of beads for bangs, the woman reached under the counter and gave her a handful of bobby pins. Jade pinned her hair and put the cap on. She pushed the corners of her eyes up.

Nefertiti, the woman said, momentarily roused from her apathy. Absolutely. And I've got just the thing to go with it — I hate to sell it . . .

She lifted a long pole with a hook on the end and brought down a full-length tunic-like dress made of a thin gold fabric so faded it was almost transparent.

It looks like nothing hanging, you have to try it on.

Claire found a skeleton-painted bodysuit, she was tugging it on when she heard Jade come out to stand before the mirror. She peeked through the curtains. Jade was stunning. A woman from another era, queenly and exotic, the outline of her body barely visible through the light material.

Yeah, the woman said reluctantly. It was made for you.

It's beautiful, Jade said. The glass beads around her face made small, rich noises when they clicked together. Light glinted off her cheekbones. I'll take it.

She saw Claire's face in the crack of the curtains then, she said, What have you got on? Come out here, let me see . . .

No, Claire said. It's nothing —

Come on, Jade said, she was already reaching in, pulling her out. Don't be shy —

Claire glanced at herself in the mirror and immediately turned away. She looked at Jade, how the costume transformed her, and felt ridiculous standing beside her, that reflection revealing nothing but painted bones stretched wide over her frame, she couldn't stand it.

It's awful, she said, I'm taking it off —

But Jade held her back, she said, Claire, it's great! Look how sexy you look —

I look fat, I hate it —

What? You're crazy —

But Claire wouldn't listen, she twisted away, fingers already tearing at the zipper, and in the dusty dressing room, the suit clung to her, the zipper caught, she thought she would suffocate, she swore, her voice strangled.

Hey, watch out, the saleswoman called, don't rip it!

Claire balled it up, she threw it in the corner.

She was zipping up her jeans when she heard someone say Jade's name, a woman's voice, low, acerbic.

. . . hope you're not spending all that hard-earned money in here, she was saying.

I was just leaving, Claire heard Jade answer. Where you headed?

Claire tugged her boots on quick, but when she came out, Jade was gone. She walked the perimeter of the store in disbelief, ignored the saleswoman's bored gaze until she spoke.

If you're looking for your friend, she said, she left.

Oh, Claire said, as if it were something she knew, something she had just forgotten, that's right.

She walked out fast, looking straight ahead, but Jade wasn't there, she was nowhere, and instantly Claire was lost, the sensation a sickening weight in the pit of her stomach. I can get home from here, she told herself, I know where I am —

It was when she turned to look for the street sign that she finally saw Jade, standing on the far corner talking to three other people, a woman and two men. Still dazed, Claire waited for her to glance back, to look for her, but she never did. After a minute, Claire walked up to them, smiling tentatively.

. . . Nothing, Jade was saying, she hardly glanced at Claire. Maybe later.

Who's your friend? The woman's face was chiseled, beautiful, the face of a lynx. She wore a black leather jacket over a fishnet T-shirt that showed the perfect undercurve of her breasts. She seemed unconscious of her self-exposure; she slouched on one hip, terrifyingly chic.

Claire, Jade said, this is Deirdre, Andrew, and . . . ?

Gregory, the second man said, and rolled his eyes, as if this were some kind of joke.

Hi, Claire said, supremely conscious of the way the first man was looking at her, eyes roving quickly down her body, then up again, a cold scrutiny, utterly uninterested.

Tina's having a party tonight, he said to Jade, at some loft over on Mercer.

Apparently she's been house-sitting for one of her sugar daddies, Deirdre said. Little does he know . . .

We heard free X, Andrew said.

They all laughed, and Claire smiled, as if she understood the joke.

You can come if you want to, Gregory said, he yawned. I doubt we'll stay long.

I can't, Jade said. Not tonight.

Oh, bring your little friend, Andrew said, as if Claire were not even there. I'm sure Tina won't mind.

No, I've got to work tomorrow, I don't want to stay out late, Jade said.

You're working? Deirdre asked, and Jade nodded, she lifted her hand in a wave, she was already walking away.

Which shift? Deirdre called after her, but Jade didn't seem to hear.

I'll see you, she called, she turned around. Claire glanced over her shoulder and saw Deirdre looking after them, saying something, and moments later, Andrew and Gregory burst out laughing.

Claire flushed hot, she turned around but Jade was ahead of her, she crossed the street against the light, moved in front of oncoming traffic, and Claire stopped, abrupt on the corner.

Move, lady — ! A skinny teenager, his head shaved, pushed past her, and Claire felt blind fury, tears stung her eyes, her arm swung back as if to hit him, but instead she turned on her heel and headed the other way.

Claire! Jade caught up with her halfway down the block, grabbed her arm. Where are you going?

Home, Claire said, although she was so disoriented she had no idea if she was going the right way, she didn't care.

Wait, Jade said, her jaw set, tense, but Claire tugged out of her grasp. Jade looked at her, wounded.

That's the second time you haven't introduced me to your friends —

They're not my friends, they're people I *work* with, Jade said, as if this were explanation enough. Claire felt her heels hard against the pavement, she said nothing, her silence hostile.

You're too good for them, Jade went on, I won't —

What's that supposed to mean?

I don't want you to know them, Jade said with a sudden violence that surprised her, I don't want you to know anything about them, or ever —

She stopped, she took a deep breath.

It's something I want to get away from, she said finally.

Claire stood with her hands shoved deep in her pockets, she could not shake her sense of alienation.

You're the one I want to be with, Jade said, she slid one

hand down Claire's arm and into her pocket, fingers unclenching Claire's fist. Believe me.

28

JADE INSISTED ON TAKING HER TO DINNER THAT NIGHT, THEY went to a restaurant that served French-Vietnamese food. It had a colonial feeling, the walls were painted pale pink, the bar dark green, heavy teak ceiling fans rotating slowly overhead. It was crowded, the tables set only inches apart.

Jade ordered for both of them, hot clear soup, sublimely spiced, fish wrapped in lemon grass, a bottle of cold wine. Their waiter had exquisite features, served them as if he did not, in fact, really work there.

Two women sat next to them, sharing a piece of cheese-cake, talking intensely. One of them wore tortoiseshell sun-glasses and a scarf that looped around her breasts, leaving her shoulders bare.

I was awake all night last night, she was saying. Panicking. Until five in the morning. I have everything in my life except, you know, happiness. Real happiness.

They both glanced at Jade, Jade who sat across from Claire, smiling as if in possession of deep joy, a joy that needs nothing to touch it off, a joy evoked by life itself, by the candle in the middle of the table, by a bottle of cold wine. Her eyes were charcoaled, they were rich-looking, she was rich-looking, luxu-rious, she possessed depths, every time Claire looked at her there was something new, another facet, gleaming and elegant, rising from an invisible source.

She asked Claire a thousand questions, she leaned forward, ready to laugh, she leaned back, listening, swept her hair off her face, smoked with deep pleasure. Her happiness was contagious, it swept over Claire and brought her in, made her feel essential. She saw other people turning their way, too, women with con-stricted faces, and men, wanting what they had, looking at Jade. Claire looked too, again and again, looked when she thought

Jade wouldn't notice, thinking if only she could pin the source of her beauty down, hold it like a picture in her mind, she could stop staring, but she knew that Jade's beauty would elude the heaviness of memory.

That costume you bought, Claire said. It makes me think of the time I saw you in the deli . . . you had a long dress on, and the cat jumped on your shoulder . . .

You didn't get anything to wear tomorrow, did you.

I don't care. I hate Halloween.

You can't hate Halloween. It's my birthday.

You're kidding.

I'm not. I wish I was.

Why didn't you tell me?

I just did.

Are you going to celebrate?

I'm going to work.

Afterwards, then — you have to celebrate, you have to do something.

There's nothing to celebrate — I'm going to be thirty years old, and I haven't accomplished a fucking thing.

That's not true.

It is true, Jade said, but who cares. It's Halloween, I'm going to be somebody else anyway — I'm going to be Nefertiti.

Claire looked at her and thought how that birthdate fit — she was the queen of disguises, her capacity to transform a fluid thing, a shifting of the ions in the air, a static charge.

Jade poured the last of the wine, she changed the subject.

What do you hear from Tommy?

Nothing.

You haven't called him?

Claire shook her head.

Does that mean . . . did you break up?

No. I can't break up with him. Even if I did . . .

She refolded the napkin on her lap, made the edges meet.

He'd wait for me, she said, and the words came slow as confession, admitting themselves to her against her will. Forever.

How do you know? Jade asked, and it wasn't skepticism in

her tone, but a craving for assurance that Claire heard, the need for guarantee. She looked at Jade, and the assurance rose inside her, solid as flesh — the way Tommy loved her, it was beyond words.

There's no one else for him, she said. There's no one else there.

There's always someone else, Jade said, that retort low and hard, but when Claire flinched she moved, her hair fell forward and hid her face, and when she brushed it back she was smiling, as if she couldn't take any of it seriously any longer.

It's just a distraction anyway, she said. Men, sex.

From what?

I don't know. Work. Real work. She smiled again. I don't know what it is, she said. I just know what it isn't.

She looked over Claire's head, caught the waiter's eye. Waiting for the check to come, Claire was seized with something like thirst, but more so, indescribable, primal — it was wrenchingly physical, it came from her body, the deepest part, the marrows of her bones. She reached for a glass of water and drank it until it was gone, knowing before she put it to her mouth that it wasn't water she wanted, and not knowing what it was.

Afterwards, they went to a place Jade knew in the West Village, it was off a narrow cobblestoned street, through an unmarked door and past a courtyard, a dark bar low-ceilinged as a cave.

No one knows this place is here, Jade said, unless they know it's here.

The bar was full, mostly men, standing, drinking beer, talking loud. A television was on, a football game, mud-stained uniforms, small moving specks of light.

Jade went to order from a bartender who stood wiping glasses in a white apron, his forearms thick, a man's man. She said something that made him smile. Hidden in the corner of that dark little bar, Claire watched him handing her the change, watched Jade turn around, and for an instant everything slowed down, the whole picture took on the quality of memory, the light, the scarred wooden tables, the sound of a radio playing in the back, and she thought, I'm alive, right now, right now, and it flowed over her in waves, she could hardly bear it.

Around her, a wild roar went up. Touchdown, the men shouted. Touchdown!

29

THERE WAS NO WORK FOR CLAIRE THE NEXT MORNING, BUT she went up to the agency anyway, waited there for hours. Eileen hardly spoke to her; she was being punished, Claire thought, for not having called in yesterday.

She was a nonentity when she finally rose to go, scooped hollow from having sat there for so long, invisible. She walked down the street with her hands in her pockets, a cold wind whipping her hair back into her face. It was late afternoon and the weather had changed, there were clouds moving in, they blocked the sun, cast the city in shades of gray. She stopped at a small nondescript restaurant and had a hot chocolate, craving the warmth of it, the comfort, but she felt conspicuous, she could not stay. She lingered at a newsstand, read her horoscope in all the magazines; none of them said the same thing, but she studied them all, hoping to divine some kind of directive from their cryptic, blithe advice. When she finally looked up, dazed, she couldn't recall a word she'd read.

Broadway was weird with Halloween; it was everywhere. Tall women with pale faces and red lips, their faces grave — witches, Claire thought, the real thing. There were small beings in demon masks, children or dwarves, Claire couldn't tell, she averted her eyes. She saw men wearing curly green wigs, sequins pasted around their eyes, their smiles distorted, terrifying, and there were eggs smashed at intervals along the street, dried-up yolk like still lifes of violence. She kept her head down. She knew exactly where she was but she counted blocks like a blind person, dogged by an irrational fear of getting lost.

She was almost at the Lebanese man's deli on the corner

when she saw a black man in whiteface shambling down an alley. He stopped in front of a trash can, picked two aluminum cans out and put them in a bag. His eyes grazed Claire's, inscrutable behind the thick grease of his theatrical makeup. She could not tell how old he was, whether he was really poor or just eccentric, and as he passed her, she had the odd feeling of having accidentally witnessed a religious act.

She veered into the deli, desperate for simple human interaction. The deli man came out from the back, wearing a Nancy Reagan mask.

Hello! he said. The mask was grotesque, his eyes brown and alive peering through the holes. Happy Halloween time! What you need!

Just this, Claire said, she was holding a package of cupcakes. And birthday candles — do you have birthday candles?

Birthday candles, yes! How many you need, I got!

Thirty, she said.

The deli man was incredulous but Nancy Reagan retained the same, fixed, horrible smile. You joke me!

It's not for me, she said, it's for my friend.

Yes, okay! he said, and then, incongruously, Just say no!

She went home, resigned to spending the rest of the day alone, but when she walked in, there was a note from Jade under the door, bold charcoal slashed on white paper.

Getting off early, she'd written. Celebrate with me.

30

THEY WALKED OUT INTO THE NIGHT, THE AIR WAS FRESH AND strong and chilly, the wide avenue glittered beneath their feet. Jade wore her costume, she'd painted her eyes with a single sweep of black liner, her scent came off her like a breeze. This must be what it's like, Claire thought, to be famous.

Diamonds and pearls! A man's voice, soaring from an alleyway, disembodied. *Stu*-pid women — *cra*-zy pussy!

His eyes gleamed in the shadows, his mustache was a dark fringe.

Baby, come over here, I got somethin for you —

Just ignore him, Jade muttered, she took Claire's hand.

You girls gonna get a nasty yeast infection that way! he shouted after them, his laughter more insulting than his words.

Men, Jade said, she wouldn't look back. I'm sick to death of them. You're my date, she said. I'm with you.

She stepped into the street, raised a hand, and beneath her coat, her dress was like a beacon. A cab braked hard.

Mars, Jade told the driver, and he nodded; he needed no other direction.

They saw the crowd a block away, a throng of people six feet deep around the stairs leading up and into a warehouse, from which two doorpeople reigned, both of them black-clad, slouched in a kind of boredom, terminally fashionable. Their eyes roved the crowd, they nodded imperceptibly here, there, ignored the hands that waved, even those fists clutching ten-, twenty-dollar bills.

You, they said. You, you.

Fuck this shit, someone in front of them said. Let's go someplace else.

Claire turned to Jade, filled with the same immediate hopelessness.

Maybe this wasn't such a good idea . . .

Look, Jade said. Look at the moon.

They both gazed up, and Jade turned, offered her profile, neck curved back, the glass beads swinging against it. When Claire glanced back at those stairs, the doorman was looking at them. He pointed.

Come on, Jade said, and they pushed through the crowd with their heads down, wearing the false humility of the chosen.

Even before they walked into the first room, the music was overwhelming, that deep bass beat throbbing through the walls, vibrating up the floor, filling her veins with a strange buzz, infiltrating her being. There was no question of liking it or not liking it; at such volumes, she was simply incorporated.

But she wasn't prepared for the spectacle inside — wild lights that played over the crowd, red, blue, strobe white, making everyone look savage somehow, making the sweat on their faces gleam, catching the shine of flesh — it was like entering an orgy, Claire thought, an assault on every sense, shocking. People were dancing, their skin gleaming and wet, throwing their heads around, ecstatic. Claire shrank back, intimidated by the hard urban beauty of the faces that posed against the walls, but Jade was in her element. She was already moving through the crowd, moving with the music, reaching back to catch Claire's hand, shouting, Let's get a drink!

She led Claire through the room and up labyrinthine stairwells, where people who looked as if they lived in clubs were draped over the banisters, young women with impossibly perfect skin powdered dead white, lips painted in Cupid's bows, their outfits outrageously minimal; one girl wore nothing but a gaucho hat, purple lace tights and a piece of black duct tape over each nipple. She met Claire's stare, blowing smoke from the side of her mouth.

There're three other floors, Jade told her. And a roof.

They went all the way up to the top, where the ceiling was close, the pipes painted neon, and dilapidated velvet couches filled the floor, the air thick with smoke.

They sat on a plush scarlet loveseat, their knees touching, ordered margaritas. Jade turned to her, those features exquisitely framed by the cap of beads, but she seemed unaware of herself, focused on Claire as if she were the only other person in the room.

I've been drawing a lot lately, she was saying, with charcoal. You hold it between your fingers — like this — it's so different from the way you hold a pen, or a pencil — remember how hard it was to learn that when you were a kid? It's all about restraint, like civilization — with charcoal, it's just the opposite — it's about instinct, it's your first impulse, it extends out from you, you can't control it — it's so black, it smudges on everything, it's like life . . .

What are you drawing?

Women, Jade said. The women at work, mostly — it's like I'm seeing them for the first time. I sit and stare, waiting for them to reveal something, I don't know what — who they really are, how it comes through in the lines of their bodies, the way they move —

Her poise had left her and in its stead was a kind of nocturnal energy, intense, compelling — it was in her voice when she spoke, in her limbs when she moved, in her restless hands.

No men? Claire asked.

Jade made a gesture, dismissive. Men are so simple — all their lines are straight and hard, they keep your wrist in the same position — they never show you anything.

Listening, Claire felt herself becoming increasingly lucid, the haze of smoke and music receding. It was like New Year's, she thought, like being on the verge of something new, unknown but inevitable, and she was filled with anticipation, for nothing but the next moment, the next hour.

I don't miss anyone, she said, she had not known she was going to say it, I don't miss any place, or any thing.

It took Jade off-guard, her smile was sudden. She looked away as if she wanted to hide her pleasure, it made Claire want to give her everything, there was not enough —

Hi y'all. A guy stood before them, a beer in his hand. What's up?

Jade burst out laughing, she grabbed Claire's hand. Come on, she said. Let's dance.

Fucking New York women, they heard him saying as they left. Fucking bitches, every one.

They ran down the stairs toward the music coming from the second floor. Over the inescapable beat, a woman's voice sang, smooth as honey.

it's our time/time today

Jade knew the words, she sang them, moved in so close their heads were touching.

the right time is here to stay/stay in my life, my life always

Claire was flushed with heat, with happiness; there was hardly any room. Jade held her by the waist, sang in her ear.

keep on movin/don't stop

They danced to songs that had no apparent climax, that never ended but blurred into each other, one after the other, and always the same beat, low, continuous. It made her think of oppression, endurance, stamina.

I'm so hot, Jade shouted, and though her face had color, her skin was cool, she wasn't sweating — there wasn't enough flesh on her body to make her sweat, no insulation between her bones and her skin. She must be cold all winter, Claire thought, cold in her bed alone at night. Jade put her mouth close to Claire's ear so she wouldn't have to shout, and her voice vibrated in Claire's head.

Let's have another drink . . . !

People lounged, artfully draped, and stood at the small bar set up against the wall, but before they could reach it a young black man stepped in front of them, lifted his hands.

If I had nothing to offer I wouldn't waste your time, he said, he was talking to Jade. I saw you on the floor out there, and you got some moves, but you gotta let your shoulders go. Like this.

He leaned back and it wasn't so much that his shoulders shook as that a line, a current of motion, passed through them, a slow wave.

You try, he said.

I was just going to get a drink, Jade said, her smile perfunctory, polite.

It's a slow thing I'm telling you, it is no big expenditure of energy, the young man said. He had an easy manner, the faint traces of an island rhythm in his voice. His skin was the color of polished mahogany, flawless in this quiet light.

Watch me. He did it again, and then he gently pushed Jade's shoulders back. Like this. He manipulated them and she started to laugh.

No, he said, you're good, you're good, you just loosen up

112

a bit — check it out. He did it again, faster this time, and then he was dancing all around her, his body was fluid, shoulders moving and his hips keeping the beat. Jade was still smiling, but she stepped back, and that slight distance made her part of the audience, removed her from his grasp. He stopped.

I seen you before, he said.

I don't think so. The smile never left her face, but there was something in her eyes — the alarm, Claire thought, of recognition.

Yeah, I know it . . . you're a dancer, am I right?

She shook her head but she started moving, back toward the dance floor, and as he followed, his grin triumphant, she threw Claire a look. Wait for me.

Claire stood at the bar, she did not know what to do with herself. She met the bored glances that came her way with a look of defiance, addressing them in her mind. I live here, she thought. This is where I'm from — but the sentiment rang hollow within her, it fell flat. A smoke machine began to fill the room with its white steam, the smell of it sickening and sweet, like the smell of anesthetic. She covered her eyes for a moment, covered her nose. I have to get out of here, the thought came over her like panic, like the inability to breathe, but when she looked up, there was Jade, walking toward her, smiling, the girl in gold, that smile like a spotlight, making heads turn to see who she was smiling at, and Claire was lifted from the crowd, transported.

Let's get out of here, Jade said.

31

THERE WAS A LINE OF CABS WAITING OUTSIDE, THEY JUMPED into the first one, Jade leaning in the window to tell him the address.

Fourteenth Street and Ninth Avenue.

Where we going?

You'll see. Jade was a vixen in the backseat, her eyes dark,

113

her dress gilded, and the fabric clung to her body, Claire could see the curve of her breast through it, the narrow line of her waist.

Fourteen an Nine, the cabbie announced minutes later. Jade insisted on paying, she wouldn't take Claire's money, gave the driver twice the fare.

Overtipping is one of the joys in life, she said, and I just happen to be rich this weekend.

They got out. They were still in the meatpacking district, the streets cobblestone, the buildings big and dark, the smell of blood faint in the air, rank. Claire looked around, could see nothing but a white-lit sign. Hot Bagels, it said.

This way, Jade said, heading toward it. Halfway there, Claire saw the black velvet ropes set up outside a closed door, a big black woman with very short hair standing just inside them.

Ladies, she said as they approached, and lifted the cord to let them pass.

They pushed through the door, Jade first, and instantly they were engulfed by air so warm it was steam, music like swamp music that seemed to rise from the floor to fill the air with sound, and barely inches from the door, a crowd of bodies was dancing, everybody close, hips swinging rhythmic and slow.

A young, pretty girl was sitting behind a table, her head shaved, her nose pierced by a thin gold ring, a rose tattooed on the top of one shoulder.

Five dollars! she said, she had to shout, and Jade gave her ten, took Claire's hand.

Let's get a shot of tequila!

They started to make their way through the crowd, and looking up, Claire saw a go-go girl dancing on the bartop, her breasts bared, wearing nothing but a pair of black leather hotpants. She looked about eighteen, her body was lithe, and she danced with her arms over her head, eyes half-closed, smiling. Shocked, Claire glanced around to see if anyone else was staring, and it was only then that she noticed there wasn't a man in the room.

Two shots of Cuervo! Jade was still holding her hand. The women at the bar smiled at them, and Claire averted her eyes, did not know where to put them. Slides were being projected from the back of the room — women kissing, women holding hands, naked women, women laughing, women flashing peace signs.

Jade turned toward her, her eyes were brilliant. Here, she said, drink this.

They downed the shots together, no salt, no lime. A woman rose from the barstool next to them, and Jade patted the empty seat.

Sit here.

The alcohol made her lightheaded, filled her with a kind of courage. She tossed her hair back, looked around. They're only women, she told herself, just like me —

It came to her then, the difference she felt, it was like being in another culture — the looks she intercepted were appreciative, they were inviting, and she realized it was her own attitude, that instinctively assumed feminine arrogance, hostile, proud, competitive, that was the foreign element; here, she was at sea.

Don't they let any men in here? she asked. At all?

Not unless they're gay.

It was weirdly disorienting, this total absence of men; she could not stop looking through the crowd for that male face, but at the same time, there was something profoundly relaxing about it, as if some subtle threat, dormant but pervasive, had been temporarily lifted.

Want to go downstairs? Jade asked. It's quieter.

The women made room for them to pass, and Claire was aware of a thousand perfumes, of the delicacy with which they stepped back, so that she only just grazed them, fabric whispering against fabric.

Sorry, they murmured, but their eyes were bold, their smiles daring.

Did you see those two, Claire heard someone say behind her. My God . . .

Downstairs was like being at someone's cool basement party. There was light, there was a television, a pool table. Women sat at little tables, Claire saw them all. There were starkly beautiful Latin women with wild black hair and sensuous mouths, young girls dressed boyish in plain white T-shirts and Levi's, and women in miniskirts and sheer blouses, their perfectly manicured nails wrapped around tall, cool cocktails.

Jade sat among them like a queen, her body made of long, fluid lines, her smile like the centerpiece of the room, the point of light toward which everyone turns during a pause in the conversation, as if for reassurance.

You've been here before, Claire said.

I come here sometimes, Jade said, when I can't stand the sight of another man.

Jade had ordered two margaritas from a passing waitress, and now she was paying again, she pushed Claire's money back at her.

I'm taking you out tonight, she said, she smiled. I'll be the man.

Claire laughed, aware of the alcohol in her system, how it heated everything.

I should be the man, she said. Look at me —

She was wearing jeans, boots, a simple black shirt buttoned low.

Clothes don't count, Jade said, her authority irrefutable. You're the girl — you're the original starry-eyed girl, Claire.

Oh, and you're just a regular guy, right?

Jade laughed, too, she could not suppress it.

I would never, she said, be regular, but.

She lifted a hand, counted off on her fingers. I am tough. I am hardened. And I am paying.

You're paying, Claire conceded, but that's it.

Oh, Jade said, she shook her head. You don't know the half of it.

Then why don't you tell me, Claire said, she sat forward in her seat, hands holding the edges of the table, she knew there was something.

116

Jade struck a match, and the sound of the flare, the sudden, sharp smell of sulfur, the light on Jade's skin as she bent close to the flame, her face full of the reverence of concentration, gave the act a sense of ritual, erotic, sacred.

I thought, Claire said, you wanted to quit smoking.

Jade looked at her, she let the smoke drift from her mouth, from between her teeth, and it rose, an ephemeral, floating mask, briefly obscuring her eyes.

It's not the smoke, she said, it's the screen I need.

Claire, she said.

Claire waited, but Jade did not continue. After a moment, she put the cigarette out, she pushed her chair back, held her hands out.

Dance with me, she said.

Upstairs, the crowd had grown, they filled the floor. Framed in the window that faced out on the street, another go-go girl danced, a beautiful black woman with myriad cornrows in her hair, her body curved and solid. Claire's eyes kept straying to her half-naked form, the routine joy she seemed to take from this steady bump and grind, and she thought it must be the audience of women that transformed the act, making it all seem innocent somehow, celebratory.

Jade moved through the dense mass of moving bodies, she had Claire's hand, she led her to the middle, turned around. She put her hands on Claire's hips, so close Claire could feel the heat that came off Jade's body.

The song was ending, turning into something else, a love song, slow, rocking, sweet as only music can be.

All around them, women moved in against each other, a warm migration, and Jade's hands came up, slid around Claire's neck, she closed the space between them.

You think you want me to tell you everything, she said, her voice as intimate in Claire's ear as a private thought, but you don't.

Yes, I do, Claire said. You should trust me more —

Sometimes, Jade whispered, I'm so . . .

She didn't finish her sentence. The song was changing again, another beat mixing in, pumping, hypnotic, inescapable. Like some great tide, the women responded, they rolled up their sleeves, tied up their hair, and, in the middle of the floor, Jade stepped back, one hip swinging out, those glass beads blurred by motion, her costume gathered up so high you could see the tops of her thighs, she danced without stopping.

32

IT WAS PAST THREE WHEN THEY LEFT THE PLACE, BUT OUT-side, nothing was sleeping. The early-morning air was fresh, gusts of wind making street debris alive, everything full of surprise. There was traffic, yellow cabs cruising past, and people drifting out of bars, an unexpected air of festivity, voices soaring, the sense of curfew banned.

Searching for a cigarette in her purse, Jade walked halfway into the intersection as casually as if it were her living room, she did not even look up as cars passed, horns pressed almost in afterthought, drifting back to them, fading like the horns of ships leaving their moorings.

The ride home was a brief hiatus, that neutral space of transport. They both sat quiet, the backdrop of their evening temporarily lifted, windows rolled halfway down to let the air blow in, eyes half closed. Against Jade's profile, Claire could see the big darkened buildings of Broadway, the wide, empty sidewalks.

Let me, Claire said when the cab stopped, but Jade was already pushing bills through the little aperture, saying, Keep the change.

Here, Claire said, she tried to press her money into Jade's hand. Please, take it —

I don't want your money —

Take it!

It turned into a struggle, both of them breathless, giggling, until finally the bills flew into the air, fluttered gently down to the street.

Jade . . .

They're yours, Claire.

Why won't you let me give you anything?

I'll take anything you want to give me, Jade said, I just don't want your money.

They looked at each other in the shadowed doorway of that building, the money scattered all around them like so much litter, forgotten.

No, Claire said, I'd want to give you much more — too much — you'd never want it all —

Words surging from such a depth of feeling she could hardly utter them, and Jade moved as if from the same instinct, stepping closer, one hand reaching up to wind itself into Claire's hair, the other grabbing her belt, and then their faces were close, they were as close as they'd ever been.

I've never, Claire said, but the sentence had no end. All she could see were Jade's eyes, a dark shine, fixed on hers, unwavering, wide.

Wait, Claire said, she could hardly breathe, and Jade let go, she stepped back.

I have something, Claire said, upstairs —

She fumbled for her keys, her hands were shaking.

Go ahead, she said when they got up to the landing, I'll meet you there.

Alone in her apartment, she stuck all thirty candles into the cupcakes she had bought that afternoon; when she was finished, she had punctured every last shred of icing through; there was no surface area left.

Close your eyes, she called from the hall.

In Jade's apartment, there was no light. She had lit candles everywhere, candles in the kitchen, in the bathroom, put on music so quiet it spread like a hush across the apartment, making them whisper.

Can I open them yet —

Not yet —

119

By the time she reached Jade's bedroom, they were blazing with light. Jade was sitting on the edge of the bed, her eyes shut.

Nefertiti, Claire said. Make a wish.

Jade opened her eyes and her hands came out to grab the mattress's sides, she made no sound.

Claire knelt on the edge of the bed, the candles were dripping pink and yellow wax on her fingers, and Jade said, I wish that you love me as much as I love you —

She blew the candles out fiercely, and for a moment, they both blinked in the sudden dark between them. Claire laughed a little, she put the plate down, but Jade kept looking at her, her eyes burning.

I want to be different from everyone else in your life, she said, words harsh in her throat, I don't want to be just another friend, some girl you met when you moved —

You could never, Claire said, her voice rose. The way you talk to me! No one's ever talked to me the way you talk to me —

The way you *look* at me . . . ! Sometimes I think it must be something else you're looking at, it couldn't just be me . . .

You're so beautiful, Claire said, words wrenched almost painfully from her. I've looked at you so much, you don't know.

It's the novelty, Jade said, she smiled but the words were cruel. It'll fade.

It won't fade! Claire seized Jade's wrists. I'll love you till I die.

Don't say that, Jade said. People have said that to me, you don't know . . .

I will, Claire said, she wanted to push it against Jade, to press the weight of that promise down, make her feel it through her ribs, force it into her heart —

There was a moment, neither of them moved, and then Jade leaned closer, Claire heard the bed creak, and she felt heat in her face, she stared down at her hands, how each freckle seemed to stand out in sharp relief. She was paralyzed, she could hardly breathe. She felt Jade's fingers brushing the ends of her hair, grazing the back of her neck, and she sucked her breath in, an involuntary sound.

She turned to say something, she didn't know what, and Jade kissed her, mouth open, Claire tasted alcohol, smelled that perfume, and her hands came up, Jade caught them, their fingers interlocked, and Jade slid off the bed to the floor, some low moan making her throat vibrate, the sound of desire, of yearning.

I want to take your clothes off, Jade said, voice hot in Claire's ear, tugging at the hem of her shirt, but when the buttons came apart, breaking their contact, Claire clutched at it, scared, and Jade let go.

They looked at each other, no sound but their breathing, Jade's eyes searching, and Claire was awed by her fearlessness, the absolute assurance of her desire.

You go first, she whispered.

I forgot, Jade said. I forgot how shy you were.

She stood, eyes fastened on Claire, and Claire stayed very still, watching. Jade took hold of her tunic and in one swift movement pulled it off; she was naked underneath.

Now, she said, and then she fell on Claire, her skin shockingly warm, silky, and they rolled against each other, their mouths colliding, legs locking together, locking and relocking, and Jade was pulling her shirt off, tugging her jeans down, hands following the curve of her body down to her hips — this is what it's like, Claire kept thinking, this is who she is — and then Jade's hand drove down, reached for her like a man, her touch electrifying, and Claire gasped into her mouth, she heard Jade saying her name, and she felt her hips pressing up, forward, movement a hard question, driving, until Claire reached too, pushing down into that shadowed triangle, and Jade's thighs tightened hard around her wrist, so much strength, how foreign another woman felt, entirely different from herself — it was terrifying, this plunge, and yet this was Jade, opening, letting Claire move beyond the glint and sway of her surface, move all the way down to her depths, and she glimpsed for the first time something raw, how she needed to be filled, desire making her

fierce, the sounds that came from her like cries, like agony, and
Claire rocked against Jade's hand too, until they found a rhythm,
their hair tangled together, breathing against each other, rocking
and rocking until they were both shuddering, Claire first, then
Jade, whose last cry was so twisted-sounding Claire pulled back
quick to see if she'd hurt her and saw instead the dazed marvel
in her eyes, and how her hair looked, spread out wild against the
pillow.

There were no words. Jade leaned over the bed and blew
out the candles. They curled up together in the new dark, Jade
fitting herself around Claire's back, palm flat on the slope of her
flank.

I'll never sleep, Claire thought, but almost instantly she
was dreaming, quick flickering images playing like cinema against
her eyelids, dreams wet with rain, a green forest dripping, and
the natives soaked and helpless as animals beneath it. They
opened their arms and she fell into their melting embrace.

33

WHEN CLAIRE WOKE THE NEXT MORNING, SHE KNEW IN-
stantly where she was. Next to her, the bed was empty. There
was something terrible in the way the sheet was thrown back,
half sliding onto the floor, as if Jade had thrown the memory
from herself, ashamed of what she'd done. Her costume lay
crumpled where she'd stepped out of it, soiled, abandoned.

Claire reached down for her shirt, and the sight of it there
on the floor, flung aside, wanton somehow, flooded her with
sexual flashbacks, outrageous, illicit, small details so sharp they
made her face burn; she could hardly believe they were her
memories to claim.

When she straightened up, Jade was walking through the
door, hair wet. She wore nothing but her robe, untied, and for
an instant Claire saw a flash of navel, of skin.

Hi.

Claire heard the smile in Jade's voice, that single word full of an unashamed intimacy, making Claire recoil. Her lust was gone, it had vanished, and when she finally brought her eyes up to Jade's face, her features looked flat, earthbound.

Claire looked away, turned to the window as if to gauge the day, though there was nothing to see there but the tarp.

What time is it? she asked, the question abrupt.

There was a slight pause before Jade answered.

Almost eleven.

Eleven . . . ! Claire stood, pressing her shirt against her chest, desperate to cover her nudity. It's so late — I have to get out of here —

She pushed her arms into her shirt fast, fingers fumbling with the buttons. As if shame were contagious, she saw Jade reaching down to pluck whatever item of clothing lay at her feet, turning her back to tug it on.

Oh, she said a moment later, these are yours . . .

Claire glanced at her, swift and guarded. Jade held Claire's jeans shut over her crotch, fingers spread taut as if stanching a wound.

It doesn't matter, Claire said, she would have said anything to keep Jade clothed. I'll get them — whenever.

She tore through the bedclothes, looking for her underwear, and all the while she could feel Jade watching, motionless. She straightened up before she'd found them, she couldn't stand it.

Never mind, she said, eyes sliding off Jade's face. It's only down the hall —

She grabbed her boots, headed for the door.

Wait — ! Jade moved swiftly, they reached the door at the same time, and standing in that high frame, Claire was excruciatingly aware of Jade's proximity, of the space between them, how they did not touch. Whatever ease of affection had existed between them was gone now, and every gesture, no matter how small, lay open to the possibility of misconstruction. They had crossed the border, and everything had changed; it was like waking in the wilderness without a compass, without a map.

I think we should talk, Jade said.

I'm not like you, the words came into Claire's mind, and with them, the manic, frantic suspicion — I was manipulated, she thought, I was betrayed.

I have to go, she said, I have to work —

You're already late, Jade said, almost pleading now. They can wait another five minutes —

No, Claire said, if I don't get there before noon, there won't be anything for me —

Jade expelled her breath, the sound involuntary, as if in pain. She turned away.

I have to work, Claire said again, and this time when she headed for the door, Jade made no move to stop her.

34

HAVE A SEAT, EILEEN SAID, SHE SMILED BRIEFLY WHEN Claire walked in. I'll let you know if something comes up, all right?

Eyes hidden behind her sunglasses, Claire tried to smile back, but she felt raw, inflamed, sure that Eileen could see right through her.

She sat in the corner, her back up against the wall, but it was long minutes before she risked a furtive glance at the woman sitting next to her. Her hair was pinned back neat, and Claire reached reflexively for her own ponytail, felt how her hair frayed around her face, how it escaped the elastic, refusing to be caught.

As if sensing Claire's eyes, the woman looked up, and Claire thought she saw something in the woman's face, a kind of twitch — revulsion, she thought, and she was gripped by the certainty that this woman, that all the women in here, could see something essential about her — the unmade bed she'd left behind herself like some sickness, her underwear still lost in the folds of the sheet.

Had they ever, the thought began, and although she wouldn't articulate the rest of it, she couldn't stop the images that rose, those vivid sense memories. *You think you want me to tell you everything.* She sat very straight, her shoulders rigid. *But you don't.* Her face burned.

The phones had nearly stopped ringing. After an hour or so, Eileen walked to the other end of the room and sat talking to another agent. Perversely, Claire imagined telling her everything, how she would recoil in disgust. Even in the corner, Claire could hear her voice, drifting back.

So he says to me, he says, that's how my mother did it, and I say to him, I say, you want to be mama's little boy you can move back to *her* house, and live under *her* roof . . .

She was a woman who knew her place in the world, Claire thought, her place among men. She had a sudden vision of Tommy in the city, what an incongruous sight he had been in his rancher's clothes, looking somehow too solid next to everyone else, and the memory was a knife through her heart.

What have I done, the thought came, it clutched her, turned her to ice. What have I done.

Be ready Monday by eight-thirty, okay, Claire? Eileen said, breaking through that tormented reverie. If something comes up, I'll send you out.

Outside, the streets were still littered from Halloween. They had the desolate look of an abandoned party, streamers strangled in the gutters, empty bottles rolling against the curb.

Entering her building, she kept her head down, slipped through the front door, then stood in the dark hallway without breathing, straining to listen for anyone else. From somewhere came music, a dog barked, but the landing was quiet. She went up the stairs, distantly aware of a vein throbbing in her temple; she didn't make a sound. Safely inside her own apartment, she took off her shoes, did not turn the radio on. It wasn't until hours later, standing in the middle of the room in her stockinged feet, that she finally believed in the silence that seemed to penetrate from the apartment next door, the lack of human presence. Wherever she was, it sank into Claire slow as the drip of an IV, she wasn't home.

It seemed to take an enormous effort to undress that evening, even brushing her teeth was a terrible chore, and beneath the fatigue, there was something else, dangerous, foreign —

What, she thought as she fell into bed, what — but already her mind was reaching for cover of darkness, submerging . . . escaping, it came to her at the last minute, and it wasn't from Jade. It was herself she did not recognize.

35

SHE STAYED INSIDE ALL WEEKEND, DRINKING PEPSI AND reading the heavy Sunday paper, still wearing the T-shirt she had slept in. The apartment was overheated, it was tropical. She ran a bath and the windows steamed. Darkness fell without warning; Daylight Savings Time was over. Suddenly, she was lost. What will I do, she thought. She stood in the middle of the room, clutching the sleeves of her robe, dumbfounded.

The phone rang. Tommy, Claire thought, and leapt for it.

Home alone? Her sister's voice was an ambush, knocking her completely off-guard.

Yes, she said slowly. She did not sit down; it seemed unwise.

Oh lucky me, Paula said, and in that faintly acidic tone Claire heard everything, how she had not been forgiven.

So what'd you do this weekend? Paula asked.

Nothing.

Oh come on. You can tell me.

Really, nothing.

I thought you were seeing someone.

That last word so carefully neutral in Claire's ear, for one wild moment she thought her sister knew, and shame swept through her all over again, burning hot, indefensible.

What's that supposed to mean? she asked, her voice sharp. Who said that?

No one said shit, Paula said, hostility rising instantly to match her sister's, I just assumed, since you haven't even been in touch with Tommy —

That's not true — I've been trying to call him all weekend, and there's never any answer.

Paula made a sound, tight, unsurprised, and Claire felt herself beginning to sweat, small prickles of moisture along the top of her brow.

I saw him when he got back from New York — his face was so bruised he was scary-looking, Paula said, and in that judgment, Claire heard the city she lived in unequivocally condemned.

It could've happened anywhere, she said, sounding defensive even in her own ears.

He said it was over some girlfriend of yours —

She lives next door, Claire said abruptly, Paula's word for Jade making her burn all over again. That's all.

What happened?

It was just a stupid bar fight — some pervert, Tommy tackled him.

Over some other girl? Who is she, anyway?

No one, Claire said irritably, I told you — she lives next door.

That's not what he said.

Claire paused, she could not quite believe what she'd heard.

He said if it weren't for that girl — what's her name, something weird —

Jade.

Yeah, Jade — he said if it weren't for her, you would've come back by now.

That's what he wants to think, Claire said, the edge in her voice a razor. He doesn't know what he's talking about.

Don't tell me, Paula shot back, tell him — if you can find him.

What's that supposed to mean?

There's someone on the other line, I have to go —

Paula, wait —

You better talk to him, that's all I've got to say —

Wait!

And if you want to talk to me, you're going to have to call me, too.

There was a click, and Claire was disconnected. She hung up, then picked up again seconds later, dialed Tommy's number.

She listened to it ring twelve, thirteen times before she gave up. She moved around blindly, cleaning, clattering the dishes in the sink, wiping counters, but the evening was shattered, she was shattered, she could hear it when she breathed, an inner rattle. Like snakebite, Claire thought, her sister's phone call had hit her, lightning-fast, venomous.

She tried to calm herself, to sit down, but the apartment converged around her, none of its shapes making sense, the furniture all too big, ill-fitted, a clumsy assortment of junk, and suddenly there were tears in her throat, filling her eyes — she jumped up. There's nothing for dinner, she thought. I have to get something to eat.

She walked down to Canal Street, where all the shops were darkened, closed, the street itself desolate, she was aware now only of a growing hollowness, a need to be filled. Farther into Chinatown she found throngs of people in restaurants washed with fluorescent light, Chinese families having Sunday dinner, their yellowed chopsticks clicking and flashing, their voices a harsh, foreign din.

Claire ordered take-out from a waiter whose manner was beyond rudeness; she was not human to him, she thought. She stood near the kitchen, waiting, and thought of nothing but the food, hot-and-sour soup, shrimp in pungent sauce, sticky white rice.

It was still hot when she turned into her building, she could feel it through the brown paper bag. She would eat it straight from the cartons, she wouldn't have to turn the oven on . . .

She had a sudden image of her sister then, how she'd looked through the tinted windows of the airport terminal, standing by the car, her hair caught in its uncompromising ponytail. Underneath the early-afternoon sun, her face had been pale, washed out save for the frown between her eyes, two deep lines that faced each other across the bridge of her nose. Saying goodbye to her sister, she could not speak. They had held each other, years of love rising speechless in their grip, but their eyes did not meet.

Claire had stared after her until the car was gone, and then she'd stood at a newsstand and flipped rapidly through the pages of a glossy magazine. The images blurred and the magazine gave off a smell, rank and sweet, sample perfumes whose smell she would later and forever associate with the sense of having been forsaken.

She ate herself full, ate until she was stupefied with MSG, until all she wanted to do was sleep. She put her head under the pillow and in the dark, under that soft weight, she was vaguely aware of the tears that still pressed against her eyes, like a low-grade storm that would not pass.

She woke up hours later, the light in her eyes, all her clothes still on. In the bathroom mirror she was stormy-faced, her eyelids puffy. She turned all the lights off and went back to bed, but sleep escaped her, it was gone, and with it her sense of safety. From next door, she heard the faint sound of music, a woman's laughter; it was not Jade's. The world was a dangerous place, it was clear, full of senseless violence, of heartbreak and bitter betrayals, a place where she could not count on anyone — least of all, it came to her now, herself.

But Tommy, she thought, Tommy had always been there for her, and the way he loved her came up like a treasure she had been hoarding, the memory of the long quiet of Saturday afternoons in bed with him, slanting evening sunlight streaking through the open window, dust floating gilded along shafts of light, rich and quiet . . . there was never anybody else there, no human voices save their own.

She took the phone under the covers, dialed his number in the dark.

. . . Hello? His voice was full of sleep, came across unclouded by static, as if he were just around the corner, and the false sense of proximity made Claire hunch even closer to the phone, filled her with the desperate yearning to be home, near this man she loved, and the flat stretch of desert it seemed she'd always known.

It's me.

Claire . . . Jesus . . . what time is it?

I've been trying to call you for days.

Mm, he said, as if he couldn't quite wake up.

I've been feeling so bad . . . and the only thing that helps is thinking about you . . . I've been thinking about you so much — it keeps me going, it's the only thing . . .

He didn't answer.

Are you there?

Yeah, he said, but he sounded strange, distant, muted.

What's wrong?

Nothin's wrong. I'm just really not up for talkin right now.

Why not?

He didn't answer, and she kicked the covers off violently, suddenly needing air.

Look, I know you didn't have a good time when you came to see me and I'm sorry, I really am — it was my fault, I had no — I didn't realize —

Yeah, whatever. It's over.

What do you mean, it's over?

Claire, he said, he spoke her name like a warning. Maybe you oughta call back some other time . . .

You're not — you haven't — She couldn't articulate the thought, not even to herself.

You still love me, she said. I know you do.

For a moment, all she could hear was the hum of the wire, miles and miles, the hum of distance itself.

Yeah, he said. Goodnight.

36

SHE KNEW THE NEXT MORNING WHEN SHE WAITED FOR THE phone to ring at eight-thirty, dressed, her hair combed back tight, that there would be no work for her today either. When she finally called them an hour later, Eileen told her to come in, that request automatic — it didn't cost her anything.

And in the waiting room, fighting against the panic of anticipated poverty, of not having enough money to buy a sandwich for lunch, she remembered the girl who used to come in every day, in her black pants and wrinkled white shirt, the girl they left to doze each morning, until it was time to send her home, and now she thought, that's me. Persona non grata.

She stood up. I have to work, she said, no one heard her.

I have to work, she said it again, louder, and this time two of the agents raised their heads, they glanced at each other.

I can't just sit here like this, she said.

Listen, everybody knows how you feel, one of the agents said, but don't get excited, okay? It's been a little slow lately, don't worry, it'll pick up —

You don't understand, Claire said, she felt something loosening inside, a terrible agitation. I'm running out of money, I have to work — you have to send me out —

She was standing in the middle of the room now, everybody was looking at her. The agent who had answered her pushed her chair back, she said, Who's your agent, hon?

Eileen, she's not here, she went out —

Okay, listen, why don't you just take the rest of the day off —

No! You're not listening to me! I can't go home! You can't send me home, I have to go out! She was shouting, she couldn't control herself. I signed up here because you said you'd get me work, you promised!

Ssh, the agent said. Calm down, okay, hon? Take it easy, okay?

Just then, the phone on her desk rang, she picked up automatically.

Perfect Temps, how can I help you?

I want that, Claire said, she stood in front of the agent's desk, tears streaming down her face. That one's for me —

The agent raised a finger, she said, Yes, sir, if you'll just repeat that address for me, we'll have someone there in half an hour . . .

She hung up, she thrust a box of Kleenex at Claire. It's only an interview, she said, so I can't guarantee anything, but if you get the job it's a permanent, all right? Can you handle that?

Yes, Claire said. Yes.

The firm was at Fifty-third and Lexington; it occupied the entire thirtieth floor of the Citicorp Building, a place that could house, Claire was sure, the entire population of Alamogordo. She stepped into an express that shot up past the first twenty floors without stopping, she felt her stomach drop. When the glass door of Berman, Gordon and Kase swung shut behind her, it was as if she had entered another atmosphere; the gray carpet was deep, and the quality of the silence made Claire think of money, plush and controlled.

The receptionist hardly looked at her, she was inhumanly composed behind the high, polished throne of her counter.

I'm Claire Stearn from Perfect Temps, I'm here for Mr. Gordon . . . ?

He's in conference. The woman drank coffee from a mug, gazed at Claire beneath pale-powdered lids. Her enunciation carried the traces of a British accent.

Oh. Do you know how long he'll be?

She lifted a hand, the universal gesture of ignorance, took another sip of coffee. Her lipstick left a perfect pink imprint on the rim of her cup.

I guess I'll just wait, then . . .

Claire sat down and folded her hands in her lap.

Fifteen minutes later, Gordon came out to greet her. He was about fifty years old, he had a kind face, a casual manner.

Sam Gordon, he said, his grip was warm. Won't you come into my office?

His office was the corner one, it was spectacular, with windows that looked south and west so you could see magnificent structures that made New York New York, converging thickly around them.

Now, he said, tell me a little about yourself.

Claire sat forward on the deep red leather couch, her hands nervous. She felt as if she were about to be auctioned.

I can type eighty-five words per minute, and I take short-hand, too —

Hold on, he said. Why don't you tell me where you're from, first?

Oh, she said, she flushed. Alamogordo, New Mexico.

Alamogordo, he said. Sure, I've been there. That's where they did the nuclear testing, isn't it?

You've been there? It provoked a sudden sense of kinship with him, as though he'd just told her he was a distant cousin.

It's a beautiful state, New Mexico, he said. They've suc-ceeded in establishing quite a few wildlife preserves out there.

He didn't ask her any questions about her abilities, her ex-perience, or her references. He told her he dealt primarily with environmental law, and then he asked her how she liked New York.

It's the biggest place I've ever been, she said; it was not an answer she had rehearsed.

Really, he said. Bigger than the desert?

It's roads that make a place big, she said, because they di-vide it up, and then you can get lost. I don't think of the desert as having any size.

You must miss that, he said.

No, she said. I know it's there.

He studied her for a moment, smiling faintly, and she re-membered where she was, that she was being assessed for a cor-porate job. She sat up straighter, trying to compose her face into the same cool lines the receptionist had worn, unflappable as a machine.

I brought my steno pad with me, she said, she lifted it from her purse. If you want to try a letter on me . . .

All right, he said, let's do it.

She looked around while he found a file. His office was warm, like a room in somebody's house, the walls lined with books with titles like *Philosophical Fragments* and *Restructuring the*

World Economy — thick volumes that seemed to point the way to a better world, ordered, thoughtful.

Ready?

He had an unhurried, easy way of speaking; as she translated the sound of his voice into small, crisp notations, each mark seemed like a notch leading her out of the wilderness and back to safety, to a place where she could feel the ground solid beneath her.

You're very good, he said when she read it back to him. Very fast.

I learned shorthand in high school. My mother made me take it.

Oh? Was your mother once a secretary too?

No, she runs a dress shop in Alamogordo. She owns it.

Sounds impressive. He took his glasses off and held them in one hand. He had deep brown eyes, a steady gaze that invited confidences.

Not really — it's just a little place, downtown. Nobody goes there anymore.

Nobody goes downtown?

It used to really be downtown, twenty years ago — now everyone goes to the mall instead, five miles north. It's huge, it has three stories, every kind of shop you could imagine. But my mother won't move. She says her customers know where to find her.

She sounds very wise, your mother.

She's just stubborn, Claire answered, and smiled, to soften it.

Well, Claire, he said, he stood. Think you can start today?

You mean — that's it? I'm hired?

You're hired.

He walked her back out to the lobby.

Lila, he said to the receptionist. This is Claire. She'll be taking over for Anna.

Nice to meet you, Lila said, as if she'd never seen Claire before. She turned to Sam. Shall I cancel the rest of the interviews, then?

Please, he said, and smiled at Claire. I'll call Ursula to show you around. I hope it won't be long before you feel at home.

Ursula was an older woman in a gray flannel skirt suit, a cameo brooch at the throat of her blouse. Her hair was sprayed into a stiff series of small waves, and though her face was pouchy with the softness of age, she was brisk, she was all business.

Ursula Perlmann, she said, extending her hand. I work for Mr. Walter Kase. Mr. Gordon has instructed me to make sure you understand where everything is. Please come with me.

She walked Claire around the office, pointed out where things were. Their heels sank soundless into the carpet, people looked up when they passed. This is Claire Stearn, Ursula told them, Mr. Gordon's new girl.

Her voice was bossy bright as she explained everything, but there was something underneath, something brittle and waiting. She was a woman, Claire thought, with no man in her life, a woman who slept alone every night, her apartment fastidiously ordered around herself, everything always in its place.

This is the case library, Ursula said, flicking a switch. It was a small room lined top to bottom with shelves and filing cabinets. There was a big table in the middle, dark and polished, no windows.

Of course, you're familiar with the standard legal filing system.

Claire shook her head.

Surely you must be! Ursula's tone was one of shock, but Claire had the feeling she was not, truly, surprised.

I've had training on the computer system, she said. In school. But not this . . .

Yes, well, the computer's one thing, but it's by no means all. Ursula pursed her lips. There were pucker lines all around her mouth, and her eyebrows were tweezed into two thin arcs.

Mr. Gordon knows perfectly well he's not supposed to hire anyone without legal training. It just means extra work for everybody else.

135

What happened to Mr. Gordon's last secretary? Claire asked timidly.

She got pregnant, Ursula said, and turned off the light.

It was the end of the day and people were leaving when Gordon called her into his office.

There was something he wanted to run past her, he said, he leafed through the pages of a file, open on his desk.

It's a pro bono case, a suit the city wants to bring against a chemical plant, he said. A friend of mine from the mayor's office has asked me for legal advice, but first the data has to be analyzed —

Usually we hire a paralegal, he said, he looked up over his glasses. But it's more a question of familiarizing yourself with the language than anything else . . . I thought you might like to give it a go.

Me? But I haven't had any experience, and I might . . . I just don't know if . . .

There's no rush, he said, I don't have to get back to them for some time. Why don't you take them, see what you think?

The only light in the office came from the lamp on his desk, throwing the rest of the room into shadows, and through those huge, plate-glass windows she saw other offices lit up, men in white shirts talking on the phone, the light of their computers reflected on their faces. It was like a glimpse into another city, quiet, efficient, a city in which things were being accomplished, in which the world was, day by day, taking shape.

Okay, she said, I will. Thank you. Thank you very much, Mr. Gordon.

No need to thank me, he said, he was smiling, it was the natural expression of his face. But there is one thing . . .

Yes?

After five, everyone calls me Sam.

37

IMMEDIATELY AFTER SHE STARTED HER NEW JOB, THE DAY
took on a rhythm for Claire, the rhythm of labor and hourly
wages, the rhythm of the mundane. Although the material in the
files Gordon had given her seemed impossibly dense at first, after a while she found that the meaning of its peculiar dialect began to yield, she started to perceive its patterns. She took it
home in the evening, and found the complexity of the case
strangely gratifying, how she had to be aware of a thousand small
details at the same time, how it seemed to order, to organize her
mind. Sam encouraged her to ask questions, he put her in touch
with the woman from the mayor's office who was in charge of
the case.

Call me Erica, she said to Claire over the phone, her
speech the clipped dialect of the New Yorker, getting straight to
business. That's it, she'd say when Claire hesitantly paraphrased
her understanding, you've got it.

It was good to feel her life settling around her, simple and
organized. First thing in the morning she opened Sam's mail,
sorted it. He got newsletters from every conceivable environmental group, interchangeable to Claire — Defenders of Wildlife, Conservation International, African Wildlife, The Nature
Conservancy, The Wilderness Society, National Wildlife Federa-
tion. She thought this proliferation vaguely ridiculous, ineffi-
cient. They all sent urgent pleas, computer-printed letters with
especially alarming phrases underlined, phrases that talked about
survival, about extinction, phrases that began or ended with *forever*. They made her uneasy, she wouldn't read any of them; he
supported them all.

His wife, Nadja, came into the office on Wednesday, unan-
nounced, a woman whose hair was nearly white, whose eyes
blazed with an immediately discernible intelligence, whose every
movement was deliberate.

You must come to dinner, she said to Claire. The first year
in a strange city can be very lonely.

Riding home on the subway the same evening, Claire let her eyes half close. The first year, she kept thinking, how it sounded — as if there would be more.

She emerged from that deep tunnel and up into the din of Canal Street, with its stores like crowded pantries spilling into the street, its buses and cars, its Chinese crowd, and moved through it all unfazed, moved as if her friends were watching, her gait brisk, sure, pictured their eyes, wide, their new respect. They could never have predicted this, she thought defiantly, never have predicted me —

Inevitably then it recurred, that night with Jade, but the thought was wearing itself into familiar grooves, slowly losing its power to shock. She had been drunk, she had been someone else. It was one night, it was Halloween, she thought, and pushed the memory into that single category, contained it there. She had not run into Jade once, not once, it had been over a week now, and Claire put all her faith into this mutual avoidance pact, she did not question it. Maybe they would never meet again.

38

WINTER DESCENDED OVERNIGHT, A COLD SURPRISE. ONE morning, there was frost. It had rained, and the puddles on the street were brittle. People came out of their houses unprepared, their hands, their necks naked. They blinked like newborns in the raw air, gathered around the newspaper stands to read the headlines, the bold black print arresting: WALL COMES DOWN, they said. COLD WAR ENDS.

She was halfway down the stairs the next morning when she saw the young woman at the bottom, and her first instinct was to turn around again, to flee — but then the woman looked up, her glance swift, and Claire recognized her immediately as Jade's friend, Olivia.

Hi, Claire said, she faked a half-yawn, elaborately casual.

Olivia looked at her, obviously still trying to place her. Have we met . . . ?

Just once, Claire said. On the street — I'm Jade's neighbor.

Olivia's hands were full of mail, Jade's mailbox open before her, and it was hard for Claire not to draw the immediate, the obvious conclusion — they were lovers, she and Jade, they had given each other free rein, given each other their keys —

Claire tried to smile, felt it strain across her face, some terrible grimace. She lowered her head, said, Excuse me —

Wait! Olivia seized her arm, her face alight with sudden hope.

I'm late for work, Claire said, desperate to be out of there, I really can't —

I remember you now — we met on the street, right?

Claire nodded helplessly.

Oh, God, you're saving my life, Olivia exclaimed. Jade asked me to pick up her mail while she was in Paris, but now *I* have to leave town, too —

Paris, Claire repeated dumbly; she could not quite process the information.

Yeah, Olivia said, looking at her curiously. She left about a week ago, right after Halloween — didn't she tell you?

Claire looked at her, she didn't answer, but Olivia rushed on, she had no interest in the true nature of their friendship.

The thing is, my sister just had her baby, five weeks premature, and I have to go down and help her, I don't know when I'll be back, so will you take this — and will you water the plant? She was already pressing everything into Claire's unwilling hands, all of Jade's mail, the keys.

What plant, was Claire's first thought, suspicion, there was no light in that apartment, nothing but those dark tarps —

This is my number at home, Olivia said, she was scribbling on a piece of paper. You can leave a message if anything comes up — listen, you're a lifesaver, she said, and slammed Jade's mailbox shut, the sound metallic, definitive. You have no idea!

Wait, Claire said as Olivia headed for the door, but either

she didn't hear or she pretended not to, and a moment later Claire was left standing in the chilly entryway, alone.

She looked at the pile of correspondence she held in her hands. There were bills, junk mail, a lingerie catalog, and a single postcard. The front was a black-and-white picture of a woman with her head back, laughing. The handwriting on the back was an androgynous sprawl: *Hey — this looks like good times, huh? Was thinking maybe you were ready for another roadtrip — first thing we'll do, burn the maps. My proposal still stands.*

There was no signature, only the single initial, *W.*

Paris, Claire thought, it was hard to believe. When exactly had she packed, at what moment had her plane left the ground . . .

She felt Jade's keys, heavy and cool in her hand. She didn't want them, and it seemed to her that even in this staged transatlantic vanishing, Jade's betrayal continued, how she'd contrived to keep Claire in the dark, to mock her.

She jammed everything deep into the bottom of her bag and headed out the door, walking fast, but all the way uptown, she was aware of that extra bulk of mail in her bag, how it bumped against her thigh. Jangling along with her hand on that greasy metal tube, she kept catching her own eye in the window, an unwelcome glint in what seemed the face of a ghost, slightly blurred, pallid.

She had been haunting herself, she thought. There was no one else.

Coming out of the Fifty-first Street station, she ran into Lila.

We're late, Lila said, and then smiled as if she could no longer hold it back. She had bad teeth, discolored, slightly crooked, and it occurred to Claire that perhaps this was more reason for her composure than actual cold-bloodedness — her unwillingness to divulge this flaw.

Look. She pulled off gray suede gloves and held her hand out to show a simple diamond solitaire.

My boyfriend asked me to marry him, she said, and, walking to the elevator, she seized Claire's arm.

Lila's diamond took center stage. All day Claire saw people bent over her hand, as if she were a bishop, and above them Lila smiled, heedless of her need for dentistry. Because some man loves her, Claire thought. Some man wants her, terrible teeth and all.

The way Tommy wants me, she thought. She sat at her desk, her hands clasped tightly together. It was still early in Alamogordo, he would be having breakfast . . .

When she closed her eyes, she could see everything, his kitchen, the rise of the mountains distant on the horizon, the dogs lying patiently by the door. It was more real than anything, more real than the office around her with all its machines humming, the click and whirr of the fax, the constant ring of the phone —

She picked it up, punched his number in quickly.

Hello? It was a woman's voice. Claire held the receiver, too stunned to speak.

Hello? Hello?

She hung up fast, her heart pounding, and thought, I misdialed, that's all. I misdialed.

She didn't call back.

She stayed at her desk during lunch and tried to read a book, her mind like a fish, darting here, darting there, she would not let herself stop and linger, everything seemed dangerous, and she read the same sentence again and again, again and again, while her knuckles grew white around the pages of the book.

By the time Sam came back from lunch, she had a headache. It grew, pounding huge and slow with every heartbeat, a roar of pain along the inside of her right eye. Aspirin did not dent it; it was inexorable, like the coming in of some great tide; it was like being blinded.

I'll call my doctor, Lila offered. He'll phone in a prescription for codeine.

I'm allergic to codeine, Claire said. She spoke very quietly, so as not to jar her head.

You should go home and lie still, Ursula said reprovingly.

Claire nodded. She had her things gathered, her sweater,

her bag, but then she didn't move; she couldn't face the screech and clang of the subway, the throng of people outside.

Go on, Ursula said again. You're not going to be any use to us around here.

I'll just wait for Mr. Gordon to get off the phone, Claire answered.

I can certainly be trusted to tell him, Ursula said.

Okay, Claire said; she only wanted everyone to be quiet. Peripherally she was aware of Ursula standing, and she had the vertiginous certainty that she was coming to tip her out of her chair. She let her hair fall forward over the sides of her face, as if for protection, and then she heard Ursula's voice again, bright and loud.

Mrs. Gordon! How nice to see you — is Mr. Gordon expecting you?

When Claire looked up and saw Nadja, she burst into tears.

Nadja took her home in a cab. I have some herbs, she said. They're very potent.

They lived in a brownstone in Chelsea, on the top floor. The floors were polished wood, there was a fireplace and in one corner, a beautiful stone Buddha, its hand lifted in calm repose.

After starting water, Nadja put Claire on the couch, took her pulse with the confidence of a doctor. Neither of them spoke. She let go of Claire's wrist and put both thumbs at the base of her neck, applied just the minimum of pressure. It was as if she were interfering with the course of the pain; though the change was subtle, it seemed possible for the first time that it would go away.

I'll be right back, she said after a minute. She turned the lamp off, and Claire felt the relief of darkness against her eyes.

The brew Nadja came back with was bitter, but not hard to swallow.

How do you know how to do all this? Claire asked.

You don't get to be my age, Nadja said, without learning a few useful things in life.

142

Claire tried to smile, she lay without moving.

Do you get these headaches often? Nadja's voice was quiet, a voice made for speaking in the dark. There was an ease between them, a lack of defenses, the simple relationship of one person caring for another.

Only sometimes, but there's never been anything I can take . . . I'm allergic to painkillers.

An allergy like that is a gift of sorts, Nadja said. Even in the darkness her eyes were warm, her face soft. Pain can be a great educator, she said. She pressed her palm to Claire's brow.

We have a guest room, she said, if you'd like a real bed . . .

I want to stay here.

She kept her eyes closed and slowly slowly slowly the pounding lessened. She was aware of Nadja's presence in the chair next to her, and she had the queer feeling that Nadja was just as attuned to the headache as she herself was. She felt no need to speak.

It's going away, she said finally. There was a vacancy where the pain had been, an awareness of its parameters.

Good, Nadja said, she stood up. Now you must rest.

Claire didn't protest, she lay immobile, like a limp girl from the silent movies, too wan to rise. She watched while Nadja built a fire, those capable hands twisting newspaper, lighting it with a long match.

I have to run a few errands, Nadja said. You try to sleep a little.

She left. There was no sound then, and no light save the warmth and crackle of the fire. When Claire closed her eyes, she could still see its orange glow.

39

THE FIRST THING SHE SAW WHEN SHE WOKE UP WAS THE Buddha's face, a sea of peace, flickering in the light. From the kitchen came the soothing, domestic sound of water running, of someone humming.

Claire moved toward it, and found Nadja cooking, chopping peppers, onion, tomatoes. The kitchen was fragrant with the smell of butter and garlic, of warm bread in the oven. Nadja pulled a stool out for her to sit on, she smoothed Claire's hair back from her face.

How are you?

I'm fine, Claire said, it was like a miracle. Where did you ever find those herbs?

They're from the Himalayas, Nadja said. A Tibetan doctor gave them to me — you must take some home with you, in case you ever need them again — although I hope you won't.

Oh, don't worry about me. I'm basically healthy.

Yes, I can see that's your natural state. When were you born — what month?

August, Claire said. The sixteenth.

An Augustian child, Najda said, nodding, as if she might have known. Have you ever had your natal chart cast? Your full horoscope?

No, why? Can you do it?

I used to, Nadja said. It used to be a hobby of mine. It got so I could guess certain particulars after a while — the ascendant, the placement of the moon . . .

Oh, Claire said, guess mine.

Nadja smiled, she looked at Claire. Such a beautiful face, she said. I think there must be Libra there — Libra rising, perhaps . . .

What does it mean?

It's the way you approach the world, she said. The mask you wear. But your moon, I think, is something else . . .

What does the moon tell you?

It signifies your emotional nature . . . your true self. With you — I think it might be hidden, it might be in the house of your unconscious . . . hidden, but deep — a Plutonian moon, that's my guess.

Tell me more, Claire begged.

Nadja laughed. I'm only guessing, she said. You mustn't take this too literally now.

But what does Pluto mean?

Pluto's the furthest planet — its power is subterranean, but stronger than any other's. It's all about death, and sex — the great mysteries.

You see that in me?

Nadja laughed again. Is it so alarming?

No, but it sounds so glamorous . . . it sounds more like my friend Jade than me.

Perhaps it's what draws you to her.

Claire watched Nadja moving around the kitchen, occasionally sipping from a glass of wine, and it seemed to her that this woman lived in a state of grace, that she understood the deepest mysteries, what cannot be spoken of.

Lila got engaged last night, she said. Did you see her ring? It's quite beautiful.

I guess she's in love.

Nadja glanced at Claire, her smile teasing.

Too bad she can't just enjoy it, she said, without all that marriage business.

What do you mean?

Don't misunderstand me, Nadja said, I love my husband, but sometimes I wonder if marriage isn't a kind of retreat from life — a way of hiding behind someone else, of choosing security above everything else.

She leaned one hip against the counter, poured them both more wine.

I think I've reached the age where one begins to wonder what other lives one might have had, she said, she smiled. What other passions.

Passions, Claire thought, another neutral word — it could mean anything. Anyone.

I tell you, Claire, Nadja said, her smile widening into a laugh, if I were your age now . . . !

But what about . . .

Nadja waited, and for a second Claire imagined telling her

everything, she opened her mouth, but she had no words for it, she could not even begin.

It's not safe, she said instead; she spoke abruptly, felt the flush rise up her face.

Well, I know, Nadja said, but the admission was reluctant, and Claire had the sense that Nadja was censoring herself now, too.

Excuse me, Claire said. I'm just going to wash up.

Nadja pointed her in the direction of the bathroom. On her way, Claire peeked into the rooms of the apartment — there was a study, the walls nothing but bookshelves, a lush Oriental carpet on the floor, the desk solid, planted wide, made of teak, dark and rich-looking, the chair behind it deep. The room had the same feeling as Sam's office, an unexpected center of calm, weighted with a sense of knowledge. There was a small print on one of the shelves on the far wall, a golden map of the world, with primitive lettering beneath. "Take good care of the Earth," it said. "It was not given to us by our parents. It was loaned to us by our children."

She saw their bedroom, simply done, a wide bed with a small table on either side of it, each with its own lamp, and she could imagine them reading there at night, reading passages to each other out loud, everything dark around them save the small pools of light falling on the crisp printed pages.

There was only one other room besides the bathroom, and it was the most beautiful room in the house. The wooden floors were bare, the walls were white. The bed was high and narrow, its frame made of iron, the spread white as the walls. Above it hung a shimmering tapestry of a goddess, gold and crimson and emerald green. In one corner was a tall vase full of flowers, purple lilies, whose sweet, delicate fragrance was discernible even from the doorway. In the other corner was another Buddha, this one golden, raised on a small white pedestal, little candle lamps burning in a semicircle at its feet.

Claire stood there for a long time, and felt her breathing deepen. It was like standing on the threshold of a temple.

Back in the kitchen, she asked Nadja about it.

Oh, it used to be my son's room, she said.

Your son . . . I didn't realize you had any kids.

She was stirring the vegetables, her back to Claire, but Claire saw her pause; she saw the spoon stop, and for a few seconds Nadja was totally still.

We don't, she said. We just had him.

She turned around and smiled at Claire, but her eyes were shrouded with sorrow, terrible and deep.

He died when he was seventeen, Nadja said.

Claire sat where she was, dumbstruck.

It's all right, Nadja said. It was years ago now. Years. We won't speak of it.

She smiled again, reassuring, but Claire saw, when she opened the refrigerator to get something, how she stared into it, unseeing, her eyes puzzled-looking somehow, as if she were still trying to understand the event, as if it were still beyond her.

Down the hall, the front door opened, and Nadja looked up. Sam was home.

He'd brought fresh mozzarella, another bottle of wine, a small tin of olive paste. Eating like this, he said later, is as close to being Italian as we can get.

Sam has a theory, Nadja explained, that everybody secretly wants to be Italian.

Why? Claire asked.

Why, Sam? Nadja looked at her husband with exaggerated innocence.

She's baiting me, Sam told Claire. They were sitting at the table, the remains of their dinner sprawled before them, luxurious, their glasses half-filled with wine, the ice cubes in the water melted.

I'm not, Nadja said.

She thinks I'm prejudiced.

Sam's theory, Nadja said, is that Italians act the way everybody else really wants to — shouting at the slightest provocation and driving too fast and pinching women and —

Eating like this, Sam said.

I've never been to Italy, Claire said.

Ah, well, said Sam. You'll see, then.

He spoke easily, as if it were inevitable that Claire, too, would travel thousands of miles someday, that she would see everything. *Gone to Paris.* She tried to imagine it, herself in some distant country, alone, and could not. Tommy, she knew, would never go with her. I would get to the end of my life with him, she thought, and we would still be on the same plot of land.

She glanced covertly at her hosts; how different it was for them. They were a couple who had been everywhere, the Mediterranean, Jerusalem, on safari in Africa, a couple who had shared a thousand lives. They told fragments of stories, stories of one-star hotels in third world deserts, of week-long bus rides with terrorists and hitchhikers, self-mocking stories in which glimpses of their youth were revealed, an eccentric circle of friends. They showed Claire picture albums, all of them leather-bound, soft and worn. There were whole books devoted to a single country — Ireland, Fiji, Brazil.

Where's this? Claire pointed at a bird's-eye view of a glittering city, the buildings tall, silvery.

Buenos Aires, Nadja said. That was the time we went to Patagonia — Sam, do you remember that penguin? The one who fell in love with you?

Love! Sam said. How you exaggerate — it was strictly infatuation.

Nadja flipped the page. Ah hah, she said. Now you tell me — is that not the picture of true love?

It was Sam in a parka and boots, turning to peer over his shoulder at a penguin in mid-waddle that had broken away from its group and given chase.

He shook his head now, stood to clear the plates.

It really was, he said, the most mysterious thing.

Naturally, Nadja said. Love always is.

She closed the books reluctantly, she sighed.

Oh, she said, how I envy you, Claire. You have it all before you still — your youth, the whole world.

Claire glanced at Sam, wondering if he knew what she meant, if he knew about his wife's doubts, and saw how he looked at Nadja, the kind of look that only exists within a marriage, intimate, beyond words. Whatever he knew or did not know, Claire thought, it was clear that they had made their peace with each other. They had survived everything, she thought, including the greatest sorrow.

Look what I have. Sam came back into the dining room, a plate in his hands. Cannolis.

Sam! How did you sneak that past me?

Anyone for an espresso?

Look at those, Nadja said. How am I supposed to keep my girlish figure when you come home with those?

I can make cappuccino, if you prefer.

No, espresso, espresso, Nadja said. With lemon.

She got up, began clearing plates. Let's have dessert in the kitchen, she said. It's cozier.

Hours later, when Claire finally rose to go, he called the firm's car service, he waved her protests aside.

It's supposed to snow any minute, he said. You're not taking the subway. Besides, we'll put it on the expense account.

The car smelled like powerful men, cigar smoke and leather. It smelled like safety, slightly stupefying, and she half slept in the back, secure in the knowledge that it would take her home.

40

SAM HAD BEEN RIGHT. SOMETIME DURING THE NIGHT, IT BEgan to snow, and when Claire woke up the next morning, the city was blanketed in white. It snowed all day, it showed no signs of abating. At the office, they took turns veering off to the windows, exclaiming, Look, look — and one by one the others would come, even Ursula, until there was a knot of people, their bodies close and warm together, sharing a brief and reverential silence.

By two o'clock, the Metropolitan Transportation Authority

had issued a warning: they couldn't say how long the trains would run. Sam let everybody go.

Claire walked out of the building and stood for a second in the middle of the sidewalk; strangers were smiling at each other, earmuffs big and clownish over their ears, hands childish in woollen mittens.

Ever see this in Alamogordo?

Claire turned around and there was Such, taller than she'd remembered, grinning his crooked grin.

I know, he said. You're shocked to see me above Fourteenth Street.

He leaned in close. I bank up here, he said. What's your excuse?

I work in there, she said, pointing at the Citicorp Building. Thirty floors up.

Brave girl, Such said, he linked his arm through hers. Going my way?

He made her walk over to Fifth Avenue with him. They've already put the Christmas windows up at Bergdorf's, isn't that disgusting? he said. I must see them.

They were an anomaly amid the crowd, ambling down the street while everybody else rushed for shelter, frantically waving down cabs.

Such pointed at the mannequins in the window, as if mindless of the snow that fell on his head, assigning each of them a role in the Nativity scene.

There's Joseph, he said. You can tell he's worried, because even with all that Armani, the Helmsley Palace refuses to give him a room.

Claire stood just behind him, surreptitiously scraping together enough snow for a snowball.

And the one in white there's Mary, he went on. Poor Mary — you just *know* black would be more flattering —

She lobbed it at him and it burst against his back. He whipped around, his eyes narrowed, and declared war.

They stayed out until their shoes were soaked through and

then, shrieking as if they'd only just noticed the cold, ran for the nearest subway.

They went to Such's apartment, a sixth-floor walk-up on East Fourth Street, a wreck of a place, the kitchen table strewn with newspapers, cassette tapes, old coffee cups, dead flowers, and everywhere else, the detritus of a single man's life, his clothes heaped high in one corner (the power pyramid, Such called it), and against the wall, a magnificent stereo system, sleek and black with blinking red lights. His record collection was awesome (if obsolete, he said ruefully), and there was one tall poster of a striking-looking young man gazing intently down toward the ground.

Who's he? Claire asked.

That's Jeff, Such answered, a very famous movie star . . . in some circles.

What's he looking at?

Me, Such said, walking past her to the bedroom. Come along, Claire. You may enter the inner sanctum — many have tried, he said, and many have succeeded.

The afternoon slid by and turned dark without their noticing. They lounged on Such's bed mauling through an assortment of chips and cookies and watching sixty channels intermittently, stopping only at the home shopping network, his personal favorite.

Listen, he said suddenly.

What?

Can't you hear that? It's deafening!

Hear what?

My phone, he said morosely, not ringing.

Oh, she said. Who's supposed to call?

No one, he said. It's hopeless.

You're in love, she guessed.

Pathetically.

With who?

Van, he said. Know him?

She grinned, she shook her head. Who is he?

He's a waiter at this restaurant I go to, Such said, *all the*

151

time . . . I've spent my life savings on Caesar salads, and he still doesn't even know I exist.

What's so great about him?

He's got this wide-open face, this incredible smile . . . he's definitely *not* from New York. He's one of those boys, one of those rare angels . . . perfect. Except, of course, for one thing . . .

No sideburns?

No sideburns, Such said, he flopped back on the bed and sighed.

But then . . . I mean . . . how in love can you be, if he isn't . . . ?

A raving homosexual?

I wasn't going to say *that.*

It happens, Such said, he shrugged.

Do you think — has it ever happened to you, the other way around?

Are you kidding? The other way around is my middle name.

I was just thinking about this friend of mine . . .

Uh huh.

Claire looked at him sharply, but his expression was guileless, listening, and after a moment, she went on.

She told me that once she and this other friend of hers, this girl . . . I don't know exactly what happened, but I guess they got drunk or something and somehow they ended up in bed —

I'm shocked, *shocked,* Such said, grinning, and Claire felt herself becoming flustered.

No, she said, you don't understand — she's not like that, she really isn't —

Like what?

I mean, she has a boyfriend and everything, she would never — she's just not *like* that.

What are you saying, she was date-raped? Such's voice was cool, but Claire could hear the amusement underneath, and she shook her head, she wouldn't look at him.

No, but maybe . . . I don't know, maybe her friend is, you know —

A crazed lesbian?

I don't mean crazy, Claire said, she couldn't seem to regain her composure. But she must be — I mean one of them has to be, or else it never would have happened . . . don't you think?

Not necessarily.

Claire glanced at him suspiciously, sure that he was holding out on her, but he raised his eyebrows, he raised his hands.

Hey, last year I had a crush on the checkout girl at Key Food . . . sometimes you just have a hard-on for someone's soul, you know what I mean?

She didn't answer, she pulled her knees up against her chest.

Tell your friend not to worry about it, Such said. He picked up the remote control, flipped the channel.

Now look at this item, he said. A porcelain figurine, absolutely charming — I think it's Little Bo Peep. Make a great Mother's Day present, don't you think?

What happened? Claire asked. With the girl?

Oh, Such said, it turned out she was only fifteen.

Jesus, he said, he pointed at the set. Will you look at that — what the hell is that?

You put it into your bathtub and it makes bubbles. It turns your bathtub into an instant Jacuzzi.

Now how could you have possibly guessed such a thing? Such looked at her with new respect.

My mother has it. Claire took the last cookie out of his hand. It doesn't work.

41

SHE WENT HOME THROUGH THE SNOW IN A CAB, HER SHOES were still wet from the day. Going up the stairs, she thought of Jade's apartment, silent, uninhabited. Without having made a conscious decision, she found herself walking past her own place to Jade's door, aware as if for the first time that she had the keys, that she could have entered here at any time.

If there was a plant, she thought, bending to unlock the door, she would water it.

Inside the apartment, it was totally dark. Claire stood in the middle of the living room, blinking; she'd never been there without Jade, and it was as if the place had lost some vital dimension, height or width or length, gone flat in some physical yet undiscernible way.

The plant was in the bathroom, a bamboo whose leaves were curled, the tips gone brown. She was overwhelmed with a cosmic sense of guilt, the unique sensation of having been responsible for some other living thing's death. Maybe it wasn't too late, she thought. Yanking the shower curtains back, she ran hot water to make steam, then poured water into the dry soil, watching the plant as if it might spring back to life before her very eyes. The air in the bathroom thickened, became humid as a rain forest. The steam felt good. She peeled off her socks, then her blouse, and felt her mind going blank. After a while, she took the rest of her clothes off and climbed in the tub, turned her face up to the spray.

She lost track of time, the water against her skin soft as the snow melting on the sill of the small bathroom window. When she got out, she saw Jade's robe hanging on a hook behind the door and put it on, cream-colored silk, soft as second skin.

She walked through the apartment to the bedroom, she didn't turn any lights on, and her foot came against something heavy, soft — Jade's little beaded evening purse.

She sat on the floor and lit the candle stubs lined along the windowsill, as if the use of any electricity might have made her presence here too real. She opened the purse, took everything out one by one: a small black flask of perfume; a bracelet, heavy links with big red stones, the clasp broken; a plum-colored lipstick, its cylindrical container silver. She felt the weight of each object in the palm of her hand, each one like a talisman whose meaning escaped her.

I should go home, she thought, but she knew there was

nothing waiting for her there, no one. She lay back on the pillows for a minute and closed her eyes.

She woke suddenly, could not comprehend the strange spaces on the wall, the lack of shadows. The dream she had been having clung to her, thick as fog, of dancing close to someone, in a room so smoky they could not see each other's faces —

It was sound that finally penetrated through, and it was only then that she realized what had woken her — someone in the hall, unlocking the door now, something heavy against the floor, and then a light, footsteps . . .

Claire sat up just as Jade came in, saw her catch herself in the doorway, stopping hard, an apparition. Her hair was bleached so blond it was nearly white, utterly shocking. Claire lost everything, her words, the prepared expression on her face.

. . . Claire! Jade said, she was just as taken aback. What are you doing here?

I came to water your plant, Claire said, words running into each other, I fell asleep, I don't know how — I think it was too late —

Too late?

I think it's dead.

Jade let go of the door, she stepped into the room. The harsh brightness of her hair was stunning against her high, dark brows, the pale olive of her skin. It made her look like someone else, and she had the deep burning eyes of a traveler, someone who has crossed time zones, who has moved beyond the natural circadian rhythms.

It's my fault, she said. I didn't think I'd be gone this long.

I didn't think you were coming back, Claire said, she could not overcome the sense that she was speaking to a stranger.

Jade's glance skidded off Claire's, as if she didn't know where to rest her eyes.

It's like I never left, she said.

Claire heard something in her voice, a kind of desperation, and she allowed the thought for the first time that Jade had wanted to escape it all as much as she had — that that was why she had stayed away so long. She wanted to say something then,

155

to acknowledge it all, but the right words eluded her, she did not know what they were.

I'm wearing your robe, she said finally, it was all she could think of. I'm sorry.

That's okay, Jade said, I have your jeans.

They looked at each other warily in that dark room, both of them standing tense, ill at ease.

Before either of them could speak, there was a noise down the landing, the unmistakable sound of male footsteps, heavy, and then she heard the door swinging open, softly, the hinge squeaking —

She had left the door unlocked, Claire thought, frozen on the spot. Jade turned, fast, moving toward the source of the sound. Claire grabbed for the phone, but before she could dial 911 she heard a hard grunt, and she dropped it, ran into the living room —

She saw the man first, he already had Jade, and her heart stopped, her throat constricted on the scream rising from her chest, she ran toward them — and then Jade turned back, her smile pale.

Claire, she said. This is Luke.

Claire stopped just in time, but when he reached out to shake her hand she knew that he had seen her panic, he had put it all together, but all he said was, Good to meet you.

She nodded, still unable to speak, her face hot. He was older, thirty-five maybe, maybe more. He wore a black jacket, a white T-shirt, blue jeans, and he had a two-day growth of beard, sunstreaked hair that fell across his eyes. When he raked it back, a quick, customary gesture, Claire saw they were blue, light and intent, eyes that didn't miss a thing; she became excruciatingly aware of her hair, a wild tangle, of her nakedness beneath the half-tied robe.

You two roommates? he asked.

She was looking after my plant, Jade said.

I live next door, Claire said. I was just leaving.

Huh, he said, and then he reached out for Jade, his arm around her neck, pulling her close to him.

And here we are just coming, he said, he kissed her mouth, the back of his head obscuring her face, and in that single gesture Claire saw the man, all will and possession, how he claimed her, and she saw Jade's hands gripping his arm, she could not tell if it was to bring him closer or keep him away.

She seized the moment to duck into the bathroom to change.

When she came back out, he was bringing in the rest of the luggage, all of it compact and heavy, worn black leather. His eyes were bloodshot, but there was an energy in him, he moved like a man with things to do in the world, a man for whom each hour counts.

Jade was in the bedroom, they could hear her stripping the bed, making the sheets snap.

I should go, Claire said, she spoke quickly. It was nice meeting you —

She started to extend her hand, but he stepped back, half crouching, and it wasn't until she heard the click and whirr of the Polaroid that Claire noticed the camera, he was so quick with it, so sly.

He pulled the picture out, handed it to her.

A souvenir, he said.

She took it, her smile stiff, formal; she wanted only to make her exit.

Please tell Jade, she began, but he was already calling her, his voice overriding, unafraid of its own volume.

We'll see you, he said, he stood in the door like the host of a party, bidding the last guest farewell.

Okay, Claire said, inanely cheerful, aware only of the cold, gritty floor beneath her bare feet. Bye . . . !

But Jade ducked under Luke's arm, one hand reaching out for Claire's, and she pressed some brief garment into Claire's hand, the motion quick, surreptitious.

I'll see you, she said, and then beneath her breath, Those are yours.

Even before she glanced down, Claire knew what it was. She nodded vigorously; she couldn't speak, but there was no need, Jade was already stepping back; she didn't say anything more, just closed the door.

Walking down the chilly hall, her underwear clutched in one hand, Claire looked at the developed picture, her face washed-out white with flash, her eyes lit red, and wondered what, exactly, it was a souvenir of.

42

ON HER WAY HOME FROM WORK THE NEXT DAY, CLAIRE walked down Sixth Avenue, somehow calmed by the broad sweep of it there, how the World Trade Towers rose like near-sighted giants up ahead, while behind her, the traffic of Canal Street was jammed with humanity, the sound of car horns musical, constant.

LeRoy's Coffee Shop was on Sixth near Walker, a place where even a woman could sit and eat alone, unpitied, largely ignored. It looked small from the outside but went back deep, laid out narrow and crooked as the rooms in someone's old house. There were tables and booths, but Claire liked to sit at the counter, slowly turning the pages of a magazine while she ate big bowls of soup with heavy bread, drank coffee from a thick white mug.

She had already ordered when she realized, the single blonde in the corner booth was Jade. She had a sketchpad propped on one knee, a cigarette burning forgotten nearby, and in the space of that brief, anonymous moment, Claire thought she could see the pallor of Europe on her face.

Jade raised her head then, as suddenly as if someone had called her name, and Claire was caught. She stood, she tried to act as if she'd just come in.

Hi.

Hello. Jade's smile was the smile one gives a stranger, distant, courteous. Her sweater was the color of sand, too big, the form of her body hidden beneath it.

What are you drawing?

Nothing much.

Women, Claire thought, *nothing but women.*

She stood there, Jade did not invite her to sit down. Under the coffee shop's bright, mundane lighting, there seemed an immeasurable distance between them, the long space of rift and miles, and nothing left to share but caution.

How was Paris?

Gorgeous. The answer came behind her, she recognized Luke's voice before she saw him. He slid into the booth opposite Jade, one hand reaching across, cupping the back of her neck, pulling her toward him to kiss her. Absolutely gorgeous.

He sat back, looked at Claire as if she were just registering in his field of vision.

It's the girl next door! he said, he made an expansive gesture. Join us.

Actually, I was just —

Miss? The waitress called Claire from behind the counter, she had curly black hair piled up on her head, an Irish accent. Would you like your coffee over there then?

Sure, Luke called before Claire could answer, and then she had no choice. She slid into the booth slowly, her eyes on the table. Jade exhaled smoke from the side of her mouth.

"A blonde to make a bishop kick a hole in a stained glass window," Luke quoted, looking at her.

I thought Chandler's women were all dames gone bad, Jade said, her cool enormous. Luke's grin changed his face, made him boyish, made Claire think of summer, skateboards, dogs unleashed at the beach.

You like the hair? he asked. I dyed it for her, in the bathroom of the plane between Paris and Berlin.

Berlin, Claire said, the information jolting, I didn't know you were in Berlin.

It came out almost like an accusation, and Jade looked at her then, her eyes hard, as if to say, You had no right.

Yeah, that's where I was headed when I met her, Luke said, and she insisted on tagging along.

Jade rolled her eyes. After you bought my ticket and had a car waiting at my door, you mean?

I couldn't just leave her there, Luke said, he kept addressing Claire. You should've seen her when I met her . . . sitting in some dark cafe, smoking, looking like she wanted to slit her wrists —

When in Rome, Jade said, shrugging lightly, but she crushed her cigarette out with quick, brutal jabs, as if to kill the subject.

In answer, Luke lifted his hand, and Claire saw the camera for the first time, though the gesture was almost careless; he used it as if it were a part of him, a natural extension of his arm, of his hand; there was no time for self-consciousness, no time to pose.

I found you, he said from behind the lens. I discovered you.

Yeah, Jade said, and though she seemed on the verge of smiling, her eyes glittered, dangerous. I didn't exist until you came along.

He reached across the table then, fast, wound his fingers in her hair, and when her head dropped back he took another picture, he said, I made you what you are today —

He pulled the picture from the camera, tossed it on the table.

A blonde, he said.

This mania of yours to document, Jade said. How many times do I have to tell you? The charmed life will *not* be televised.

He laughed, he tried to hide it, but Claire saw how he looked at Jade, and she thought nobody had ever looked at her like that, she couldn't even find a name for it — a look like thirst, and revelation.

Speaking of the charmed life, he said, I told Taylor we'd meet him at the Lion's Head for a drink —

He turned to Claire. How about it?

Oh, no, that's all right —

Come on, Luke said, do us a favor — keep old Taylor

from feeling like the third wheel — I'm buying, you can't say no. One drink, I promise, and then you can go, what do you say.

He was already standing, throwing money on the table for her coffee, his assurance supreme, unquestionable. Claire was swept up by it, there seemed no appropriate moment at which she could pull back, and then they were out on the street and he was stopping a cab, stopping traffic, only for them to join the flow moments later, to be carried straight into its heart.

43

THE LION'S HEAD WAS IN THE WEST VILLAGE, OFF SEVENTH Avenue. It was a big journalists' hangout, Luke told them, they all went there after work, and it wasn't until then that Claire realized the obvious, that Luke was a journalist, too.

When they walked in, Claire was immediately struck by the noise — although there was music, it was barely audible. The level of conversation was a dull roar, laughter an occasional brief spike, lifting and falling. They stood at the bar, waiting to be served, and Claire eavesdropped on the pair of young men standing next to them, how sure they sounded, trading opinions with the conviction of those who are in the know, who are just ahead of the rest of the world.

I met Qaddafi's mistress last night, one of them was saying. At a dinner party. I'd been warned beforehand, who she was, but I imagined a devout, mysterious woman with a veil . . . I'd been talking to her for ten minutes before it dawned on me, this was she.

Thoroughly modern Millie? His companion was suave, incapable of surprise. He drained the last drop of beer from his bottle.

Parisian, his friend answered. Dior, from top to bottom.

A man approached them, raised his voice over the din. Hey, Elliot — who're your friends?

Luke grinned. Jade, Claire — this is Taylor.

He was tall, too, taller than Luke, and younger. His face

had the look of hunger, of ambition, slightly gaunt, his jaw strong.

Ladies. He bent his head in mock reverence when he shook their hands. What are you drinking?

They ordered martinis, and Claire and Jade sat on barstools, facing the men. Another one of their colleagues had stopped to talk, he did not introduce himself, spoke in a kind of shorthand, with a sardonic air that seemed to be standard currency, as if delivering the news somehow put them all beyond it.

You see the wires? Luke asked him. Czechoslovakia's coming down, too.

There was no sarcasm in his voice, just a certain controlled excitement that gave Claire the strange sensation of being pulled into the sphere of history, of huge events.

It's unbelievable, the man said. Can you imagine what it must be like there right now?

Fuck imagine, I got a camera, Luke said, he looked at Jade. You wanna go to Romania with me?

He was like a boy, his hair falling into his eyes, asking.

I can't afford it, she answered.

Money's no object, he said, I got enough frequent flyer miles to take you to Kathmandu and back —

Well, if it's Kathmandu, Jade said, I'll reconsider.

Christmas in the Himalayas, he said. Let's do it.

That was the excitement that surrounded him, Claire thought — his talk was propulsive, it was the direct prerequisite of action. It made her mute, she kept sipping her martini instead, the gin thick and silvery in her mouth, burning warm all the way down.

Taylor leaned on the bar, he focused on her.

So, Claire, what do you do? he asked, and the question sounded patronizing in her ears, full of an avuncular condescension.

Nothing, really, she said, she didn't want to tell him she was just a secretary.

Ah, he said, a trust fund baby.

What?

Just kidding, he said, he lifted two hands. A comedy joke!

Oh. She tried to smile, thinking she did not know how to do this, how to be glib, flip, thinking she was out of her depth. She turned instinctively toward Jade, all at once overwhelmed by the peculiar sensation of having missed her friend while she was gone, of missing her still, but even though Jade sat only inches away, she seemed almost unaware of Claire's presence, she had one leg crossed high on the other, a cigarette burning between two fingers.

She loved me once, Claire thought, and realized how distant it all was, from here, how hard it was to believe that anything had ever happened between them. She seemed like someone else entirely now — the queen of disguises, Claire thought, has found the jack of hearts.

Where's the bathroom in this place? Jade asked, standing.

I'll show you, Luke said, his hand on her elbow.

Claire was left alone with Taylor, she couldn't think of anything to say.

This place is jammed, Taylor said. Packed.

Claire smiled as if he'd just told her something funny, an inside joke, and finished her drink.

It was only one night for her, too, the thought came then, with all the exaggerated urgency of a sudden alcohol infusion, I have to tell her I was wrong, I have to tell her everything —

Excuse me, she said, she slid off her stool. I'll be right back.

It took her five minutes to maneuver her way through the mass of bodies, and she had just turned the corner that led to the back when she saw Luke, his back to her, his body blocking the way. She was about to say something and then she saw Jade: his arms on either side of her, she was flung up against the wall, her bright hair splashing to one side while he pressed against her, one knee up between her legs, his mouth on hers like he was drinking her.

Claire stepped back, she didn't make a sound.

That was fast, Taylor said. You run into our friends?

They're coming, Claire said, and heard her words sliding together. But I have to go, I just remembered . . .

What? I thought we were going to grab a bite to eat —

I can't, Claire said, she had her jacket on. There's someone — I'm supposed to meet someone, I'm late —

Taylor shrugged, he lifted a hand. See you.

There was a letter from her mother waiting for Claire when she got home, brief, on two square pages of pale lavender stationery.

I don't see much of your sister now that she's working on base, it ended. Sometimes she doesn't come home until nine. I've had to stay at the shop evenings myself, to finish the inventory, but then again, my dance card hasn't been too full lately, ha-ha! so it's not a real tragedy. I never realized how much extra help you girls were in here, the way you used to turn that radio up and sing, it used to drive me crazy. Whoever would have thought I'd miss that!

— The last word underlined twice, the writing that particular flowing cursive they used to teach girls in grammar school when her mother was young, every "i" meticulously dotted, every "t" well crossed; it broke Claire's heart, she could not have said why. On the bottom of the page was a careful imprint of her mother's lips, the vivid orange-toned lipstick slightly smeared now from the envelope.

A fierce wind blew outside, she could hear it as it turned the corners of the buildings, a high rushing whine. She stood by the window, put her hand flat against the chilled glass. Down on the street below, there was no one. Long minutes passed. She stood where she was, she did not move, staring so fixedly that after a while, it all began to look strange, unrecognizable even.

In the distance, there were sirens.

What, the thought came, what am I doing here?

A car stopped at the corner, and for an instant, Claire thought the woman emerging was Jade. Something inside her leapt forward, and she had a vivid flashback of what it had been like before, being with Jade — how everything had changed, how the city had opened, dark and glamorous, offering everything.

She woke breathless from a dream that night, herself alone surrounded by nothing but space, black and empty, stars a cold and distant map of lights a galaxy of miles away, and she had to sit up, both hands over her heart. My mother, she thought. Oh God, I want my mother.

44

IT WAS SATURDAY, AND CLAIRE HAD NOT SEEN OR HEARD from Jade since the night they'd gone out to the Lion's Head. They could be anywhere, Claire thought, Paris or London or just farther uptown, holed up at his place, ordering take-out, never getting dressed. She wouldn't think of it.

The afternoon dragged by. She picked up the files she'd brought home from work, a list of questions Erica from the mayor's office wanted answered, but she couldn't focus, she couldn't make herself concentrate.

She occupied herself with menial tasks instead — scrubbing the tub, wiping the windowsills, sweeping the floor. The effort provided her with some pale comfort, the slight bead of sweat along her upper lip, the sense of virtue that cleaning invariably bestowed.

Darkness fell quickly, like a curtain. She made peanut butter toast and turned the television on. There was a nature documentary on the public channel: the effects of drought on large African game. She saw starving lions, their manes too big for their skeletal, feline bodies. Fires smoldered and burned for days. It made her eyes hurt to watch it. If they could photograph the beasts, she thought, why couldn't they feed them, too? The mere act of watching seemed complicitous; she turned it off.

She sat curled up in her chair; she wanted desperately to be good at solitude, she was not. She tried to remember what she had been like before she had come to New York, and she recalled the impatience with which she'd moved through the world, the way she'd walked down the streets of Alamogordo, contemptuous of the men who honked their horns when she crossed in front of them, but she could not identify herself with that person now, could not remember what that certainty felt like.

She remembered Saturdays in Alamogordo, how she and Tommy would go riding in the evening, after the heat had begun to subside, the horses' hooves kicking up the ground — she remembered how it smelled, that earth, how it caked the creases of her jeans, settled over the toes of her boots.

Sometimes, when they'd had some fight the night before, Claire would stay in town, punishing him with her silence, making him wait, refusing to take his calls. She would hold out till midnight maybe, and then she'd wake him, speaking low into the phone, and he'd drive the hour in from the ranch just to see her, she standing by the road waiting when he got there, hands in the pockets of her jeans, acting as if nothing had happened. Too late to drive back, they'd blow eighteen bucks for a motel room, drink warm champagne, push a pillow between the headboard and the wall to keep the bed from knocking, and Claire's hair would be everywhere, in his eyes, across his chest, dim and burning red, while underneath the window, the crickets sang.

She lifted the phone to her lap, though she'd sworn to herself she would not call him — always wait for a man to call you, her mother used to say, never let him know how interested you are.

Claire remembered how her mother used to look, evenings she was waiting for a man to come by, sitting in the kitchen, smoking, then nervously picking imaginary flakes of tobacco from her tongue, drinking her highball before the ice had any time to melt. Always when they came she would make them wait, make them ring the doorbell twice, and then when she opened the door her voice changed, from its nervous, sharp brightness to a low, sultry swell.

Bye girls, she'd call, and Claire remembered how desperately she had loved that woman as a young girl — the woman her mother could call forth on any evening, with her darkest red lipstick and her favorite new dress.

She closed her eyes, and it was only then that she discerned it — the faint sound of music, an unearthly chorus of female voices, wailing, surreal, like background music for a dream. She put the phone back down.

Jade was home.

45

COME IN, SHE SAID; SHE DID NOT SEEM SURPRISED.

I brought you your mail, Claire said, she held it awkwardly in both hands.

Thanks, Jade said, she took it without looking at any of it, her air distracted.

Claire stepped inside, and immediately she had the impression of having walked into the wrong place, although she recognized individual objects, the lamp, the chair . . . she stood where she was, she could not place it. Jade was already walking toward the bedroom, stopping to pick up scattered items of clothing, her movements brisk, efficient.

I would offer you something to drink, she said politely, but I don't think there's anything in the fridge.

That's all right.

Claire trailed behind her, stopped in the doorway.

Jade's bedroom was a chaos, it was the room of someone in transit, the baubles of travel strewn on the floor — Claire saw airplane liquor miniatures, foreign candy bars, thick, glossy magazines, the earphones of a Walkman tangled around a scarf.

Are you going somewhere . . . ?

I guess, Jade said, her back to Claire as she took clothes from her closet. I haven't even unpacked from Berlin yet, but Luke wants me to go to Czechoslovakia with him —

It was only then that Claire realized what it was.

You took the tarps down.

Jade turned, her arms full of sweaters.

Yeah, she said, it was so dark when I came in today — and then I thought, if they can tear the Wall down in Germany . . . of course, I'll probably regret it the next time I try to sleep here. She shrugged, as if she weren't sure what had possessed her, or at least, Claire thought, as if she wouldn't tell her.

I guess you haven't been home much.

I've been staying at Luke's place, Jade said, her tone maintained the same guarded neutrality as she knelt to repack her clothes. Over on Second Avenue.

Claire nodded, all at once overcome with misery; she had nothing left to say. I should go, she thought, but she stood where she was, she didn't move. Through Jade's blank, denuded windows, night was like a shroud, pulling itself over the city.

Oh, God, Jade said, as if to herself, I forgot I had this.

She lifted something wrapped in a towel. It was a piece of broken-off brick, a scrawl of black paint jagged across one side.

The Wall, Jade said. That's all that's going to be left of it.

You're in love with him, aren't you, Claire said then, and though she meant it as a question, it came out like a statement, abrupt, inappropriately personal, and for a moment, Claire thought Jade wasn't going to answer. She met Claire's eyes for the second time, that look wary, gauging.

I don't know, she said, I still don't know him that well.

She stood up, crossed the room to rummage through her coat pockets.

I was thinking, Claire said, maybe we could go out for a cup of coffee or something . . .

Thanks, but I have to pack, Jade said, she concentrated on lighting a cigarette. Everybody smokes in Berlin, she said. You wouldn't believe how far a pack of cigarettes will get you there.

Claire nodded, incapable of making small talk.

When are you leaving? she asked.

Tomorrow morning.

When will you be back?

I'm not sure.

Claire nodded again; she could feel the same unshed tears pushing behind her eyes, swelling her throat shut.

Thanks for getting the mail, Jade said then, and Claire understood she was being dismissed. You don't have to worry about it anymore — I'm having it forwarded to Luke's place.

Okay, Claire said, and burst into tears.

She could feel Jade's shock from across the room; she pressed her hands against her eyes in a futile effort to control herself.

Claire . . . don't. The unexpected anguish in Jade's voice only made her cry harder, she could not stop.

Come here . . . sit down.

She felt Jade's arm coming around her shoulders, holding her.

I'm sorry, she said, she kept repeating it. I'm sorry . . .

It's okay, Jade said, she smoothed Claire's hair away from her face, but Claire kept her hands over her eyes, she wouldn't look up.

It's just . . . you're leaving, and . . .

Jade waited, still at her side, and it was that stillness that finally made Claire regain herself. She wiped her face, stared down at her hands.

That night, Jade said. You misunderstood.

But I never — there's never been another girl — I thought you were, that something . . .

You want to make everything black and white, Jade said finally, but it's not.

I just want to be friends, Claire said, the way we used to be.

Jade crossed her arms at the waist, she didn't say anything. Her face looked small, her eyes dark.

We never should have, Claire said, groping for the words that would reconnect them. That night —

Jade's look stopped her, those piercing eyes, making Claire stammer.

It's just that we were both —

What? Jade said, she wouldn't let Claire off the hook.

It was Halloween, Claire said, helplessly.

Jade shook her head.

169

I keep forgetting, she said, her smile twisting up to one side, cynical, how young you are.

But all Claire heard was the forgiveness in her voice, and her own smile was wide, she could not repress it.

Call me, she said, when you get back.

At home that night, Claire took the airline ticket from the drawer she'd put it in the day Tommy had left; it was the first time she'd looked at it. Open, read the reservation, the letters all capitals, they seemed to shout. Open. She pictured herself landing, how small Alamogordo would look, engulfed by the wide tracts of desert on either side, and nothing hidden under those vast, inarguable skies.

Tommy would be there, he would be waiting, his feet planted solid, wide, his pickup parked outside. I could have him, Claire thought, I could have him still.

She had an image of Luke and Jade then, in some hotel in Europe somewhere, Luke lying back against the pillows. Even unshaven, uncombed, he would have a glamour, an aura of nights past — it would be no novelty for him, Claire thought, this finding himself in some foreign country in the midst of civil unrest, a beautiful woman undressing before him. She imagined Jade letting the shirt fall from her shoulders, her smile all seduction, promising everything. They wouldn't bother peeling the bedspread back — it would all happen, they would be oblivious to their surroundings, to the rain outside. Maybe later Jade would take a bath and Luke would stand in the doorway and watch. Maybe he would kneel next to her and wash her back, warm water slipping down her shoulder blades, fingers on her spine . . . he would not be able to keep his hands off her.

What other passions.

She put the ticket back into its drawer, shut it. I should get up, she thought, and turn off the light.

She dreamt that she was in a big house, dark, full of stairways. She wore an outrageous costume made of ostrich feathers, curving just barely to cover her crotch, paraded topless in rooms that glittered with strange men's eyes. She walked downstairs and found a large double bed. It had no sheets. Luke lay along one side, he was watching her as if he had known she would come. She lay next to him, careful not to let their bodies touch. He started talking about Jade. None of his sentences were comprehensible, and yet she knew what he meant, and she answered him in kind. He moved closer and closer until finally he lay on top of her, and still they were talking about Jade, feverishly, saying everything they knew, everything they had ever thought, describing her body, the way it looked in different light. He started showing her how they made love. Like this, he said. Like this. They moved against each other. Suddenly Claire became aware of someone watching. She turned her head and saw Ursula standing on the stairwell.

But it isn't me, she cried. Can't you hear him? It's Jade!

Ursula said nothing, but her eyes were half-lidded, disbelieving, mocking with some knowledge of Claire that Claire herself did not possess.

46

HI SUCH, IT'S CLAIRE.

Claire who?

Claire, she said. We worked together once, remember?

Yessss, I think it's coming back to me now . . . you're the little redhead number picked me up at Battery Park, am I right?

She smiled into the receiver, said, I think it was you who picked *me* up —

Sorry, but the last time I picked up a woman was in the seventies, and she was my date for the senior prom —

The foil for your manhunt, you mean.

. . . I beg your pardon?

What about the checkout girl at Key Food? The one who was only fifteen?

Oh, great — if there's one thing I can't stand, it's being quoted back to myself —

I can't help it if I remember.

The curse of youth.

Claire laughed. Such, I'm so glad you're home.

Why, what are you doing?

Nothing.

. . . You admit it just like that?

Well, I was going to eat some ice cream, but then I thought —

Claire, you did the right thing. I'm here for you. Just put that spoon down, and *step away* from the refrigerator.

— that maybe, if you weren't busy . . .

Well . . . I'd have to make quite a few phone calls first . . . a lot of people are going to be very, very disappointed . . .

I'll pay.

Where we going?

I don't know . . . somewhere with a view? . . . But cheap . . . can you think of anyplace like that?

Half an hour later, he was in a cab outside her building, holding the door. When she got in, he threw a fake fur across her lap. She lifted the edge incredulously.

Where *are* we going? she asked. Siberia?

Wouldn't be caught dead, he said. The Cold War is *over.*

They were headed south, winding through the narrow, spooky canyons of Wall Street, where invisible currents lifted litter into wild eddies that swirled up and around, around and around. There was no other sign of life.

They reached Battery Park, and the driver stopped in front of the South Ferry Terminal Building.

You're paying, Such cried cheerfully, he jumped out. He took her up the long flight of stairs that led to the terminal, insisted she wear the ratty fur around her shoulders. They got there just as the Staten Island ferry was docking.

I'll get this one, Such said grandly, then put a quarter in the turnstile and pushed her through.

What's on Staten Island? Claire asked dubiously as they followed a thin stream of people on the boat, the smell inside of heavy fuel and brine.

172

Don't ask me, Such said, his hand on her elbow. It's not as if I've ever *disembarked* there.

But then why are we . . . ?

You wanted a view for cheap, am I right? Such asked, his eyebrows arched, his accent gone native. So, enjoy!

They sneaked looks at their fellow passengers, young women with big breasts and big hair, their dates in jeans and plaid jackets, faces chapped red from the cold, all of them sedated from happy-hour drinking, with nothing to look forward to now but the inevitable ride home.

The engine chugged beneath them, making the floor vibrate, and Claire felt the thrill of motion. Come see, Such said, and led her out through the doors to the back promenade.

The city was right there, the south end of Manhattan rising fantastic and gleaming in the black night, and Claire gripped the wooden balustrade with both hands, consumed by the sight of it, unable to look away though her teeth chattered in the cold. Such leaned next to her, both of them watching in silence as it receded, the boat issuing a strong white wake behind them.

Look, he said. There's the Statue of Liberty.

Claire saw it, ghostly and silent in the dark, the torch raised high, and it sent a shiver down her spine.

From his back pocket, Such pulled a flask.

Let's go get some coffee, he said.

He spiked the coffees generously and they cupped their palms around the Styrofoam and sipped at it, watched the people file off when they reached Staten Island minutes later.

You've never gotten off? Claire asked.

Too scary.

They walked around the whole ferry on the way back, the decks wide and empty.

This is one of the old-fashioned ones! Such told her, he had to shout over the wind. They're like Checker cabs now — an endangered species!

Look, he said as they reached the front deck, Emerald City!

There it was again, Manhattan, that dense, three-dimensional skyline, hard to believe. The city of my dreams, Claire thought, she said nothing.

They'd finished the flask by the time they docked again, and she felt charmed, inviolable.

Where to? Such asked as they emerged into the street.

Anywhere, Claire said, I'll go anywhere.

Oh, I wouldn't take you just anywhere, Such assured her, flagging a cab. But I do know of a very cozy little place in the East Village that I think you're really going to like . . . I know *I* do.

Second Avenue and Fourth Street, he told the driver.

The sign outside simply said BAR. Such opened the door for her.

Real ladies first, he said.

The place was a dive, nothing but a room with a pool table and a jukebox, the reek of stale beer.

Such, the bartender said when he saw them. What's up?

Got a date, Such said, he put his arm around Claire. Claire, meet Arthur. Arthur, Claire.

Arthur smiled at her, he kept having to shake the hair from his eyes. Nice to meet you.

Claire glanced around while he served someone else; the place was full of men, and none of them were looking at her. She touched Such's sleeve.

Is this a gay bar?

A *what?* Such said, as if shocked. People turned and looked. Claire shaded her eyes, mortified.

It's okay, Arthur said. We like women, too.

Do not, Such said. Anyway, listen, Arthur. Can't stay. We just stopped in to say hi.

Hi, Arthur said.

Really, I'm serious. No amount of *free booze* could keep me here.

Arthur rolled his eyes, lifted a bottle of tequila.

Oh no, Such said. Not tequila. If you loved me, Arthur, if you really loved me, you wouldn't point that bottle at me —

Shut up and swallow, Arthur said, he poured one for Claire, too.

I really shouldn't, Such said. He looked at his empty shotglass mournfully. Tequila goes straight to my asshole.

Arthur burst out laughing but Such covered his mouth, looked as shocked as if someone else had said it. Good God, Claire, he said. Tell me to shut up.

I would, she said, but then who would talk to me?

Arthur would, Such said, but Arthur had turned to serve somebody else, he didn't hear them.

Is he a good friend of yours?

Well, I've only known him about a year now, Such said, but that's like seven in gay years. Which is not to say that I *know* him, really, Such said, loud, making Arthur turn around, I just bump into him when I come here, stricken with *la nostalgie de la boue*.

What?

A longing for the mud. It's kind of the reverse of aspiration.

His middle name, Arthur said. Another round?

Absolutely not, Such said, he lifted his glass toward the bottle. I've had enough.

Never say uncle, Arthur said, pouring again.

Never do, Such said, he grinned.

They knew each other well, it was perfectly clear, and it occurred to Claire only then that they had slept with each other.

Oh God, Such muttered, he glanced away from someone coming in. Nightmare trick from the past.

Claire started to turn but Such's hand clamped down on her arm, he said, Don't look. He might talk to us.

She leaned against the bar with him, she didn't want to think about how late it was getting, or the files she'd promised herself she'd get through, stacked on the kitchen table.

Such, she began, but his eyes were fixed on another man just walking in the door.

Move away from me, he whispered theatrically. *Quickly*.

175

She picked up her coat. I was just, she said, her tone matching his, leaving.

Such caught her just outside the door.

Wait a second, where are you going? Come back in and meet my friend —

No, I have to go home, she said, I have to work tomorrow.

Well, if you're going to start using four-letter words . . .

He walked her to the corner for a cab, insisted on waiting with her, coatless — I'm not cold, he said, he leaned over to kiss her cheek as she got in.

You need anything, he said, you know where to find me.

47

THANKSGIVING AT SAM AND NADJA'S WAS AN ODD ASSORT-ment of strays and rarities — Rinpoche Lobsang Tetyong, an older Tibetan monk in scarlet and yellow robes, his face like the face of a Navajo, wide-planed, beautiful, his smile dazzlingly white; a woman in her mid-thirties with very short hair and no makeup, who introduced herself simply as Jim; and Ursula, looking unusually soft in a toffee-colored sweater, a pair of topaz stones dangling prettily from her ears.

Claire brought Such, they arrived in the middle of the afternoon. Nadja greeted them at the door, a wooden spoon in her hand.

I'm mashing potatoes, she said.

I'm Such, he said, and Claire saw how Nadja laughed, how instantly she liked him.

The apartment was beautiful, shining. There was a fire in the fireplace, candles, food everywhere — silver bowls filled with walnuts, with chocolates, with pears, and in one corner, a magnificent Christmas tree that soared up to the ceiling; it was like a piece of forest, transplanted, dark green and vibrant, hung with small golden balls and real candles, the wax dripping like snow. They had placed the stone Buddha just in front of it, and from a certain position across the room it seemed as though the tree were sprouting out of the statue itself, a living masterpiece.

I can see, Such said, that you're not the people responsible for flooding the suicide hotlines during the holidays.

No, Nadja said, she was still smiling at him — an amusement, Claire knew, that would last all day. Why, are you?

Only if I spend it in Palm Beach, he said, with my mother.

Come into the kitchen, Nadja commanded. And entertain me.

Sure, Such said. Can I mash, too?

Everybody was in the kitchen save Rinpoche.

He likes to wander off, Sam said. He was wearing old khakis and a gray sweater with a small hole in one elbow, basting the turkey. His smile was the kitchen's center; everyone gravitated toward it, they crowded around with glasses of wine in their hands, getting in the way, apologizing, unwilling to leave. He assigned them menial chores, putting butter on the table, laying out spoons, the pepper grinder, and they fulfilled each request with the eagerness of children who have been deluded into thinking their tasks essential. All the while he chopped apples and onions and celery and raisins and almonds and bread and parsley to make a huge pan of stuffing.

We always make extra, Nadja said. It's the best part.

No, Jim said. Nothing's better than whipped potatoes. Whipped potatoes with butter and gravy. I could live on it for the rest of my life.

She spoke quickly, had the accent of one who has been born and raised in New York City, slightly coarse, altogether human. She was the lighting designer for a theater company in SoHo — We used to be avant-garde, she said, but now they just call it alternative.

Alternative to what? Sam asked.

Cats, Jim said. *Oh, Calcutta!* Don't ask me — I just work there.

Ursula came walking back into the kitchen and automatically Claire looked up, the sound of that brisk step making her guarded, ready to receive orders. Sam saw it, he laughed.

What can I do? Ursula asked.

I refuse to make any requests of you today, Ursula, he said. You have to stop working or you'll make me feel guilty.

Ursula laughed, high and girlish. I like to work, Mr. Gordon —

Sam!

— Sam, she corrected herself, at once officious and embarrassed. If I didn't have my work, I'd feel a complete wretch of a human being.

I've heard people say that before, Such murmured, lounging against the kitchen counter. I've never understood it.

What do you do? Nadja asked.

Temp, Such said.

He plays the piano, Claire said. He's an entertainer.

There's a slur in there somewhere, Such said. But it's Thanksgiving, Claire, and I'm not going to take the bait.

We used to have a piano, Sam said.

Really? What happened to it?

Oh, Sam said. It stopped getting played, so . . .

Nadja shot him a glance, and he paused briefly.

We got rid of it, he finished.

Nadja looked down, Claire could not see her face. There was a peculiar silence for a moment, and then Such spoke.

I know, he said, it's funny how they seem to grow when they don't get used. I've been thinking about charging mine rent.

Here, Nadja said, thrusting the masher toward him. Mash. I'm going to make sure Rinpoche's okay. Come with me, Ursula — you're his favorite.

My goodness, Ursula said, following her. What a thing to say!

Did you play? Such asked Sam.

My son did.

He was amazing, Jim said, coming to stand closer. He played Scott Joplin like no one. Incredible.

He play still? Such mashed forcefully, the tip of his tongue showing.

Well, Sam said. He died.

Such's arm stopped in mid-motion. Claire clutched the counter with both hands. Sam smiled, he shook his head.

We don't live in recognition of death, Jim said. Our lives would be different if we did.

He played it so fast, Sam said. You remember how fast he could play it?

Who could forget?

Sam put an arm around her. What a blessing you are, Jim, he said.

Over his shoulder she raised an eyebrow, she said, I've been called a lot of things, but . . .

Sam laughed, he let her go.

Okay, he said, he put the last pan of stuffing in the oven. Forty-five minutes and counting . . .

He clapped his hands against each other; it was the sound of something finished, satisfying.

Come on, he said. Let's go sit with the tree.

I can't believe you work for that man, Such said to her when they finally left, both of them loaded down with leftovers. He's a miracle. They're both miracles.

I know, Claire said.

And Jim! What a name, he said. What a dyke.

What? You think so?

Listen, honey, it takes one to know one, and I can't believe you didn't notice the looks Jim was giving you — I know you're still new in town, but get a grip, will you?

. . . you think she thought *I* was . . . ?

In her dreams, Such retorted. I was talking about *me*.

You're deranged, she said, she tried to cover her embarrassment. Seriously deranged.

Especially during the prayer, she was so jealous that Ursula got to hold your hand and she didn't.

I can't believe, Claire said, that that's what you were thinking about all night.

Believe it, Such said. They were riding downtown in a cab, an old Checker, the back roomy as a carriage.

This makes me think of old New York, Such said. Back when Washington Square was the height of chic — can you imagine. Now it's just the best place to buy nickel bags.

Claire gazed out the window, she saw the city's history in all of its great, wide buildings, gone dark now with years of soot, and she was comforted by the size of them, the age. They had witnessed decades, she thought, centuries even — they had witnessed thousands of people, and now her.

She reached across the seat and took Such's hand.

48

IT WAS A WEEK LATER BEFORE CLAIRE SAW JADE AGAIN, AND there were Christmas lights everywhere, white and shaped like giant snowflakes hanging in the middle of Fifty-seventh Street, covering all the stripped-bare branches of the trees that lined the middle of Park Avenue, multicolored and flashing in the windows of people's apartments.

Claire had joined the YWCA uptown; she swam every night after work, sat in the steam room for fifteen minutes afterward. She loved the way the heat felt hours later; even out in the frosty, winter air, her face retained its flush, her muscles stayed warm and loose.

She was just outside her building, fishing in her pocket for the keys, when the door swung open. She and Luke collided, and though she hadn't seen his face, she knew instantaneously it was him. She reared back fast, but her hair was caught on the zipper of his jacket, she couldn't pull away, and the claustrophobic nearness, the smell of him, confused her; she could not extricate herself, could not form a single cohesive sentence. He said, Here, let me —

But their fingers only fumbled together, making her snatch her hand back, and she was ready to yank her head away, let the hair rip, when she heard Jade's voice.

Wait, she said, and Claire felt her touch, soothing, quick. Just wait one second . . .

She unwound the hair without breaking a strand, it was over in moments.

Sorry, Luke kept saying, I didn't see you there —

You should watch where you're going. Jade's voice was grave, but Claire knew she was amused, though nothing in her face betrayed it.

You're back, Claire said, she acted as if she'd already forgotten the incident, as if it hadn't thrown her in the least. When did you get back?

The three of them stood inside the chilly entryway, Jade in a man's overcoat, her face devoid of makeup, beautiful.

When was it? Last night? She looked at Luke. We just woke up, I'm so disoriented —

Yeah, Luke said, he rubbed his face. Last night, right. He stood for a moment with one elbow up against the wall, and though he was obviously tired, his gaze still made Claire nervous; there was something unblinking about it, unrelenting, and she thought this must be the gaze he wore when he was working, observing detail and committing it to memory.

A couple came running down the stairs, Luke had to move apart to let them pass, he grabbed the door before it could close again.

Listen, we better pick up that Chinese, he said, I called half an hour ago, it's gonna be cold — you eaten yet?

This last addressed to Claire, and she shook her head, taken off-guard, started to say something, but Luke held the door wide for her, he said, Come on, I got my car parked just down there.

They walked down the street, Jade between them. She smiled out from the luminous face at anyone who looked at her — truck drivers, garbagemen, shopkeepers, cleaning ladies. Her beauty was like a drug, incendiary. She wore it like a veil of light, a halo that preceded her; it made Claire want to shake Jade, to tell her to discriminate, to say, Anyone can ask to be looked at like that, any whore! But she also knew that Jade asked for nothing — everything was given her, showered on her. She held her hands up against the barrage, murmured thanks, her gratitude a pale thing.

It was so cold in Prague, she said now. You could always see your breath, even when you went inside . . .

Claire nodded, she could think of nothing to say; nothing in her own experience compared to the places the two of them had just been, the things they had seen.

We'll make a fire when we get home, Luke said, he put his arm around Jade's neck, grinned at Claire. Warm you women up.

His car was an old black Fiat with two leather seats slung deep and low; it felt like a cockpit, and Jade sat in the middle, legs straddling the gearshift, laughing, her happiness apparent. She was like a favorite child, getting everything she wanted, riding through life without disappointment.

She and Claire waited, the engine idling, while Luke ran in to get the food.

How have you been? Jade asked her, and Claire could hear, whatever hardness had been there the last time was gone. This was the woman she'd met, Claire thought, this was her friend —

I've been working, she said, I got a job.

Really? A real job?

I'm just a secretary, but I'm learning something. And I like the man I'm working for. He and his wife had me over for Thanksgiving. She'd turned to face Jade; they were only inches apart. The dark closeness of the car was at once intimate and anonymous, made for confidences.

How've you been? she asked now. What was it like over there?

Insane. The streets were mobbed, every day — there were so many rumors, the wildest stories, it was hard to know what to believe, but Luke had a sixth sense about what was true, it was amazing — the students were demonstrating and the police went in, tear gas and clubs and worse, students killed . . .

Weren't you scared?

I should have been, Jade said. But there was this feeling, I can't explain it, of being in the middle of something else — I couldn't sleep, I couldn't eat —

You look so thin, Claire said.

She did, her bones seemed to glow under her skin, but it suited her, made her limbs long, clean, elegant lines. She shrugged. She was beyond ordinary needs, Claire thought; she had been inhabiting another sphere altogether. Just looking at her made Claire hungry, she was starving, she craved red meat, bread, chocolate.

One Delirious Chicken, Luke announced, his sudden appearance intrusive, prescient. And two Empress Shrimps, coming up.

49

LUKE'S PLACE WAS ON SECOND AVENUE NEAR FIFTH STREET, at the top of a nine-story building. It had a slow-moving, old-fashioned elevator with an iron grate. The corridor was narrow, everything was dirty.

Jade opened the door with three keys, newly minted, while Luke parked the car. Welcome to the pentshack, she said. Isn't it glorious?

It was, in fact, a shack, a little house built right on top of the roof. His living room had glass doors that led outside, where there was a view of the Empire State and the Chrysler and the Pan Am buildings on one end and lower Manhattan on the other, with its rickety six-story tenement buildings. Inside, bookcases seemed to line every available wall and the books spilled over into everything; they lay open and face down on the couch, on the kitchen table, they piled up from the floor, as if he had just been reading them yesterday, as if he were about to return and pick them up again at any moment. Claire turned one over. *Diary of a Seducer,* read the title, by Søren Kierkegaard.

The whole place had a dilapidated look, the couch was ancient, there were dirty glasses in the bedroom and a mound of laundry in a corner of the bathroom, but there was color everywhere too, color from other countries, Peruvian rugs, African sculptures, Mexican blankets, Tibetan calendars, and among these things, all kinds of equipment — an old-fashioned typewriter, two high-tech microcassette recorders, a laptop computer, and cameras of every size, 35-millimeter, Super 8 film, Polaroid. Together, his possessions exuded a sense of mobility, of creativity, a feeling that, at any moment, plans could be implemented, secrets discovered — that, at any moment, they could change the shape of the world itself.

Make yourself at home, Jade called from the kitchen, and Claire took it as permission to walk farther back, and into Luke's bedroom.

It was a bachelor's bedroom, there was nothing but a bed and a bureau, the surface bare but for some of Jade's jewelry, silver and gold spilled carelessly across; otherwise there was nothing decorative, no pictures, nothing extra, except, unexpectedly, a white mosquito net hung over the bed. It gave the room a certain mood, romantic, but also the feeling of camping out, of being on safari.

She heard the front door open and shut, the sound of his voice in the kitchen, low, the intimate tones of a man conferring with her, his other, the woman of his dreams. They're talking about me, Claire thought, she was suddenly sure of it — as if she were an inanimate object, she thought, or some wayward homeless child, a poor relative —

She backed out of the room fast, she could not bear it.

There you are. Luke was piling wood in the fireplace, Jade was twisting newspaper. They both smiled at her and she was ashamed of her own paranoia, but she did not disbelieve it.

Here I am, she said. She stood in the middle of the room, her coat in her hands, and almost as if by accident, she met Jade's gaze. Neither of them said anything, but the look that passed between them was unguarded, direct. It made Claire lower her eyes, she said, Where can I hang this?

But even as she turned away from them, she realized that the sense of being extraneous had evaporated, been lifted clean from her system. Across the room, the radiator hissed and clanked. Jade stretched luxuriously. Oh, it's so wonderful to be warm again!

They ate on the floor by the fire, watched it burn, inexorable, hypnotizing. Luke had opened a bottle of red wine, he kept jumping up to pour more, he told stories, outrageous stories that tested the edges of belief —

He had been tailed by some men in Prague, he said, they followed him for days —

The third night they cornered me in this alley, started closing in. I was up against the wall, one guy came at me and I swung at him —

What? Jade sat forward, she had not heard any of this.

They would've killed me, he said, he opened another bottle of wine. They were both huge, like tanks — and then suddenly there was this gang of kids, teenagers, all of them in dark pants and black jackets, they saved my fucking ass. Take off, one of them told me, in *English*.

Who were they?

Who knows. Never saw any of them again.

Jade laughed, her cool was gone, and in its place was an ardor, she was flushed with it, her eyes burned.

What about those pictures of what's-his-name, Jade asked. That playwright — what's his name, it sounds like a Greek dessert —

Vaclav Havel.

Yes, that's right — are they going to print them?

Luke nodded. They're running an interview next week, he said. He's a bright guy. Charismatic.

How do his plays end? Claire asked, and they both laughed at that, though she had not meant to be funny.

I don't know, Luke said, but it's a good question.

They drank the other bottle, it went down so smoothly Claire was hardly aware that she was getting drunk, but she could see it in Jade, her movements becoming volatile, unpredictable. Claire and Luke were both watching Jade, she realized, their backs propped up against the couch at either end of the

185

coffee table, Jade the single point on the other side, her back to the fire.

There's only one fortune cookie, Jade said. We'll have to share it.

Here, she said, she offered it to Claire. You open it.

Claire cracked the varnished pastry and unfurled the little piece of paper.

"You can have what you want if you really want it," she read. "Just move toward it, and reach out."

If you *really* want it, Jade said, she laughed. I guess that must be the key —

What is it? Luke asked, he had his own volatility, his energy rose to match hers. What do you want?

Intoxication, Jade said, she made to reach for the bottle but he pulled it back, and her hands landed on his shoulders, she pushed him until he was up against the wall.

I want — She held him there, her heels coming off the floor.

Say it, he said, and for an instant they were still, eyes locked, brilliant.

She seized the bottle and let him go, laughter a breeze that came off her. Ask Claire, she said. Claire knows —

She fell back on the floor next to Claire, poured the rest of the wine in her glass. Have some, she said, get drunk with me . . . !

She picked up the slip of paper, closed it in her fist, said, If you really want it . . .

She put an arm around Claire's neck, her lips to Claire's ear. What is it, she whispered, that you really want?

Claire felt her face turn hot, she was suffused with a violent embarrassment, and she reached for her glass, drained it. The wine was harsh at the back of her throat, made her eyes close. When she opened them again she saw Luke, standing across from them, his arms at his sides, naked-looking somehow, rudderless, but Jade didn't seem to notice, she put her mouth to Claire's ear, she was whispering, The way you smell . . . I bet he misses that most of all . . .

What's going on, Luke said, he cleared his throat. What are you two whispering about —

Jade leaned her head on one arm, looked up. None of them said anything, and Claire was aware of a sudden density in the room, an almost suffocating sense of possibility. She could hardly move.

Hey, Luke said. His voice was soft, his face only half lit, sharp in the shadows.

Come here, Jade said, the words cracked with tenderness. Come down to our level . . .

Claire was overcome with a flash of fury, a sudden, murderous instinct — she would have liked to slap him, to stab him, to push him through a window —

He bent toward Jade, and Claire fled.

In the bathroom, she shut the door, locked it, and cool white-tiled air filled her lungs, light washed over her, bright electric illumination, making her freckles stand out, her face pale beneath them.

She leaned over the sink and put her wrists beneath cold water, watched it run, a clear and steady stream, the sound ordinary and soothing.

Claire . . . Jade knocked on the door, her tone gone contrite, quiet. Are you okay?

I'm fine, Claire said, she used the voice she would have used with Ursula, with anyone she didn't want to know her. She opened the door, kept her eyes down.

I really should get going, she said. It's late —

No, stay, Luke said, Claire heard the same apology in his voice. You can sleep here if you want to — this couch is the best sleeping couch in the world — it's more comfortable than the bed.

Claire kept her back to him, she yanked her coat from the closet.

No, she said, and it took everything she had to add, Thanks.

50

SAM WAS ALREADY IN THE OFFICE WHEN SHE GOT THERE THE
next morning, fifteen minutes early. Lila had not yet arrived,
Ursula was filing, the phones were quiet. Claire sat at her desk,
overcome by a desire for invisibility so strong it was like hunger, like thirst. She dreamed of disappearing, going anywhere,
changing her name, arriving in some distant, foreign land as
somebody else, the future a pristine blank upon which she would
tread lightly, lightly, so lightly perhaps she would not even leave
a mark.

Can I get you some coffee?

She looked up; Sam was standing just outside his office, his
hands in his pockets. She had the feeling he had been standing
there a few seconds before speaking, watching her.

That's okay, I'll get it —

No, he said, please. Let me.

He didn't ask her how she took it, but when he came back
it was just the right color, not too light.

Erica tells me she's very impressed with my new paralegal,
he said. I just spoke to her last night.

Really?

In fact, she called to ask if I could spare you for some conference they're having the first week of January. "Indispensable,"
I believe, was the exact word she used.

She looked at him, surprised.

I don't think, he said, raising an eyebrow, I like the sound
of it.

Come into my office, he invited then. Nadja went to
Zabar's yesterday, I have a box full of babka.

The heavy winter sky loomed large through Sam's windows, Bach played quietly from the small stereo he kept beneath
his books. The babka was sweet and doughy, layered with sug-
ared cinnamon. Sam spread napkins out on his desk, he let the
crumbs fall; he was a man at home, unconcerned with the ex-
ternal, his ease apparent.

How's everything with you, Claire? he asked.

Okay, she said, it was the best she could do.

He leaned back, he sipped his coffee. His attention was quiet, absolutely focused; it made her want to tell him everything.

It feels strange sometimes, she said, living here.

Change is never easy, Sam said.

No, she said, she tried to smile, could not. She picked up her coffee cup and put her lips on the rim, but she couldn't swallow.

Sam swiveled slightly in his chair and looked out the window.

I'm always amazed, he said, at how different everything looks in the morning.

Claire nodded, though he couldn't see her.

It never really gets dark, though, he said. I guess that says something about this city, doesn't it?

That everybody who lives here's scared of the dark?

That's one way to look at it. He swiveled back around, smiling. Tell you what I think, he said. I think you're homesick.

She smiled a little, she could not admit it, even to herself; she didn't have that luxury.

Christmas is just around the corner, he said. If you want to take a week off . . .

But that conference, she said. I still have to get through the rest of the files —

Take them with you, Sam said.

I don't know, Claire said. But thank you anyway. She stood up. And thank you for — the babka, and everything.

Riding home on the subway that evening, Claire kept catching her own eye reflected in the window, and she recoiled each time, as embarrassed as if she'd been caught looking at a stranger.

She stopped at the Lebanese deli on the way home, asking for Tiger.

The deli man grinned broadly at her. Tay-gur out!

189

You shouldn't let him go like that, she said. He could get killed out there, run over by a cab or something.

The deli man shrugged. He want to go, he go! He got head of his own — what I can do?

I don't know, Claire said disconsolately. But you should do something.

The deli man made a long face, he pointed at her. Why you sad!

I'm not sad.

Yes, you sad! What, you tell me — you got love trouble?

Claire shook her head, she smiled weakly. No, she said, I'm just hungry.

Oh, he said, he threw his hands up. Then you come right place!

Crossing the street to go home, she was aware of her heartbeat in her temple, a pulsing throb. She climbed the stairs the way an invalid would, stopping on the landing, hand on her throat. But the hallway was quiet, there was no light beneath Jade's door. Claire opened her own sneaky as a thief, she shut it noiselessly.

Inside, she found the message light blinking.

Hi . . . It took her a second to recognize Tommy's voice because he was speaking so low, as if he didn't want anybody to overhear.

Claire heard the long pause that followed, and she could feel his struggle in that silence, how he was shuttling back and forth between love and pride.

I was just wonderin, he said finally, if you were ever comin home.

She sat down, her coat still on, her gloves. It was another life, she thought, another life entirely that waited for her there.

She closed her eyes and imagined the babies they would have, sunny sturdy-legged blond babies with freckled knees, solemn faces, children who would grow up under that endless desert sky. She imagined growing old, Tommy sleeping in the bed beside her, his back broad and solid, the warmth of his eyes unwavering, and it came to her that she could spend an entire life with him and never once doubt herself.

THEY DROVE TO EL PASO FOR HERRADURA SILVER, THREE women piled into Bonnie's El Camino, doing eighty-five, ninety, and it felt like nothing on that straight long stretch of desert highway, no one on the road but them and the radio on loud, the chorus of last summer's popular song rising faintly from a steady hiss of static.

Claire drove, it was she who'd commandeered the raid, she kept her foot pressed all the way down on the gas, and crowded up next to her, Bonnie sang, they both did, loud as children, voices swallowed by the wind.

Your legs are strong/ and they're so so long/ and you don't come from this town —

One elbow out the window on the other side, her hair whipped back, Paula was silent, squinting in the rush of air. It was Christmas Eve.

Ninety-nine miles later, they reached the first traffic light and Claire slowed, she said, The metropolis!

She pronounced the words ironically, thinking of where she'd come from, and she felt how Bonnie kept looking at her, a series of quick glances, as if Claire had become somehow suspicious.

She held the tip of her tongue between her teeth, wanting to tell what it was like, New York, but she stayed quiet; they all did. She drove through the outskirts of town, streetlights just come on against the dusk, drove on new paved road past half-lit neon signs advertising topless dancers, men outside staring as they passed, dull eyes widening with lechery, and they all pulled in, elbows and hair; they turned the radio down, aware of themselves suddenly as white women, hated, desirable, rich.

They stopped in front of the liquor store and it was Paula who hopped out, their collected money fisted in her hand.

Silver, Bonnie called after her, don't forget!

She did not deign to answer, she disappeared inside.

Outside, the slow-baked air standing still, the car streaked with dust, and in the Texas night nothing happening but drink, women sitting on stools outside open doors, skirts hitched to let the air move against their legs, bodies wide and coarse, their eyes rimmed dark with homemade kohl.

Well, Claire said, I guess some things never change.

She jumped out, she didn't say what was foremost in her mind — how she could measure herself, finally, for the first time since she'd left, against these familiar landmarks. How far she'd leapt beyond. Bonnie jumped out after her, she sensed it in Claire instinctively, this new fearlessness, it was like a charge, and she came to stand close to it, something new in her laughter, nervous.

Paula came out, already twisting the top of the bottle off with one hand.

One hit now, she said, it was what they always said, and they sat on the back of the car, feet swinging, took the first sip of that Mexican tequila, illegal to sell past the border; they called it silver and that's how it felt going down, smooth and heavy and bitter, then rising mercurial to one's head, making foolish people brave.

Okay, Paula said, I'm driving back.

She had her own authority, distinct from Claire's, forbidding, inarguable; handing her the keys, Claire thought she seemed taller than she really was. It was her posture, upright as a dancer's, as a soldier's. Even her austere ponytail only enhanced her classical lines. Her beauty was not something she advertised, not something you noticed immediately. She wore no makeup, no jewelry, and still, men turned to look at her in the street. It was the clarity of her gaze, Claire thought, that made her striking, and the equally clear, uncompromising way she looked at the world. She had always been that way, she had always been the same.

She was the opposite, Claire thought, of Jade.

They shot back, with Paula driving just as fast as Claire

had, faster, through El Paso and then the small border towns, Canutillo, Anthony, everything dark there save for the cantinas and the brief snatches of Mexican music that came from their open doors. The traffic light at Las Cruces the last light between El Paso and home — after that it was nothing but miles of desert and its scrub, juniper and sage dark clumps, and overhead the stars so clear they could see the swirl of the Milky Way.

Where we going? Bonnie asked.

White Sands, Claire said before Paula could answer, she looked at her sister. There's still time before dinner, isn't there?

They made it to the dunes in half an hour, parked along the side of the fence, long loud furor of high-speed wind gone now, their voices strangely resonant in that crystalline, chilled air.

The sand slid into their shoes, cool and fine; it looked silvery in the night, the dunes shifting under their feet, making those perfectly ridged spines slither into another shape.

Bonnie held the bottle out for Claire. Take another hit!

She lay back next to Claire, and for the first time, Claire was aware of something else in Bonnie's posture, in her proximity — the possibility of invitation, a certain, if unconscious, physical curiosity. Claire lay back, aware of her own ease now, too, but it was totally different from what she felt near Jade; there was no urge here, no electricity. She gazed covertly at her sister's best friend. She was beautiful, married; she had two small children and they all rode together, the baby pushed up on the saddle against her own lean frame, that mother's body still young as a teenager's.

So you seein any guys out there, Claire? Any New Yorkers? She put a spin on the word, it made them all grin.

No. I slept with one guy once, Claire said, Rich Pepper.

Was it safe? Bonnie asked, she raised an eyebrow. Paula took the bottle, she shot Claire a look, Claire read it with perfect accuracy, an older sister's warning: it better have been.

Yeah, she answered, but it wasn't worth it.

Even as she said it, she knew she didn't really believe it; or rather, that if she had to do it all over again, she would have fallen for him the same way, disbelieved the same clues.

How's Hank? she asked now, wanting to change the subject.

He's fine, Bonnie said, she spoke breezily. He said he was going to the Roadrunner for a beer, you want to see him. Think Tommy's with him.

At the mention of his name, Claire felt herself stiffen, and she was aware of the glance her sister threw out, sharp, inquiring.

You miss Tommy? Bonnie was looking at her, too, her elbows draped around her knees.

Sometimes, Claire said, she shrugged, and then Bonnie looked away, as if she didn't want to hear any more. Neither she nor Paula asked Claire any more questions, about where she worked, what she did, who her friends were — they didn't want to know, they didn't want to hear that their lives might be different, too, that they still had a choice. They had made their choices already, Claire thought. They didn't want to question them.

Remember when we used to come here, Bonnie said, at night, in the summer? Remember how we used to sled?

Yeah. Claire remembered everything, how they tore the cardboard boxes to make them flat, took turns sliding down the dunes, rolling off into the sand, how later they would find it everywhere, in the creases of their legs and in their navels, gritty on their mothers' kitchen floors.

It was on one of those nights that she had met Tommy, she couldn't remember who had brought him, only that every time she'd looked at him he'd been looking at her, his gaze steady, unwavering, but he hadn't spoken to her until they were leaving, stumbling back down to the fence. Your hair, he'd said, and reached out to touch the ends, your hair is wild.

Paula capped the bottle. It was too cold to stay out any longer; it was too late. They all rose as one, brushing the sand from their backs.

We goin to the Roadrunner? Bonnie asked, and Claire was silent, waiting for her sister.

We can stay ten minutes, Paula said, and that's it.

The bar was just down the street, Hank's car was in the parking lot.

They're here, Bonnie confirmed, she jumped out first. Even before she'd gotten out, Claire had already zeroed in on Tommy's shape inside the bar, and just as instinctively, she knew that he had seen her, too.

She let Bonnie and Paula move past her, she hung outside the door, saw Tommy get off his barstool, come toward her; he didn't want the reunion to be public either. She felt her heartbeat, not a pounding so much as a thick, almost suffocating, rush of blood, like some slow, driving tide, rising.

Hi. She spoke low, so no one else could hear.

Hi. Tommy's hands thrust deep in the pockets of his jacket, his face closed, wary. He stopped a foot from her, but she defied his border, she stepped over it, she put her arms around his neck and pressed her face against his shoulder. He cleared his throat, for a moment he did not move, but she held on to him, she used all her strength, and finally his hands rose, he put them on her back, on her shoulders, his ambivalence a palpable presence, how he wanted to hold her, how he wanted to push her away. She let go.

In the dark, their eyes met.

I called you, she said. You weren't home.

Guess not, he said, he glanced away, and it was then that she knew for sure he was sleeping with somebody else. She swallowed hard, as if to push the thought back down, to stifle that grueling surge of adrenaline. She said nothing, she nodded, her face did not betray her.

I used your ticket, she said. I'll pay you back.

He shrugged, as if to say it didn't matter, money meant nothing to him. You want a drink? he asked. They turned back toward the bar, he reaching naturally forward to get the door.

Okay if I hold this for you? he asked. Or would that be an insult to your independence?

You're the one, she said, who's playing hard to get now.

His only answer was a kind of laugh, an exhale full of effort, and it occurred to her that he had already gone through all

195

this, that he had been working hard to get through it, to get over it; to get over her.

The bar was dark, they were all standing together, Hank and Bonnie, Paula and someone else, she had never seen him before.

Hey, he said, he extended a hand. I'm Reno.

He had the straight, stiff back, the close-cropped hair of a military man, and she guessed he was from the base.

Claire, she said, wondering who knew him, who had invited him, but a second later she knew, when he grinned, said, Yeah, I know — Paula's little sister.

That's right, she said, she looked at Paula, and though she felt sure her sister was acutely attuned to this brief exchange, she acted as if she hadn't heard any of it, she was unbuttoning her jacket, she wasn't even looking their way.

Two shots, Tommy called to the bartender, Herradura.

Drinking it quick, with one neat gesture, she had a sudden flashback of the last time she had done this — with Jade, on Halloween. She stood close to Tommy, she could feel the tequila warming her limbs, making her nerve-ends tingle, and she had a sudden urge to tell him everything, how Jade had taken her, and how it had pushed her to some other, as yet inarticulated level. The compulsion to confess was like some strange defiance, brief, gripping; she had to fight to keep the words from spilling over.

You belong to me, she thought fiercely, she wanted to grab him, but she pushed her hands in her pockets instead, an act of self-containment, of self-sufficiency.

They finished their drinks, they paid. It was Christmas Eve; they all had to go home to their families, but walking back to the car, Claire was aware of the buzz in her head, how it filled her with a kind of recklessness, the sense that she had nothing to apologize for.

Where's your truck? she asked Tommy, glancing at him sideways, flirting with him like he liked it, as if there were nothing wrong between them. Broken down again?

Why, he shot back, you want to get underneath it?

No, she said, you must be thinking of your *other* girlfriend.

She tossed her hair back, she didn't look at him. They lagged behind the others, stopped before they reached them, and then they were standing just inches apart, the San Andres, the Sacramento Mountains on either side, hills like elephants protecting the desert plateau, closing in around them.

Who is she? The question leapt from her involuntarily, harsh, demanding. Do I know her?

His breath came out again, the same effortful sound, as if this were physical labor, back-breaking. He fixed his eyes on the horizon, he didn't answer.

You don't love her, Claire said, and even as she said it, she thought of herself, of Jade, of everything he knew nothing of. Hypocrite, she thought, but a terrible willfulness had come over her, clenching in the muscles of her jaw, making her challenge him. I know you don't.

He looked at her, and for a moment she thought he wasn't going to answer that either, but then he said, simply, She loves me.

Anything, she thought. A migraine, appendicitis, broken bones — I would take anything over this —

But she stood where she was, she held his gaze.

I came back to see you, she said, her words very clear in the high, cold silence. You're the only reason I'm here.

Yeah? For how long?

She looked at him, she had no answer.

Claire! Paula's voice, slicing between them. Mom's waiting — let's go!

Tommy stepped back before she could say anything else.

I'll see you, he said, and turned around.

It was Reno who drove them home. He drove very fast, with just two fingers on the steering wheel, sitting all the way back in his seat, and something in his posture, the back of his near-shaved head, was like a hand around Claire's heart; it was, she realized, the way her father used to drive.

Are you a pilot? she asked.

Yup. He glanced at her in the rearview mirror. How'd you guess?

The way you drive.

I'm not makin you nervous, am I? he asked, he was already slowing down.

No, no. It's okay. I like going fast.

He grinned. So do I.

In the front seat, Paula looked at him, Claire saw it, a look of possession, protective, guarded, a look that said everything. She's in love, Claire thought. My sister's in love, and she never told me —

The slam of betrayal, of confidences kept. Claire slid over to the far side of her seat, out of Reno's rearview range, and leaned her head against the window, wishing the cold would penetrate through the glass to her brain, and numb her thoughts.

52

CHRISTMAS DAY. THE TREE WAS LIT, THE TURKEY WAS cooked, it was cooling, waiting to be carved. Moving through the house, Claire had the sense that she was on some kind of false stage, that any minute it would all crumble, it would roll away, and they would be exposed. As what, she could not have said.

Who's carving? Claire asked, she sang it out, as if this were in fact a holiday, carefree and warm, full of love. This was her role, she accepted it unthinkingly. She would do anything, everything. She picked up the heavy silver knife.

I'll do it, Paula said. Claire surrendered it without protest, she held the platter at her sister's side.

Mom, she called, you better come in here and whip up your famous gravy before everything gets cold . . . !

Ginny came in, her heels sharp-sounding on the kitchen floor. She stirred cornstarch into the turkey juices, a cigarette in her mouth.

It smells so good, Claire said, I'm starving.

Takes all day to cook, Ginny said, Claire could hear the bitterness of alcohol in her tone. Five minutes to eat.

Claire smiled, as if this had been meant lightly, and watched Paula slice the turkey's breast.

They were carrying the food into the dining room when the phone rang. Ginny stopped in her tracks, a bowl of mashed potatoes in her hand.

Whoever it is, she said sharply, she already knew, tell them we're eating.

Claire picked up, her mouth was dry. Hello?

Merry Christmas, sweetie!

She turned her back to the open door, she lowered her voice. Hi, Daddy.

Did you get the present I sent you?

I'm wearing my scarf right now, Claire lied. It's beautiful.

Carlotta helped me choose them, he said. Did Paula like hers?

She loved it.

From the dining room, Ginny's voice, taut as wire. Claire, hang up, we're about to say grace!

Just a sec, she called.

That your mother?

Yeah, we're just sitting down to dinner.

All right, sweetheart, he said, and the quickness with which he acquiesced was worse than anything.

Is Paula there? he asked, the last, perfunctory question; Paula had not spoken to him since he'd left, and still he would ask, every time he called, and each time Claire would say the same thing —

I'll see if I can find her.

She walked to the door, receiver in her hand. Ginny and Paula were seated, Ginny's silverware glinting in her hand, her wrists tense and poised on the edge of the table.

It's Dad, Claire said, she wouldn't meet her mother's gaze. He wants to say Merry Christmas.

Paula stood. I'll take it in there, she said.

She took the phone, she did not speak into it until she was

199

out of audible range. Claire stood in her wake as if paralyzed, an interminable moment passed before she dared to raise her eyes, to look at her mother.

Her face was white, it was crumpling. Claire could hardly bear it, she didn't know what to do.

Mom, she said, her voice weak as a child's. She stretched a hand out, the gesture of a blind woman, but her mother was standing, her chair scraping hard against the floor. She went into the living room, straight to the bar, and made herself another drink. Claire followed.

Mom . . . She watched her mother, her hands hanging helpless at her sides.

Ginny kept taking sips of the liquor, a tight and measured gesture. She was not going to cry, Claire could see that.

Let's go sit back down, Claire said, she did not hide the plea in her voice. Before everything's gone cold . . .

They could both hear Paula's voice in the kitchen, an indistinct murmur.

What's she saying? Ginny asked, her voice so brittle Claire was sure it would crack. What's she got to tell him all of a sudden?

Mom, it's Christmas, Claire said, as if this might be reason enough.

Ginny laughed, a harsh sound, shorn of amusement. Oh, sure, she said. Sure.

Looking at her mother now, at the deep lines etched along the sides of her mouth, Claire remembered the last time her father had come to see them. She'd been sixteen years old, a junior in high school. He'd shown up unexpectedly, he hadn't called, just materialized on their front step. Claire had opened the door, and the sight of him was like what she imagined losing gravity felt like — everything in her leapt up, kept rising, and for one wild moment she was sure he'd come back to them, that he'd come back for good.

I'm just on base for a few hours, he'd said, I thought maybe we could go get some hamburgers and a shake somewhere, you and me and Paula . . . maybe go up for a spin, what do you say?

But Ginny hadn't even let him come into the living room, she'd become hysterical, crying and screaming, You can't just come in here like this and kidnap my daughters — !

Paula had put her arms around her mother, she'd refused to leave.

No, she'd said to her father, she'd kept saying it, I'm not going with you.

Claire could still remember the look on his face when he turned to her, his cap in his hand; she could not have refused him anything.

They'd gone out for lunch, he'd taken her up in the plane, but the afternoon was bleached, it was joyless. He'd dropped her off after dark, on the corner.

She could still recall her mother's face the day after, her eyes red from crying, how she'd stood with her arms crossed in the kitchen while Claire ate her breakfast, defiant, refusing to apologize, withstanding the silence.

Ginny hadn't spoken to her for a week.

They both heard Paula saying goodbye, the click of the receiver being replaced.

Please come to the table, Claire said again. Please, Mom.

Ginny drained her glass, she poured another inch. All right, she said. Fine.

Paula was already sitting at her place, refolding her napkin on her lap.

Well, Ginny said, did you have a nice talk with your father?

Paula was reaching for the turkey, as if nothing, but Claire could see her hands were shaking.

It was fine, she said, she cleared her throat. They both watched as she slid a piece of white meat on her plate, and then all three were looking at it, as if it were the focus of their conversation, the answer.

When Paula spoke again, she was still staring down at her plate.

I told him I was getting married.

From the corner of her eye, Claire saw her mother's knuckles go white around her glass, but for a moment, they were both too stunned to speak.

Well, Ginny said then, congratulations.

Thank you. Paula's voice held the same strain her mother's did, and Claire felt her stomach contracting into an ever-tightening knot. She picked up her silverware, put it back down.

To Reno? she asked, stupidly, she knew, but she couldn't help it, she could not quite grasp the situation.

We've been together almost six months, Paula answered, defensive, and Claire nodded quickly, her eyes wide, as if to negate any blame.

That's how long I'd known your father when I married him, Ginny said, her laugh sharp, and though she added nothing else, they could both hear the end of that sentence — and look what happened to me.

They're going to transfer him, Paula said, her tone almost accusing now, and he wants me to go with him.

Of course, Ginny said, and though she meant, Claire knew, to sound as if she'd expected that, too, it was a loss she was wholly unprepared for. She dropped her fork to reach for her cigarettes, it clattered against her plate. She thumbed her lighter again and again, but it just sparked, refusing to yield flame.

Goddammit — ! She slammed the lighter down, picked up her glass.

We're only going to Albuquerque, Paula said then. It's not very far.

Well, you're not gone yet, are you, Ginny said, she finished the rest of her drink, blinking rapidly.

No, Paula said, so low Claire could hardly hear her.

Ginny took a deep breath.

This food is turning to *ice,* she said. Claire, will you please say grace?

Lowering her eyes, Claire had a flashback of Thanksgiving at Sam and Nadja's, how Nadja had asked Rinpoche to give the blessing. Without a trace of hesitation, with the unself-consciousness of a child, the Tibetan monk had bowed his head, closed his eyes, and began a low almost singsong chant in a language Claire had never heard before. When the blessing was finished, Rinpoche had bowed slightly lower, opened his eyes.

Now Okay, he'd said, and in the space of that brief, sacred moment, hands still clasped in a ring around the table, everybody smiled. These are the people, Claire remembered thinking, my chosen family.

She went outside after dinner was over, into the small, neglected backyard, and sat on one of the ancient swings, the chains rusted, it came off in her hands. Overhead, the sky was midnight blue, the new moon a brilliant sliver of crescent light. She could feel the deep chill of the earth coming up beneath her feet, through the soles of her shoes, even through the thickness of her socks.

My sister's getting married, Claire thought, she'd been saying it to herself all evening in an attempt to comprehend it, but it wasn't till she was alone that it occurred to her that Paula would change her name; that they would no longer share the same last name, that last thought the most piercing of all.

As if sensing it, Paula came out through the kitchen door, and for a moment, Claire saw her sister's profile in the yellow light.

Cold out here, she said, she came to stand by the swings, her arms crossed against her chest.

Where's Mom?

Upstairs, watching TV.

She okay?

Paula shrugged. I guess so.

You going over to the base tonight?

In a little while.

I had no idea, Claire said then. You never even mentioned him to me.

Yeah, well. We've been out of touch, I guess.

They were both quiet for a while, but the silence was a shared one, and Claire had the sense of having been, at long last, forgiven.

What about you? Paula asked. You going to Cloudcroft to-night?

I wasn't exactly invited.

Paula looked at her, she raised one shoulder, as if to say, So what.

He's going out with somebody else, Claire said, and though she meant to sound matter-of-fact, the words fell abruptly into the space between them.

Paula didn't answer right away, and Claire knew for certain that she had known, that she had wanted to tell her sister weeks ago, but Claire hadn't let her; she hadn't wanted to hear it.

You know he'd take you back, Paula said finally, if you really wanted him.

Her words made Claire remember Jade, the pressure of Jade's arm around her neck, the sound of Jade's voice in her ear. I miss her, the thought came then, overwhelming, but she kept turning in her swing, she didn't say anything.

Anyway, he's having dinner at his sister's, Paula said, and then he's going home. That's what he told me when I asked him, so . . .

She stood up. I'll see you later.

See you, Claire said.

She had turned until the chains were twisted over her head, and she could turn no farther.

53

ALAMOGORDO WAS DESERTED, IT WAS A GHOST TOWN, nothing but fast-food places, closed up but still glowing with fluorescence; they made Claire think of morgues, freezers full of meat, she could not look at them. She drove, her hands tight on the steering wheel, her foot a steady pressure on the gas. She kept trying to imagine her, the other woman — she tortured herself with visions of a fresh-faced young girl with flowing hair, narrow hips, a wild glint in her eye. Please God, she thought, the speedometer creeping up, but her prayer had no end.

It was all just as she'd imagined it, everything — the road, the drive, the way the land stretched out on either side, fences that always needed mending. How many times had she ridden out with Tommy, held the posts while he wrapped barbed wire, nails clutched in his mouth . . .

She saw his truck first, parked just where she knew it would be; there were no other cars.

The house was quiet beyond it, dark except for a string of red lights shaped like chili peppers hanging in the window, and she felt an almost physical rush of love for that structure, for the thickness of its walls, its sheer solidity.

She pulled up next to the truck and the dogs came rushing up at the sound of her car, yelping, leaping at the window. She opened her door and they climbed all over her, pushing their snouts into her face, their tails frantic with joy.

It's me, she said, she buried her face in their fur. It's me, here I am . . .

When she looked up, Tommy was standing in the driveway, watching her. He stood there, he wore nothing but a pair of jeans and a short-sleeved T-shirt, as if oblivious to the cold, and she remembered the furnace of him, how he would kick the covers off in the middle of the night, in the middle of the winter . . .

I brought you a present, she said, but she sat in the car still, hesitating.

Yeah?

From New York.

My favorite place.

For a moment, they just looked at each other, neither of them moved. She wanted him to invite her in, she wanted to be sure that he was alone, that he wanted her there, but he wasn't going to make it easy for her, it was clear; it was her turn to suffer.

You eat too much? he asked her finally, his lips twitching into a smile, and she knew that that was all the invitation she was going to get. She picked up the gift-wrapped box next to her, and followed him inside.

They stood in the kitchen, the sudden, stark brightness of electricity too much, they avoided each other's eyes. She saw the faded paint stains on his jeans, so familiar she could have traced their shape with her eyes closed.

He ripped the paper open, unfolded the sweater inside.

It's cashmere, she said.

It was black, fine, she could have paid him back for the airplane ticket with the money it cost. He shrugged his shoulders into it as if it were something he owned, as if he'd already worn it for years.

How's it look?

It was beautiful on him, Claire thought, and looking at him with the perspective of distance, she saw what a beautiful man he was — strong and comfortable, at home under the stars. She swallowed, she couldn't say anything, aware only of her need for him, like a wound, gaping, profound.

She stepped toward him, and he looked at her, his eyes guarded. She reached out and ran her hand down the soft fabric, from his shoulder to his sleeve, her touch unsure, trembling. She let her fingers graze against his, but he gave her no response, nothing.

You don't want me anymore, she said, words anguished. He shook his head, as if to say no, he didn't, but his hand closed around hers.

It was all the opening she needed. She reached for him, pulling herself in close, pushing her knee between his legs, trying to close all the space between them.

Claire, he said, his voice raw, but she pressed her mouth against his shoulder.

Don't say anything, she said, she surprised herself with her own vehemence, and before he could answer she kissed him, her hands on the back of his neck, desperate.

He walked to the bedroom with her legs wrapped around his waist; she wouldn't let him go.

She fell into his bed, into the deep luxury of that silence, of his arms around her again, as if she'd never left — how he found her rhythm, how he'd never lost it. She said his name, it was all she could say. Her lips against his, losing her breath, Tommy. He moved slow beneath her, slower and slower, until she was crazy.

Tommy, she said, Tommy.

He twisted his fingers in her hair and pulled her head close, closer.

You forget this? he asked. You forget me?

No, she said, she could have cried, how deep she felt it, how long it seemed now, from here, to have gone without. She was falling over the edge, she couldn't control it. She felt herself reaching in her mind, reaching up to catch herself and slipping, slipping —

Stop, she said, her whisper harsh in his mouth, but he didn't, he held her hips down, held them hard against his, and would not let go, until the sound that came from her was like pain, sobbing; until he made her come.

She lay over him, her face in his neck.

I'm here, she murmured, I'm here . . .

She didn't remember falling asleep, but she knew when she woke up that hours had passed, that soon she would be able to see the first faint outlines of the Sacramento range through the bedroom window.

She'd been dreaming, it all came rushing back to her when she turned her head, the memory of that surreal voyage vivid, startling.

She'd been flying, driving low first, then swooping off the road, taking off. The exhilaration of leaving the ground, how her stomach lifted, fell. It was night, there was nothing but darkness, and then, suddenly — New York City, rising up out of the ocean, jeweled and fabulous. She felt that landscape viscerally, how it gripped her with the indescribable ache and yearning of a lover, sexual, urgent.

Next to her, Tommy moved; he was awake, too.

What time is it? she asked.

Why? His voice as quiet as hers. You got someplace else to be?

No, she said, thinking even as she said it of her dream,

how she could not recount it. She was a traitor, the thought came to her, irrefutable, and it made her defensive, made her add, Do you?

He got up, he didn't say anything. He came back from the kitchen with a beer, sat with his back against the wall to drink it.

She sat up, too, she pulled the sheet around her shoulders like a mantle. They shared the beer in silence.

So how's life in New York? he asked finally.

I got a job, she said, it was the only answer she could manage.

You still hangin out with that girl?

Some, she said, she wouldn't pronounce Jade's name, either. She's been away a lot.

Huh, he said, his voice betrayed no interest.

She went to Berlin, she said, as if in defiance. She was there when the Wall came down.

She gets around, he said. She closed her mouth at this, she would not answer. There was a long pause.

Guess you two're still pretty good friends, he said then; it was an acknowledgment of sorts, she knew, but she was at a loss as to how to respond to it.

I've met other people, she said instead, and immediately thought of Such, how impossible it would be to explain him.

Guess you're adjustin pretty good, then, he said. Guess you're gonna be all right.

Guess so, she said, realizing only after she said it that it was, finally, the admission they'd both been avoiding: she was going to leave again, it was clear. His reference had been to her future, and she knew as well as he did that it was a future imagined without him. She had imagined it, there was no going back; it lay before her, unknown, unpredictable. It was the rest of her life, and it wasn't here, on the ground she had already covered.

Tommy, she said.

He didn't answer, he leaned over, and she heard the bottle roll across the room until it hit the back wall, that sound echoing empty, hollow.

She reached up to kiss him, but he took her hand, he took both her hands and held them down.

No, he said, his voice fissured. No more.

She looked at him, both of them trying not to cry. He was no longer hers, she knew that now, but he had never seemed more precious.

Outside, the sky was lightening.

The mountains remained unmoved.

54

THE DAY BEFORE SHE LEFT, SHE HELPED HER MOTHER TAKE the tree down, they wrapped each ornament in newspaper, put them all away in the same frayed cardboard box that had held them for the last ten years.

This is the worst part, Ginny said, shaking her head; the tree was bare, its needles were turning brown.

It's like having a corpse in the house, she said. Let's just get *rid* of it . . . !

Claire took it outside, she carried it over one shoulder like a man, and the needles fell everywhere, into her hair and down her shirt, even into the cuffs of her pants.

When she came back in, Ginny was standing in the middle of the living room, her hands on her hips, facing the corner where the tree had been.

Mom . . . ?

Ginny's gaze fell on her, her eyes focused.

Let's get out of the house, what do you say? Let's go to the movies.

Oh, Ginny said, she waved a hand, I don't want to see any movie.

We could just sit there anyway, Claire said, and eat pop-corn.

No, Ginny said, I'm too old to eat popcorn. I'm going to bed.

How can you go to bed so early? It's only eight o'clock!

I told you, I'm old, Ginny said, she reached out and took Claire's hand, her palm felt dry and powdery.

Come upstairs, she said. Help me do the crossword.

In her bedroom, Ginny turned the television on automatically, she did not even look to see what was on.

Have you spoken to your sister? she asked, as if she were asking about the most inconsequential matter, the time, the weather; Paula had not been home since Christmas day.

I had lunch with her today, at the commissary. She asked me to be the maid of honor.

That's nice, Ginny answered, she could not keep the bite from her voice. Nothing like a wedding to bring people together.

Claire shrugged, she refused to be drawn in.

I just hope she's thought this thing through, that's all I can say.

I think she has, Claire said.

What she didn't tell her mother was how changed Paula had seemed on base, not just in manner, but even in the way she looked, the way she walked — there was a kind of giddiness in her that Claire had never seen before, she was like a sixteen-year-old who has just gotten her first driver's license, she could not contain herself.

Reno and I, she kept saying, she began nearly every sentence that way. They were going to go to Las Vegas, they were going to go to Sun Valley —

He's going to teach me how to ski, she'd said, she'd laughed. I already know how to gamble!

Well, I wish her the best of luck with that pilot, Ginny said now, reaching for her robe, God knows she'll need it.

Oh, I don't know, Claire said mildly, he seems like a nice guy.

Nice, Ginny snorted. Sure, they're all *nice* — just wait ten or fifteen years down the road, when she's got a handful of kids, and she finds out how nice some woman who lives in Flagstaff, Arizona, thinks he is, too!

Oh, Mother, Claire said, she sighed.

Just remember, Ginny said, I've lived a lot longer than you have.

Claire looked at her mother's body as she wrapped her robe around herself, at the fine, wrinkled skin, the sagging upper arms, the loose thighs — it was as if her body were literally losing its grip on her bones, engaged in some inexorable contest with gravity, and doomed, Claire knew, to lose.

She turned away.

Now, Ginny said, adjusting her half-glasses on her nose, what's a five-letter word for trespass?

Claire sat on the foot of her bed, comforted momentarily by this familiar picture, and the smell of her mother's room, a talcumed perfume. Behind her, the television projected image after image, all of them bright, impossible to believe in.

I don't know, she said.

Okay, I'm going to throw you a bone, let's see . . . here we go, fourteen down — a three-letter word for snake, begins with an "a."

Claire shrugged.

Asp, Ginny said, she looked at Claire sternly. You're not trying.

Paula's the one that likes crosswords, not me.

I guess that's true, Ginny said, she put her magazine down. You never were the bookish type, were you.

Claire stretched out on her stomach, she put her cheek on top of her hands. Ginny reached over and scratched her head lightly.

No, she said, you always wanted to *do* things — even when you were a little girl, two, three years old, you couldn't wait to get out the door . . . we'd be leaving to go somewhere and you'd disappear, we wouldn't be able to find you anywhere . . . and there you'd be, already sitting in the car, waiting.

I don't remember that, Claire said, her voice muffled against her hand.

Oh, you were so cute, Ginny said. You were the apple of your father's eye.

Ginny's hand lay quietly on her head now, and Claire felt a wave of grief wash over her, intolerable. She sat up.

Okay, she said, ask me another one.

Ginny looked at her, uncomprehending. Claire picked the magazine up. Fifteen down, she read, "Sacred, inviolable" — six letters.

Nothing, Ginny said, absolutely nothing.

Claire put the magazine back down, she reached over to hold her mother's hand. N-o-t-h-i-n-g, she counted. Doesn't work — that's seven.

Through the glasses, Claire could see her mother's eyes magnified, blurred with unshed tears. She held Claire's hand very tightly, and smiled.

WINTER HAD SETTLED IN, THEY WERE IN ITS GRIP; AT THE OFfice, everyone was sick with variations of the same bug, something bronchial and lingering.

Snow fell, and the soot of the city, its exhaust, covered it before it froze again, solid as concrete. Homeless people wandered through the streets, palms turned up, the tips of their fingers blue. The sky was overcast and the wind blew, sharp and mean as a nun.

And then we're going to a little bed-and-breakfast up the Hudson. We're going to spend New Year's Eve alone, just the two of us — Walter's already arranged everything, all I've got to do is pack my valise, Lila was saying, she seemed to mention her fiancé's name every time she spoke, as if he were some novel acquisition she could not get over. She smiled, her hand rising reflexively to cover her teeth. He's so romantic!

They were sitting in the conference room, taking a coffee break. Lila had an oversized fudge brownie with walnuts, she unwrapped it with obvious relish. She ate like a man, roast beef sandwiches with french fries for lunch, never gained an ounce. I've got my dad's metabolism, she'd told Claire once, with the carelessness of one for whom the concept of dieting is totally foreign.

Claire had black coffee, nothing else. She sipped it and nodded; she didn't feel like talking, but Lila was oblivious to her mood, and her voice was loud in Claire's ear, grating.

What are you going to do?

Claire shrugged, as if she hadn't quite decided; she had no invitations, no plans.

What about that girl — your friend — is she back yet?

No.

Where did she go — Timbuktu, was it?

Kathmandu, Claire said, controlling an urge to snap.

She's got an exciting life, doesn't she, Lila said, biting into her brownie. Mmm.

Yes, Claire said, she stood. She does.

She pitched her empty coffee cup into the garbage and left the room, all at once irritated to the point of tears. PMS, she thought, and wanted to walk back into the conference room and snatch the rest of Lila's brownie from her mouth. She went to the bathroom, pressed cold water against her eyes, and just then remembered a fragment of the dream she had had that morning, right before waking: hard blue skies, clean, pure air. Vast spaces.

This day will never end, she thought, her hair crackling with static cling against her sweater, though it was, in fact, almost over. It would be dark in a matter of minutes, she knew, and the evening lengthened before her, the jolting ride home that would only take her to the overheated enclosure of her apartment with its hissing radiator, its unmade bed, the files she had yet to get through.

Shall be construed in accordance with, she thought. She leaned against the sink, overwhelmed with a longing for the sun. In breach thereof.

The door swung open.

Here you are, Ursula said, and Claire braced herself against that familiar tone, laced with faint disapproval, the implication that the time she was wasting was not her own, but all Ursula said was, Someone's here to see you.

Wearing faded Levi's and a black leather motorcycle jacket, its buckles gleaming new and silver, Jade was difficult to comprehend in the context of the office, an exotic animal who'd suddenly wandered tamely into the square.

Her smile was dazzling, her grip fierce.

I've come, she said, her voice low in Claire's ear, to break you out.

Still holding her friend, Claire was intensely aware of Lila's presence behind them, watching. This, she thought, words as loud in her mind as if she'd spoken them, this is my life.

56

THEY WENT OUT FOR DINNER THAT NIGHT, TO AN INTIMATELY lit French restaurant on MacDougal, full of people, and Claire thought, Here, this was winter in Manhattan — people converging together over hot food and cold wine, emerging from their separate hibernations, touching each other's hands.

The maitre d' knew Jade, and he steered them to a good table, near the corner, from which they could see everyone else. He smiled, he spoke to her familiarly, in French. She laughed, she kissed both his cheeks.

I think for the ladies champagne tonight, he said, his imperiousness was wonderful, I will tell your waiter — not too expensive, but good, he said, and made a sign of certainty with both hands, *Good* champagne.

They sat close together, the candle flickered on the table between them, and Claire was aware of the aura they created together, two young women, beautiful, intent, alone. She did not look at anyone else.

Tell me everything, she said, only then allowing herself to realize how starved she had been for this, Jade's conversation, and how she perceived the world.

It's an incredible place, Jade said, a medieval little town — they have more temples per square mile in Kathmandu than anywhere else in the world, and they all have these eyes painted on them — I wish I could describe the expression they have, this half-lidded slyness, with black liner like Cleopatra's — anywhere you turn around you can see them, watching you, but it's not like censorship, it's more like an invitation —

An invitation to what?

I don't know — to *ascend,* somehow, to rise above it all . . . it's the aesthetic of the sixties, it still haunts the place — the whole town is a sixties relic, like some living period set — you can buy incense in all the little stores, and teenagers follow you around offering to sell you drugs — they mutter behind you in the street, hashish, coke, cocaine — once when I walked past one, he shouted down the block after me, *brown sugar!*

Did you do any of it?

Jade laughed. What do you think?

I didn't think Luke was the type.

He said he's tried everything once, Jade said. But with opium, she said, she grinned, he said once wasn't enough.

You bought opium on the street?

We never bought anything, Jade said, but one night someone offered us some. This Irish Ph.D. who had a little house up in the hills — it was Christmas Eve, and he was lonesome, he said, for his language. He invited us over to share a bottle of Irish whiskey, and then it turned out he had this opium, too . . .

The waiter came with their champagne. He was blond, he spoke with a French accent, he had the sleeves of his shirt rolled up, an efficient white apron that came to his shins. He lifted the open bottle to them both in a brief, businesslike toast before pouring, but Claire saw how he glanced at them, quick under his eyelashes, having to look again.

What was it like? she asked.

It took forever to feel it, Jade said, I was expecting something else — to be overwhelmed, I guess — but it's more subtle than that . . . it wasn't till we left that I really — it was dawn, there was this mist coming up from the ground, thick and white, absolutely surreal . . . and there I was, walking down the street, I had no idea where I was, and I thought, This is a dream . . . I felt myself the way you do when you're dreaming, you know, how you can't feel time . . . everything was foreign to me, I had never seen any of it before — I kept thinking I was going to wake up, and then this Nepali man with a rickshaw came out of it and took us back to our hotel . . . it was a dream, I can't describe it, Jade said, but even those words spilled out of her, part of the same luminous torrent that seemed to flow effortlessly through her, unending.

Mesdemoiselles? The waiter poised his pencil over his pad, stood ready.

Claire reached over, put her hand next to Jade's, knowing Jade would take it.

You order, she said.

Jade questioned the waiter, she made him smile. She ordered lobster bisque and oysters, salmon grilled on cedar, a salad of bitter greens. She had the air of one who knew exactly what she wanted from the evening, who was sure to call it forth. When the champagne was gone, she would order more. She was heedless of ordinary concerns, she didn't ask the price of anything, she drank without getting drunk. People looked at her, alert to this instinct, greedy to latch on, but her focus was on Claire, there was no one else.

I don't know what it is about you that makes me talk, she said, and though she pronounced the words with her usual ironic air, Claire sensed the excitement that ran beneath it, a palpable current, transmitting. Talk and talk and talk.

They clinked glasses. The champagne tasted like gilt in Claire's throat, dry and feathery.

What was your favorite thing? she asked. What was the best part?

The Tibetan monasteries, Jade said, her answer immediate. There was one up on a hill that we went to, blindingly white, and inside, a thousand little butter lamps, and these monks, they sit in rows beneath an immense golden statue of a goddess — Tara, they call her, and she's ten feet tall, I'm not exaggerating — at the base there's just a riot of flowers, and dye, nothing but powdered color, and shiny copper bowls filled with water, and coins, and food piled up on plates — I always thought Buddhism was ascetic, but this temple! And the monks just sit and chant all day, their voices go so deep the room vibrates, and they have bells, and little drums, and the most amazing faces . . . There was a Tibetan refugee camp, we went and bought yak sweaters and incense, the people were incredible — they wear turquoise and fuchsia and deep yellow, colors that can stand up to the sky, to being so close to the sun — their people are being decimated, they're exiles from their own country, and still they have this radiance . . .

Claire thought of Rinpoche, and remembered him the same way.

I want to take you there, Jade said, to the Hotel Eden, where you can stay for six dollars a night and eat breakfast on the roof every morning, facing the Himalayas — and the blue of that sky! Nothing, no oils, no acrylics, could ever capture it — I wanted to suck it down, to hold it in my lungs — I wanted to memorize it, but every day it shocked me all over again, every morning.

Watching her, Claire thought she might have been describing herself — how her radiance eluded you, how you had to keep looking and looking at her, hoping, almost, for some flaw to snag the eyes, and hold them.

It sounds like the sky in New Mexico, she said, and her dream flashed through her mind again, brief and vivid. It sounds like the desert.

I thought of that, Jade said, I thought of you — especially at night. There are no streetlights in Kathmandu, and the moon was just a sliver, it was so dark — there was nothing but starlight.

Claire had a sudden memory of Tommy then, of the last night they had spent together, and she flinched inwardly, she looked away. Jade fell silent, watching her.

What's wrong?

Nothing, Claire said, she didn't want to talk about it. I just miss the stars, living here. I miss the stars at night.

You're a star.

Yeah, Claire said, her smile halfhearted. Sure.

Yes, Jade said, her smile a swift flash, brilliant. And I'm the one who discovered you.

You didn't discover me, Claire said, I saved you —

Jade lit a cigarette, her eyes were shadowed by the palm of her hand. Yeah, she said, her voice was low. You saved me.

The waiter came and took their plates away. He offered them dessert, crème brulée, pastries, mousse. Claire shook her head but Jade said yes, bring us something very rich.

He smiled as if she had chosen him; he was in love with them, Claire could see, and this time she caught the sidelong glance he threw their way. She leaned over so her hair fell forward to hide her face, so no one but Jade could see her eyes.

Where's Luke? she asked, finally coming to the question that had been in the back of her mind since Jade had first walked into the office. Are you meeting him later?

No, Jade said, she drank the last of her champagne. He's in Romania. He flew straight from London, and I came here. Ceausescu was executed on Christmas day.

Before Claire could answer, the waiter reappeared with a thick wedge of chocolate covered in whipped cream, two forks.

East Germany, Czechoslovakia, and now Romania, Jade said to him, Europe's going crazy.

But here in America, he said, he raised one eyebrow, we eat chocolate!

He spun away, satisfied when they laughed, and Jade took a forkful of cake, brought it to Claire's lips. Try this, she said. You have to try this.

You first, Claire said, but before she could close her mouth, Jade had filled it with chocolate, dense and sweet.

Don't, Jade said, argue with me.

Claire took the fork, she said, Now you —

Looking up, she caught sight of the waiter standing by the kitchen door; he was still watching them.

What are you looking at?

That waiter, Claire said, I think he wants to marry us.

Jade glanced over, she caught his eye, and instantly he came forward, he could not suppress his smile.

Is there something more, he asked, you would like?

No, but my friend here was just wondering, Jade said, if you would like to marry us.

He misunderstood, both eyebrows shot up. Well, I am not a priest, of course, but if you like —

They both laughed, surprised, thrilled with his misunderstanding, but he had already assumed an air of solemnity, he didn't break character, and it occurred to Claire then that he was an actor, that he would be famous one day.

Before the eyes of God, he said, I will now — how do you say — I will now pronounce — pronounce, yes?

Jade nodded, she glanced at Claire. Their eyes met and something flared between them, inchoate, deep. What is it, Claire thought: she felt the flush rising up her throat, in her cheeks, but she could not speak, and the waiter went on.

I pronounce you *femme et femme,* he said, he opened his eyes, and for a moment, nobody spoke, but then he smiled, he raised his hands.

But with no kiss it does not work!

They both laughed again, Claire's color high, but it was Jade who leaned across the table, she seized Claire's hand, the gesture unequivocal.

Kiss me, she said, and though Claire could still hear the smile behind the words, there was something else, something urgent. She moved toward it, she could not hold herself back, and they kissed, once, hard.

The waiter shook his head, he bit his lip.

C'est ça, he said.

57

IT WAS MIDNIGHT WHEN THEY WALKED BACK OUT INTO THE frigid night. They stood on the corner, Jade held out her hand.

Well, she said, where shall we go for our honeymoon?

Someplace hot, Claire said, her fingers lacing through Jade's.

The beach, Jade said.

And cheap, Claire went on.

Where they don't speak any English —

And no one knows us.

Each statement a pronouncement, their desire irrepressible, triumphant, and all around them was New York City, dark and glamorous, wide awake, holding nothing but promise.

I know a place, Jade said, she raised her hand for a cab. It's like being on a ship —

Claire didn't care how late it got, she didn't care if she slept at all. She felt lifted from the ordinary stream of life, freed from her own imposed rhythms, so that even something mundane, riding in a cab on a winter's night, became extraordinary, because it was in the deep hours before dawn, the hour of nightmares, of clutching for warmth. It was the way Jade lived, Claire thought, she had desires, she obeyed them fearlessly.

The bar was on Lafayette Street, it had the emblem of what looked like a gold dragon lizard embossed on a dark green door, red velvet obscuring the windows on either side.

Claire waited for Jade to go in first, and she felt the brief pause they created simply by entering the room, it was like a clean pocket of air; Jade seemed wholly unaware of it, the slanted looks, how men caught each other's eyes.

They sat down, Claire glanced around surreptitiously. The place was like the inside of a cruise liner, the walls made of dark, rich teak, with velvet drapes hiding windows, closing them in, the light golden, muted. Everybody there seemed possessed of the unerring sophistication of city dwellers, arrogant, sexy, impossible to surprise. They drank martinis, huge and silver, the air was laced with smoke.

Their waitress was Asian, she had black tape over each eyebrow. Jade ordered a bottle of champagne, she sat back; she was like some gorgeous, feline beast of prey, contemptuous, powerful. She wouldn't let Claire take her wallet out, she put her credit card on the table.

If I'm going to max out, she said, I might as well do it in style.

No, Claire said, she pushed Jade's card back toward her. You always pay —

Let me, Jade said, she put her hand over Claire's. It gives me pleasure.

Her voice low, something so intimate in the enunciation of that last word that Claire could not answer, she could not argue.

I have to go back to work, Jade said then, and as if resisting the sudden intrusion of reality, she passed a hand over her eyes, that gesture like a mortician's gesture, eerie. Tomorrow night.

But it's New Year's Eve, Claire said, she could not keep the dismay from her voice. Can't you get out of it?

I didn't even try. I have no leverage left there — none. I've been disappearing for weeks at a time, I've abused them endlessly — the first time I just called them from the airport, I didn't even ask. They're on the verge of firing me, I know it — it would probably be the best thing that ever happened to me . . . except that I'd be unemployed, and broke.

You could always do something else.

Like what?

I don't know, Claire said. What about art school?

Jade glanced at her as if to see, was she really that naive.

I mean, what were you going to do when you got out? I remember once you said you wanted to know everything, you wanted to have —

Forget it, Jade said; she reached across Claire abruptly, lifted the bottle. I was probably drunk.

She filled their glasses, squinting against the smoke of her own cigarette. She lifted her glass before Claire could answer — she would change the subject, Claire knew it, as if the possibility of her own talent were too fragile a topic, subject to being jinxed.

Where do you work, Claire asked impulsively. Maybe I'll come and sit at the bar tomorrow night, and then when you get off —

No, Jade said, her tone so sharp it made Claire flinch.

I have to work, Jade said, she tried to soften it. I can't talk.

I don't care, Claire said, she kept thinking of it, being with

221

Jade when the new year began, it seemed the most important thing, she could not let it go. I'll wait.

Oh, Claire, Jade said, and it wasn't the beginning of a sentence, of any question, it was just her name, pronounced softly, like a blessing.

Claire leaned forward, she was becoming intoxicated, and it made the light seem to shimmer, it made everything recede except Jade's face, those fine, fine features, her eyelashes dark against her cheek when she looked down.

We could be anywhere, Claire said, when we get off —

Jade catching on immediately, saying, Cairo, or maybe Jamaica —

Mexico, Claire said.

Their champagne was gone.

Or just, Jade said, home.

They fell into the back of a cab, Jade gave the driver their address, and then she told him they were married.

She's my wife, she said.

The driver inclined his head, he was from India, skinny, his accent humorous.

It's very good to have a wife, he said. My mother, she is all the time telling me the same thing! He glanced at them in the rearview mirror, his eyes lascivious. You know some girl for me?

I only know one girl, Jade said, her head fell against Claire's shoulder. And she's mine.

The cab seemed to stop abruptly and they were out in the cold, they were in the doorway of the building, and Claire was overcome with the realization that they were alone now, she was overcome with clumsiness, she could not get hold of her keys, they kept slipping through the hole in the lining of her coat pocket.

Never mind, Jade said, her laugh barely audible, the man always has the keys.

It was impossible not to think of it then, the time they had gone out before, Jade sitting among all those women, paying for

222

everything — You're the girl, she'd said, You're the original starry-eyed girl.

Claire clung to the memory of those words the same way she clung to the landing going up the stairs, Jade just ahead of her, neither of them speaking.

They reached the second landing.

Well, Jade said, she stood on the top step, do you want to —

Jade . . . !

Both of them were startled by the cry that seemed to rise from the dark, and then Olivia emerged from the shadows, struggling up, apparently, from Jade's doorway.

I've been sittin here, waitin on you — She was drunk, the words slurred in her mouth, and when she reached them, Claire could see how tears had smeared her eye makeup down her cheeks.

Olivia, honey . . . what's wrong?

It's over, Olivia said, Javier's moving out, he said —

She fell against her friend, the rest of her sentence strangled by sobs.

Come on, Jade said, her voice soft with compassion, let's get you into bed.

Well, she said to Claire, looking at her over the top of Olivia's head as if to say, What can we do?

It was only then that Claire became aware of how much she wanted to keep walking down the hall, to be admitted into Jade's apartment — to lie next to her as the sun rose, to fall asleep in Jade's bed . . .

She stared at Jade, she couldn't say anything, and the look stretched between them, weighted, excruciating. Finally Jade's laugh, as if to say it didn't matter, any of it —

Claire looked away, and then Jade kissed her, those lips so soft, the charge of that kiss so strong, it sent a wild shiver down to the crux of her, inflammatory, unimaginable.

Wait, Claire said as Jade pulled back. Isn't there something . . .

But Jade was already shifting her weight to better accommodate Olivia's, she was hoisting her friend up.

Next year, she said, she smiled. I'll see you next year.

58

WHEN CLAIRE WOKE UP THE NEXT DAY, IT WAS SNOWING again.

She stood by the window, drinking a cup of coffee. It was New Year's Eve, she had nowhere to go.

I could call Such, she thought, or Sam and Nadja . . .

But she knew there was only one person who would do.

She walked down the hall, knocked on the door.

Yes? A voice, wary on the other side. Who is it?

Me. Claire.

Olivia opened the door, her eyes still puffy from crying, bruised-looking in the wintry light.

You just missed her, she said.

What do you mean? Claire asked, it made her desperate, and she stepped inside, as if to ascertain that it was true, that Jade was really gone.

She went to work, Olivia said, she let the door swing shut, lit a cigarette.

So early?

It's not that early.

I can't believe it, Claire said, she could not accept it. I told her —

Olivia slouched against a wall, she blew smoke from the side of her mouth, and her glance seemed to defy Claire to finish the sentence.

She was supposed to let me know, Claire said, she did not know what she was going to say until she said it. How to get there.

Where? Olivia asked, and when Claire hesitated, she said, *Zeitgeist?*

. . . Yes, Claire said, as if she had just now remembered

the name, Later, but — the thing is, I can't remember where it is, exactly . . .

Yeah, it's a little tricky, that part of TriBeCa, Olivia said. Even cabdrivers get lost.

Can you tell me . . . ?

Sure, Olivia said, and Claire was taken aback at the ease of it, for a moment she didn't say anything.

Want me to write it down?

She printed the address on a piece of paper, told Claire the cross street.

Thanks a lot, Claire said, I didn't want to ask Jade — she doesn't know I'm coming, I wanted to surprise her —

Does Brannon know?

Brannon . . . ?

The doorman — if you're not on the guest list, he won't let you in. Members only, they're really strict about it.

Oh . . .

Listen, never mind — I'll call him up, I'll take care of it — I owe you one, right?

Thank you, Claire said again, it did not seem enough. Thanks a lot.

She took a long time dressing that evening, she had nothing else to do. She soaked in the tub, covered her body with rich lotion, put perfume in the crooks of her elbows, the hollow of her throat, behind her knees. She wore a simple black dress, sleeveless, the front scooped out low. She pinned her hair up, made her eyes dramatically dark, her lips red.

She studied herself in the mirror, slightly surprised by the image reflected back, sophisticated and sleek.

Here I am, she thought.

It was the last night of the year.

59

SHE LEFT THE HOUSE JUST AFTER ELEVEN, CAUGHT A CAB. IT was very cold out, the snow was still falling. Driving down Broadway, she kept hearing disembodied shouts, music, and somewhere farther south, the low thud of fireworks.

New Year's Eve, the driver muttered, his radio tuned to some evangelical call-in show. Amateur night.

He followed her directions down to Hudson, the cab rumbling along cobblestoned streets, turning finally to stop on a small side road.

There was no sign, no light, nothing but a wide black door and a man in a heavy dress overcoat standing in front of a blue velvet rope, a clipboard under one arm.

Can I help you?

Are you Brannon?

Yes. His tone, perfectly polite, icy, did not change. He was thin, his eyes deep-set, dark.

I'm Claire Stearn, Olivia said she was going to put me on the guest list . . . ?

He studied her as if she were some scientific specimen who had come to present herself for inspection, and then he checked his clipboard, running one long finger down the side of his roster. His nails were manicured, impeccable.

Stearn, he said, Claire.

He lifted the rope, the movement unexpectedly rapid, startling. For a moment she just stood there, and he said nothing, just looked at her, the rope still up in the air.

Oh, she said, only then realizing. Thank you.

She was in.

It was another door, she knew it even before she'd stepped through, another anonymous door that opened into New York City to reveal the outrageous — she could not have, no matter how many years she might live here, she could never have guessed.

The music so deep, coming up like persuasion from the floor, the room very dark, lit up only by specific beams of light, brilliant gold, deep red. Immediately before her was the bar, smooth polished pewter, the drapes behind it velvet the color of burnt umber, candles in heavy iron frames flickering from the folds. The only other light came from below the bar, a single running strip of it, warm. It illuminated the faces of two waiters putting drinks on a tray, both of them young; it wasn't until one of them turned that Claire saw she'd mistaken her for a man. They both wore the same tuxedo, the cut superb, European, but distinctly male. They could have been related, Claire thought when the waiter moved by, although she was sure they were not. Their faces were chiseled with an androgynous beauty, the woman's brows thick, perfect, her hair slicked back severe as his, the man's cheekbones high and feminine, his eyes the eyes of some feline animal, elegant and predatory.

Claire's eyes roved the crowd for Jade's bright hair moving through it, she looked for an upraised arm, a tray, but the bar blocked her vision; the clientele seemed taller than the average crowd. Like the staff, they looked as if they all came from the same tribe. They slouched against the bar, their chic was wealthy, world-weary, their money folded discreetly in their hands; though some of them stood together, their focus was distracted, they kept glancing around the side of the bar toward the back of the room, faces tilted up, and Claire felt the single concentration of that distraction, how it pulled her forward.

The floor was mahogany, the walls curved. She walked up past the crowd to see what they were looking at, and stopped still.

The back of the room was cavernous, the roof vaulted. Beautiful, elaborate platforms had been dropped from the ceiling, the walls made of chain, the same heavy pewter, the platforms themselves covered in black leather. The dancers were separated by twelve or fifteen feet of space, their outfits made of more leather, the costumes of bondage. There were two women, one man. The women's breasts were bare, encircled by leather, the straps crisscrossing in the back, between their shoulder blades. Their shorts were cut high as could be, the crotch cut out, and beneath, a fine mesh of fishnet stockings. The woman standing closest to Claire had a pierced navel, the thin hoop of it glinting in a ray of diamond-sharp light. She kept turning, posing in various attitudes of flagrant submission, flinging her head back, dropping to her knees. Her face was made up in the style of thirties cabaret, her skin powdered white, her eyes painted black, her lips the color of blood.

The man, made up the same way and encased in leather from head to foot, only his arms bare, suddenly swung up on a steel bar, and the far dancer faced him, her hands holding the metal on either side of her, her legs extended. She let her head fall back and it was only then, when Claire saw the wet gold shine of it, that Claire recognized her.

She looked like a mannequin version of herself in that makeup, her face mask-like, flawless. The last song had not yet ended and people were already stepping forward, pushing bills into the finer mesh that ran along the bottom. Claire saw how Jade looked down at them, her smile remote, her eyes distant, never really focusing. Claire moved back fast, that reaction instinctive, knowing only that she could not be seen, that Jade could not see her.

The music was changing into something else now, entirely different from what had been playing before, a Mideastern wail with a backbeat; it made the hair on the back of Claire's neck stand on end. Hanging from the bar by his knees, the male dancer began to swing, the motion controlled, but wild. People swayed back, then forward again. Peripherally, Claire was aware of a couple, two men, moving closer, their hands moving below her level of vision. Her eyes were riveted on Jade's form, she could not move.

Suddenly, in mid-arch, the male dancer flipped himself over, and when the swing came back toward Jade, his legs were out. He locked them around her pelvis and then she was on top of him, leaping high to keep the trajectory going, and Claire saw that the back of her shorts was cut out, too.

They performed to the music, simulating the act, Jade gyrating symmetrically down the length of his body while the other woman kept up her series of poses, all of it perfectly choreographed. The people below were coming closer, but Jade's eyes were closed, she no longer acknowledged the money they were waving, it fell like litter at her feet. She swung her hips from side to side, wide, powerful, and dropped her head back, so far Claire could see the pale arch of her throat and the fringe of her lashes against her cheek, a slick hank of hair escaping the gel's hold to brush her bare waist, the long curves of her thighs now high up around her partner's neck. Her arms floated up, sinuous, her wrists going around and around, her hands like swans in the white light, curved and elegant, while her smooth navel made its own circles, circles of a slave girl, so practiced it made Claire's throat dry to see.

Then her hands came down, to the top of her leather shorts, unsnapping the sides, taking them off, the beginning of a total nakedness that made Claire lean forward with the rest of them, made her hold her breath, wanting what everybody else wanted — for Jade to reveal herself.

With a smooth, unexpected movement, she hooked a thumb in each pocket and her shorts came off in her hands, leaving nothing but the black leather straps that still crisscrossed her body, and a red velvet G-string, minuscule.

It was the man who rode her then, his heels hooked on the bar on either side of her, his face in her crotch. People laughed, they clapped. Claire could not take her eyes from Jade's figure above, her hips making slow figure eights, everything tuned to that music and how it grew, a frenzied building. Her skin had a sheen to it, an ivory patina, but she did not sweat. When the song reached its zenith, the man was hanging by his knees again and sitting up between them, she was a whirling dervish, her head moving around and around, so fast her hair was nothing but a bright, slick blur —

People, men who could have been women, women who could have been men, waved money in the air, Claire saw twenty-dollar bills, and the male dancer took them, fingers deft, sliding the money into the slits cut along the leather of his pants.

It was, she thought, like having walked into someone else's dream; she felt her own paralysis like something involuntary, the quality nightmarish, mesmerizing. The music never stopped and, woven through it, Claire perceived the same recurring chant, disturbing, like sabotage, or some drugged invitation to orgy.

The first song segued into the next, strung together by the same low beat, the sex beat, a pumping continuous rhythm that never wavered, never died, and the dancers kept finding new ways to move against each other, submitting to it, transcending it, pairing off in every combination before finally coming together in the ultimate ménage à trois. Claire's side was electrified with awareness of the two men that stood beside her, but she could not spare even the briefest of peripheral glances, could not miss any of those wild angles, flank, ankle, nape.

She had no idea how much time had elapsed when the show ended, when the dancers slid through an invisible trap door in the far wall; she was in another state altogether, beyond numb, unfathomable. The men beside her had gone, she had no idea where.

Beside her, a waiter stopped, spoke, his suave voice making her jump. Excuse me, he said, he handed her a glass of champagne. Compliments of the gentleman at the bar.

Claire held it dumbly, she looked where he nodded. A man inclined his head toward her, the movement almost imperceptible. His face was thin, tanned, the face of a man with money, a man who knows how to be ruthless. His hair was already going gray at the temples, his suit was made of fine wool.

Claire looked away fast, aware now only of the overwhelming desire to leave, to get out —

She walked to the bar to put her glass down, and instantly the man was beside her.

Bonsoir, Mademoiselle, he said, his voice unctuous, his accent rich, French, 'Appy New Year.

All at once she was at a complete loss as to how to behave; some reflexive attempt to smile stretched as a grimace across her face. He leaned back against the bar, watching her.

This is your first time here, no?

She lifted her glass, as if to say, No, I'm perfectly at home, but she didn't speak, she wouldn't meet his eyes. He didn't say anything either, but she could feel his gaze on her face, on her body. She willed him to leave, and miraculously, he did.

She stayed at the bar another minute, and then she turned, wanting only to leave, but as she did so, the man caught her eye. He was at the other end of the bar now, looking at her as if he'd been waiting for her glance, and it was only then that she saw Jade, standing next to him, still in costume. He murmured something to her, leaned in, and Claire saw the money in his hands, and then Jade's smile as she accepted it. She stared, she couldn't look away, and then Jade looked up, the money still in her hands, as if she could feel the heat of that gaze. Their eyes locked, and for a moment, Claire saw the violent flash of shock cross Jade's face, creasing that expressionless mask. Claire opened her mouth, she started to move toward her, but Jade moved first, moved so fast she seemed to vanish altogether.

Claire stood in the middle of the room, while above her, on the platforms, three new dancers positioned themselves.

She was your favorite, no? The man's voice came in her ear with all the unwanted intimacy of the uninvited, and this time she turned toward the door and fled.

60

IT HAD TURNED BITTERLY COLD OUTSIDE, BELOW FREEZING, the wind had picked up. Claire stood on the curb with her coat open, gesticulated in the street, in vain; there were no cabs, they were all full. She was aware of the doorman watching her, and she started walking, a kind of limping, backward crawl, her arm still out, eyes straining for the light on top of the taxi that meant it was free. The sidewalk was treacherous with ice, there were lumps of frozen snow piled on the curbs. She kept walking, six, seven, eight blocks, but no cabs would stop, they were all full.

She turned around finally, shoved her hands deep in her

pockets, headed north. She could not bring herself to comprehend what she had seen, it refused to be assimilated.

She tried to see the other face, the woman she had known from the beginning, Jade in blue jeans and a baggy sweater, her face scrubbed, translucent. She tried to piece them together, to see how one emerged from the other, she could not reconcile the two; it was as though her eyes were crossed and she couldn't shake the double vision.

A car came barreling toward her, and a man shouted something out the window at her, unintelligible, terrifying.

Although she kept her eyes straight ahead, she saw nothing but the same image, over and over: the Frenchman sliding money into Jade's hands, Jade smiling as she accepted it.

Ten . . . nine . . . eight . . . !

She looked up, startled. She was at Canal and Hudson, traffic so thick it had stopped moving.

Seven . . . six . . . five!

People were honking their horns, they were leaning drunkenly from car windows, shouting.

Four . . . three . . . two!

She had to cross the street, there was no getting around it. She lowered her head and started, her teeth were chattering uncontrollably.

. . . *One!*

A terrific roar went up in the streets, and she heard the flat, nasal sound of hundreds of noisemakers unfurling. She tried to move fast, but there wasn't enough room between cars, and people's hands reached disembodied to claw at her, snagging the sleeve, the hem of her coat as she ran past.

Leave me alone, she shouted, but her lips were numb now, gone purple with cold, and the words came out a croak.

She reached the sidewalk that ran along the tunnel, and then Claire saw that it was raunchy with prostitutes, some of them men wearing white plastic miniskirts, stubble growing around thickly painted red lips, they came out of the shadows, laughed when they saw her.

Hey, baby, one of them called, suck you off before you go back to Jersey?

Claire heard them hooting behind her, she didn't care. She broke into a run, careened off Canal, walking blindly, eyes tearing with the cold, tears streaking down her cheeks, nose running.

Nothing that had happened between them seemed real anymore, and the woman who had been her friend no longer existed — I don't know her, she thought, I never knew her —

Move — *!* A shout distorting past her, a bicyclist speeding by so close he clipped the buttons of her coat, and she stopped, bent over, hands on her knees.

You okay, lady? An Asian man peered into her face, his teeth long and yellow. Her head snapped up.

Okay, he said, grinning over-wide. Okay, lady, I not want scare you —

She nodded, yes, yes, she backed away, started walking again, head up this time, looking for a landmark, a street sign, for anything familiar —

It was then that the yellow cab pulled up beside her, and the driver leaned out.

Hey, he said, he had the face of a thousand New Yorkers, grizzled, real, comforting. You need a ride?

61

SHE WOKE UP FULLY DRESSED; SHE DID NOT REMEMBER having fallen asleep. Jade's face was already in her mind, and she realized she had dreamt of her — obsessive, repetitive dreams, her face powdered dead white, all her features exaggerated, and her breasts thrust aggressively forward by that black leather costume, shocking amidst the well-dressed crowd.

In the bathroom mirror, her face was creased with lines from the sheet; she blinked and could not recognize herself. It was almost five in the morning, the dark absolute, and dawn a

233

fiction, impossible to believe in. Her stomach was empty, it was growling, but her own hunger seemed distant, unimportant.

Just then, something in the hallway, a noise, something heavy, sliding. She froze. It stopped at her door, then faded. She was compelled toward it, as if against her will. She opened the door. A box, enormous, filled with books. She knelt to look at them. They were Jade's beautiful art books, and something else, wrapped in a silk scarf. Claire knew what it was even as she reached for it, picked the weight of it up with both hands. That brick, with its diagonal of black graffiti; the Wall.

She looked up, and it was only then that she saw Jade's door was open, a suitcase jutted out, the sight of it there like an invitation to anyone, strangers, vagrants; it gave Claire a curious vertigo, the sense that she was falling. She walked down the hall noiselessly in her stockinged feet, stopped just outside the door.

Jade was kneeling on another suitcase in the living room, trying to make it shut. Her head was bent forward, and her neck looked very frail in the overhead light; Claire could see the roots of her hair, growing out dark. At the sound of Claire's footsteps, her shoulders went rigid, but she didn't raise her head. For a moment, neither of them said anything.

Where are you going? Claire asked finally, her voice pallid, foreign in her own ears.

Someplace sunny. Words harsh as she threw the suitcase lid back and began taking things out again, throwing them on the floor. Her eyes were still black, though the rest of the makeup had been scrubbed off. Claire kept her own glance averted.

With Luke?

No. That single monosyllable sharp, unequivocal.

More than anything, Claire wanted to leave, to turn and walk back out, but she stood as if rooted to the spot, she didn't move.

I'm not going to explain myself, Jade said. Their eyes met for the briefest of seconds.

I just want to know, Claire answered, the words coming slow, why you couldn't before.

I saw the way you looked at me, Claire, Jade said, the edge

234

in her voice sharper, she was all bitterness now. I knew that's how you'd look at me, I knew what you'd think — that I'm some kind of whore — that sex means nothing to me —

She stopped speaking abruptly, as if waiting for Claire to say something, to contradict her perhaps, but Claire could not deny it. You're right, she thought, but she couldn't say that either.

Jade knelt again, her back to Claire, and started shoving at the contents of her suitcase. Claire saw the glint of silverware, a chipped porcelain cup, stockings, wadded up.

If you want anything else in here, she said, her voice strained, take it.

She waited, her shoulders hunched, tense, for Claire's answer, but Claire only nodded dumbly, though she knew Jade couldn't see her.

Stop looking at me, Jade said then, the edge in her voice knife-like. Stop fucking *looking* at me — !

Claire turned around, and walked out the door.

She lay down in her dark apartment, pulled a pillow over her head. All she wanted was to lose consciousness again, but she knew sleep was impossible now. It was almost dawn. Sirens wailed through the street.

After a while, she got up and found the bottle of champagne she'd bought earlier that day, thinking that she and Jade might drink it when Jade got home.

The cork flew across the room, its gleeful energy ludicrously inappropriate. She drank straight from the bottle, as if it were medicine.

What matters? she asked herself, it was the only question, and though she was sure she knew the answer, it remained obscure, refused to come forth.

She clasped her elbows, closed her eyes. What matters?

When the memory finally surfaced, she knew it had been there ever since she'd walked into Jade's place twenty minutes ago.

Her father, walking out the door. He had one suitcase in

each hand, his shoulders were bent with the weight of them. His cap, tilted back on his head. She remembered everything, how she'd stood back near her mother, her sister, thinking, He'll come back. He'll come back. All the while another voice saying, Go, go with him —

She consumed half the bottle in ten minutes, it made her head spin, made her heart pound. He never had come back. I knew it, Claire thought, I knew it even then.

From the hallway, she heard the sound of footsteps, a door, shutting.

I may never, she thought, see her again.

Still not knowing what she was going to do until she was there, standing interception between Jade and the stairs, waiting for she didn't know what until she saw it — Jade's face, caught off-guard, and the wide look of hope that came up in her eyes.

Wait, Claire said then, and her next words rang out into the quiet building, charged, inescapable, stopping everything.

I'm coming with you.

62

THEY FLEW TO MEXICO EARLY THAT MORNING, JADE criminal-looking in her black leather jacket and sunglasses, and Claire saw how the official flipped through her passport, thick fingers lingering on the documented pages, multicolored stamps, Berlin, London, Prague, Kathmandu, heard him asking, What is the nature of your business?

Pleasure, Jade answered, impassive.

Mexicana's DC-10, the stewardesses beautiful and dark, their teeth white as daylight. *Buenos días, señoritas.*

Claire leaned up against the window. The euphoric rush of champagne had faded into a dull, thudding headache.

What am I doing? she thought, what am I doing here — ?

She had to shut her eyes against the sudden, terrible misgiving, and when the stewardess came by with drinks, she only curled tighter into herself, away.

She sat up finally when they served breakfast, and now Jade was the one who did not move, she had her face pressed against the chair, her knees up. Sitting next to her, eyes burning in the dried air, mind in overdrive, Claire knew Jade was not asleep; her wakefulness carried like radio waves transmitting a song whose chorus you can't stop singing, even when the refrain has become senseless. Not six inches from her, Claire knew better; they were worlds away.

Hours later, the plane inclined, they circled for landing.

Bienvenidos al Benito Juárez Aeropuerto Internacional, said the stewardess. *Bienvenidos a Mejico.*

Claire wasn't ready for it, Mexico City, third world roar of exhaust and heat the minute they walked outside, heat that slammed into her, making the hair heavy on the back of her neck, her calves chafe inside her boots.

Riding the airport bus through the outskirts into town, they saw the rubble of a city razed by catastrophe, children playing in buildings whose long, jagged cracks seemed a still reenactment of the earthquake, their windows black holes.

Along the sides of those cracked roads, there were blankets strung up on ropes, shawls, sombreros, women calling after them in the dust, *venga, venga,* their wasted mongrels barking, and Claire looked away, the peculiar nausea of not enough oxygen in her head.

They drove down narrow side streets, old men pushing carts right down the middle, impervious to the clamor of horns behind them, and cars rode half on the sidewalk, refusing to slow down, swerving around buses overflowing with people, belching black exhaust so thick you could feel it on your skin, hot and gritty.

The bus stopped finally, and they got out in the middle of a square. Dusky women in blazing turquoise, hot-pepper red, grass-green skirts stood behind pyramids of fruit, mangoes, papayas, pineapple, the cheerful, relentless hysteria of salsa playing loud on their tinny radios.

They stood where the bus had left them, and all around

them small children with gummy eyes clamored at their elbows, holding up bright cloth dolls, straw hats, cheap beaded necklaces, shouting prices, jumping up and down like wind-up toys.

Where's the hotel, Claire said, first words she had spoken in what seemed like days, I thought there was a hotel . . .

Jade didn't answer, she passed a hand over her eyes, and even from where she stood, peripherally, Claire saw the shakiness, knew for certain then she had not slept. She looked like a vampire under this bright light, with her white face, her exhausted eyes, and all at once Claire realized she probably looked the same way. No, Claire thought, I'm not like her, and though she was aware of Jade's glance on her, she kept looking away, as if distracted, by the country, her fatigue, as if she could hardly be aware of Jade at all.

We can't stay here, Jade said, it was like begging. It's terrible, all these people, it's so dirty — it's worse than New York, it's worse than anything —

What do you mean? Claire asked, she fought a sudden rush of panic, I just want to find the hotel, or wherever —

The ocean's not much further, Jade said, her voice rising. If we just go a little further, we'll get to the water —

Claire turned away from the hysteria she could hear under those words, she went rigid against it. No, she thought silently. You can't.

Quieren un coche? Lady need a car? A young urchin with a dirty face tugged at Claire's elbow, his Spanish so rapid she could only catch every third or fourth word.

No! she said. No, I'm sorry — *gracias* —

But even as she turned away, Jade was bending toward him, her wallet already out, asking, How much?

63

THE VW THEY RENTED WAS RUSTY BLUE AND DENTED, THE air-conditioning didn't work. Jade seemed heedless of it all, she lit a cigarette and drove, she was single-minded, she had one desire, and she focused everything on the road ahead, driving fast, turning sharp to miss chickens and goats and small children, never looking back.

It was better when they were out of the city, up on those high, twisting mountain roads, bougainvillea growing bright and wild, the air thin, sweet.

Where are we going? Claire asked, trying to keep the accusation from her tone. Do you know?

South, was all Jade said, and Claire heard the gravel of sleeplessness deep in her throat. She seemed very far away, wore a sense of solitude so strong it came off her in concentric circles, like the whorl of a thumbprint.

Claire slid back in her seat. She felt frayed at the edges, unable to make the simplest of connections, an exhaustion that went bone-deep. She leaned her head against the door.

It wasn't so much sleep as a slipping down, down and down into strange dreams like memories of life, and she woke thinking she was in Tommy's truck, riding that high vibration, but it was Jade driving, again, and Claire thought the image would be burned in her brain, dark glasses and her profile, a knee hitched up to steer, shoes kicked off and her bare feet dirty, all of it bending and turning with the car, as if it was her body, the force of her will itself, that was propelling them.

Outside, the terrain was beginning to look different — there was more cactus, less green. Claire's lips were cracked, her mouth dry as drought.

I'm thirsty, she said. Is there someplace . . . ?

Jade spared her the briefest of looks.

There's a Coke in the back, she said. And some food.

Claire blinked, bewildered. We stopped somewhere . . . ?

You slept through it.

I can't believe it . . . I only slept . . . it felt like a few minutes . . .

Hours, Jade said, her tone almost bitter. If I could sleep like that . . .

Claire said nothing, would not take responsibility for anything so simple. She reached back and found the Coke, drank it so fast it made her eyes water. Next to her, Jade lit another cigarette.

The afternoon wore on and Jade kept pushing ahead, a map spread out on her knees; she wouldn't let Claire drive, and every time Claire asked how much farther, she said not much. Nothing stopped her, she barreled past other cars, so close Claire had to shut her eyes. She watched the needle on the speedometer climbing, seventy, seventy-five, eighty.

Goddammit, *move* — !

There was a car ahead, full of men. Claire could see their faces looking through the back, she tried to duck down, didn't want them to see they were two white girls. Every time Jade started coming up the side, they weaved in front, blocked her. It became a game, torturous and sinister, until Jade was blasting the horn, pounding on the steering wheel, which only made the men slow down, to thirty, to twenty-five miles per hour.

That's it, Jade said. Her jaw was set, very grim. Claire clutched her seat.

Jade, don't — it's not worth it, she said, but Jade wasn't listening. She pressed her foot on the gas and the car leapt forward with such a jolt Claire was thrown back. Immediately the men swerved to move in front, but Jade didn't stop. They were wedged between the men and the mountain, Claire screamed. She felt the car riding up, the right wheels grinding wild in the earth, and then they were neck and neck, and Claire saw the long muzzle of a gun, she heard them shouting, and over that, her own voice high above, the disassociated sound of pure fear.

They shot past and the car came crashing down, so hard Claire felt the frame shift, and then the engine sounded different, as though it were rattling out of place. Clutching her own throat, Claire looked at Jade; her face was ashen.

Jade, she said. Stop. Stop.

She saw Jade's eyes closing and she grabbed the wheel, pulled them over to the side of the road. Jade opened the door, fell out. She was on her hands and knees, Claire thought she was going to throw up, but then she let her head drop to her arms, a miserable creature seeking solace in the dirt, finding its most basic level.

But all Claire could think was those men, those men with their gun were going to catch up, they were going to kill them, she would die an anonymous death somewhere in Mexico, she didn't even know where. She dragged Jade into the back of the car, her body was limp, heavy, she didn't respond when Claire kept saying, It's okay, just go to sleep, go to sleep. She got behind the wheel, could have cried with gratitude when the engine turned over.

They had knocked the car out of alignment, and it felt intrinsically familiar, seemed to echo some hitch and twist in Claire's own skeletal frame, some hidden crippled state which, once known, would banish the simple, thoughtless ease of the body forever.

They were just outside some little town, clusters of little shanties and the inevitable tourist lures, young girls minding embroidery hung from tall cactus, the flash of silver and turquoise spread along the ground.

Gringa, she could hear kids shouting as she drove past. *Gringa!*

She pushed on through the town and toward the ocean, used the last of the light and then in the dark was comforted by the smell of it, a saltiness in the air, something in it to save your soul.

Where are we? Jade shot up suddenly, as if from a bad dream, making Claire jump.

I don't know.

Nothing around them but the sound of the engine a loud throttle rolling down the road, and then Jade was saying, Let me drive — let me drive —

She climbed into the front, there was no refusing her.

Claire sat in the passenger seat, back tensed, one hand up against the dash, but Jade was fine, she seemed alert, and only minutes later the road veered right and there were lights, women standing barefoot in front of their shacks, watching after them open-mouthed. The smell of frying in the air too much for Claire — she had to say it, Stop, I'm so hungry.

There, Jade said. Look — !

Claire saw it then, the sand, and beyond that the dark water like a long gash in the horizon you could escape through, the sound of it a steady over and over wash.

They had come to the end of the road.

64

OUT OF THE CAR AT LAST, HER BODY VIBRATED STILL, THE MIrage of forward motion in her feet, in her legs, all the way up in the back of her eyes. Ahead there were little stalls and the smell of food, they could hear the slap of meat in a pan, the burble of coffee.

They walked up, gap-toothed men in hats falling silent as they approached, and nobody moved. Claire had to say, *Perdon, perdon.*

Jade stood behind her while she asked what there was.

Carnitas, the women said, voices warm, tinged with laughter. Claire knew this, these women, this Mexican sidewalk food. She ordered two, she spoke Spanish, ignored the men who watched them like an audience, brief semicircle of dark eyes. She addressed the women, asked them the name of the town.

I've never heard of it, she said, surprised when Jade nodded, as if this were it, their destination.

We're almost at San Jeronimo, she said, spoke under her breath, as if it were some kind of secret, and Claire said Oh, though it meant nothing to her; she had never heard of San Jeronimo, either.

They ate standing up, hot tortillas wrapped around small pieces of meat cooked so long it was all soft, covered with tomatoes and onion, spiced hot with chili. The women smiled, knowing how good it was, asking, *Le gusta? Es bueno?*

Around them the men smiled too, one of them came forward with one spindly stool, made a big show of wiping it off with a bandanna.

I don't think, Jade said, they get too many tourists here.

Turista, sí! one of the men said, he was older, he had two teeth only, one of them gold. *Turista surf!*

Surfers, Jade repeated, and they all laughed, *sí, sí, sí.*

Y hotel? Claire asked. *Hay hotel aquí?*

More laughter, they all started talking at once, and while Claire leaned forward, straining to understand, one of the women tugged on her sleeve from behind.

Venga conmigo, she said.

Usted tiene hotel?

The woman assented vigorously. *No se preocupen,* she said. *Tenemos cuartos para todos los Americanos.*

When they walked back to the car, the three women came with them, some of the men trailing behind. Claire said they would drive, told the woman who had spoken to her to get in front, but when she opened the door they all moved forward, pushing to get in, and Claire had to block the way, saying, Only one, only one, but in the end two of the women were in the front seat, their skirts a wide tumble of color in the dark. They introduced themselves: *Lourdes y Pepita.*

They drove slow as walking, down a narrow dirt path that wound between little houses made of wood so weathered it was silver, the roofs corrugated tin. There was no illumination but their headlights, not even the smallest sliver of moon.

Aquí, the women said at last. *Aquí!*

It was a little shack like all the rest, just farther back from the road. They parked the car along the side, shut the engine off.

How much? Claire asked.

Cinco dolares, Pepita said, and though she kept her round face straight, it was clear she had just named the most exorbitant sum she could think of.

Claire knew she should haggle, but it was too cheap, and she was too tired. Pepita's eyes widened when she gave her the five, and she tucked the bill under her skirt very quickly, as if afraid they would change their minds. She led the way inside, extravagantly welcoming.

The room was spare, cool, very clean, but Claire's heart sank when she saw there was only one canvas cot in the corner, barely big enough for both of them. There was no other furniture save a small wooden table and a chipped white porcelain jug. Pepita bustled around, she took the jug outside, came back with water, a Mexican blanket, a towel.

Okay? she asked after she'd set everything up. Okay?

Yes, Claire said, Okay.

Pepita left, and for a minute, they just stood where they were in that small room, their baggage between them. There was no place to sit but the bed, and it came over her as before, a sense of total alienation —

She stood by the edge of the bed; she didn't say anything.

Can you hear the ocean? Jade asked, tentative. It sounds like it's right there, doesn't it? Right outside the door . . .

Claire stared out the window.

I can't see out, she said, she felt like a prisoner. I can't see anything.

Jade's arms crossed tight over herself, alone in the middle of the room, her pose the pose of a child, following Claire's eyes.

There's nothing to see, she said. It's dark.

She reached over, she touched Claire's shoulder.

You're tired, she said. You need to sleep.

Where? Claire cried, she gestured at the cot. Here — ?

Jade sat down on the edge of it, her back stiff, hands clasped tight between her knees.

I thought it would be better here, she said. I thought —

Claire shook her head, pressed her hands over her eyes.

Everything will look better in the morning, Jade tried, standing again. You'll see . . .

Just lie down, she went on, she could not keep the plea from her voice. Just for a minute . . .

Claire sat at the foot of the bed; there was nothing else to do. Neither of them said anything.

Jade sat on the floor, she leaned back, she didn't move. Her face the dimmest light, the rustle of her hair. Claire rolled over so that she was facing the wall, but even then she could feel the blackness of the night outside, how it closed them in, and she had the sense of being on a desert island, far-flung, absolutely isolated.

65

SHE WOKE TO THE SOUND OF WATER THE NEXT MORNING, A day dark as evening, and instantly yesterday's long, harrowing journey came flooding back to her, all of it wild and unlikely from here, impossible to retrace. What, she thought, what the hell am I doing here?

She sat up. Jade was sitting at the little table by the window, a game of solitaire spread before her. She'd put on clothes, jeans and a T-shirt, and though it was humid in the little shack, tropical, she looked cool and dry, wholly absorbed by her game. She looked up when she heard Claire, the cards poised in one hand.

Hi.

It's raining, Claire said, in the tone of one who hopes to be contradicted.

Jade nodded.

It doesn't look, she said, glancing outside, as if it's going to clear up.

Claire sat with the blanket wrapped around herself, and all she could think was there would be no phone, there wasn't even any electricity, how far would she have to travel just to reach civilization . . .

She had called the office from JFK, spoken to the machine — personal business, she had said, the message deliberately brief, vague, and she imagined Ursula calling her apartment in New York again and again, how her lips would purse:

I have no idea, Mr. Gordon, there's no answer. Shall I call in a temporary? But Sam would remain unperturbed, he would say No, we'll wait, confident that she would show up eventually, his faith in her unshakable.

She got up, agitated.

I have to find a phone, she said.

Outside, the sky rumbled, then broke.

It's raining pretty hard, Jade said, I don't think —

I have to, Claire said, she was still wearing yesterday's clothes. There are people waiting for me — I can't just disappear —

She shoved her feet into her shoes, she didn't lace them, but it wasn't till she opened the door that she realized the full extent of the storm. Wind lashed the palm trees, making them bend so low it seemed they would break, it had turned the ocean wild, nothing but gray foam. Just standing there, her face, her hair, everything was wet in seconds —

Jade came up behind her, she shut the door.

It'll stop, she said, the voice like a parent's, measured, reasonable. And then you can take the car.

Claire didn't look at her, she didn't say anything. Jade went back to her game, and Claire stood by the window, staring out as if her concentration alone would stop the rain.

Lost again.

Behind her, Jade shuffled the cards, the small thwack and ripple of it a pleasurable sound, soothing.

Want to play rummy?

It was a long moment before Claire turned, defeated.

Okay.

She sat with one foot on the floor, half-facing the door. Jade dealt, they did not speak. Hearts, diamonds, spades. Clubs. They focused on the cards, kept score, small notches of lipstick on the back of an envelope, and slowly, Claire was calmed, by the monotonous drumming of the rain overhead, by the neutrality of the transaction between them.

You're winning, she said finally, the score having gone long between them.

Jade folded her cards, she stared out the window.

It's like a monsoon, she said. Seems like it's never going to end.

It's got to end, Claire said.

Jade didn't answer, she got up and retrieved the bag she'd put on the table, found an orange. She came back to peel it, the citrus smell filled the room. She extended half and Claire accepted it, she was starving. They ate in silence, their backs against the wall, listened to the rain, relentless, loud.

It used to rain like this in the Philippines, Jade said, they were both looking out. For months at a time.

You never talk about it, Claire said. Where you lived, any of it.

I try not to think about it, either.

She got up, rummaged through her bag until she came up with her last pack of cigarettes, half-crushed. There was only one left.

I started smoking in the Philippines, she said.

She pushed the window open a crack and Claire felt the surge of warm, damp air against her skin, the strength of the storm.

I started dancing there, too. She blew the smoke out. First American topless they ever saw at the Girl Girl Bar. I made so much money I didn't know what to do with it.

She looked at Claire directly then, for the briefest of seconds, but even in that fraction Claire could see the defiant teenager she must have been, disobedient, unapologetic, self-enclosed.

What did you need money for?

Nothing. My father bought me everything I needed — nothing cost anything over there, anyway.

Then why did you do it?

I don't know. Because it was the worst thing I could do, I guess, she said. But nobody ever touched me.

Neither one of them said anything after that, and Jade smoked her cigarette, long minutes.

If someone had told me how long I would end up doing it, she said finally, I never would have believed them.

Jade opened the window a little wider and threw the cigarette out, then just stood there. The rain was coming through the window, her T-shirt was getting wet.

Never, she repeated, and it was only then that her expression began to crack, like a hairline fissure, making her chin tremble, her brows knit.

Oh God, she said, she turned away. I've lost everything.

She still wasn't crying, but Claire could see the struggle in her face, it was worse, it was terrible.

You haven't, Claire said, it was all she could think of, but Jade shook her head, tears spilling as if wrenched, still fighting it.

Everything, she said, Luke . . . you, everything . . .

What do you mean? Claire said, helpless in the face of such misery. It's not true, don't say that —

But Jade hid her face in her hands, her crying a tortured sound, like seizure.

I have no one, she said, hardly intelligible, I'll end up alone, I know it — I'll die alone, without anyone —

Claire's own throat closing, she said, How can you say that when I'm right here?

You wish you'd never come — you can't wait to leave, I know you can't —

Claire took Jade's wrists, she pulled them down.

You're the one who walked out, she said. You're the one who left —

And I'll never go back — never, ever —

Jade's face twisted up, she could not stop crying. She tried to pull away, she tried to hide again, but Claire held her hands, held them and would not let go.

I came with you, didn't I? Didn't I?

Holding her against her will, pushing her head against Jade's, pushing in as close as she could get.

You could do anything, Claire said. You could be famous.

Jade's laugh a croak, her eyes were blurred, red, eyelashes

matted. They held each other a long time, they didn't let go. Claire didn't know how long it was before she noticed, but Jade said it first.

Listen, she said.

Outside it was still dripping, but the rain was over.

66

CLAIRE SHOWERED BEFORE THEY HEADED OUT TO GET SOME breakfast, to find a phone. The stall was crude, made of wood, and the water dripped out of the rigged-up shower head as if each spurt were its last. Claire stood beneath it until all the grime and the sweat of yesterday had washed away and she was clean.

Jade was waiting in the room when she came back, dressed in white, a thin white cotton dress knotted at her waist, white sneakers. Her hair was pushed high and off her face with a cloth band, her face shaped tight around those perfect bones.

I saw the woman from last night, she said, Pepita. She said there's a market just down the road . . .

It was the market of Mexico everywhere, makeshift stalls and piles of exotic fruits, guavas, mangoes, papayas, avocadoes so big you had to hold them in both hands, so ripe they were splitting their own skin, their fragrance heady, intoxicating.

Jade bought everything, tortillas still yellow with corn flour, limes and tomatoes and shiny jalapeño peppers, they spent almost nothing.

Children trailed them through the market, half-naked and shy, thumbs wedged into their mouths, eyes huge. Jade turned and gave them her change, a handful of coins, making sure to divide them evenly. They gazed up at her as if she were from another world, incomprehensible.

They had moved beyond the stalls now, they were on the edge of the little village, in front of a small building the color of mud, the door wide open, and Claire could see the handful of men gathered around inside, dark shapes.

The bar, Jade guessed. Maybe someone here knows the nearest phone . . .

She was just asking the man behind the bar when they were accosted by a voice from behind, female, piercing.

Eeeh, rubia! Rubia! The voice belonged to a gnome. She couldn't have been much over four feet tall, and her face was brown and shriveled as a walnut. It was Jade's bright hair, Claire understood, that had sent the woman into such a tizzy of excitement, and now she caught Jade by the elbow, she wouldn't let her go.

Pero mira! Mira que rubia!

Claire stood there uncertainly, waiting for Jade to disengage herself, but then the woman grabbed her too, her strength surprising.

Y tu tambien, venga conmigo!

She pulled them both past the stupefied men, around the bar and through a doorway in the back so small they both had to duck.

The room they stood in was dark, and at first Claire couldn't make anything out save the smell, so pungent it made her nose wrinkle, an aroma unlike anything she'd ever smelled before, earthy and acrid, on the verge of foul but not quite, inescapable.

The little gnome was lighting candles, small white votive candles, they were everywhere, and Claire saw that each one had a cluster of little statues converging around it: the Virgin in porcelain, the Virgin in clay, the Virgin with her hands outstretched and with her hands together, her robes flowing and white here, straight and pale rose there, and scattered at her feet were dead dried rosebuds, tied clumps of dark herbs, twisted pieces of bark, jars of dark liquid. Beneath the shrine, a pot simmered over a bed of coals, and Claire detected it as the source of the smell.

Mama, the gnome was saying now. *Mama, mira quien te traigo . . .*

It was only then that they both saw the woman who lay on a straw mattress in the corner, her head turned toward them, her eyes clouded and white. She struggled up on one elbow, those blind eyes searching for focus.

Quien es? The frailty of her voice was only, Claire sensed immediately, her great age; beneath that there was an undercurrent of power, a force that would have made itself known in any language, and it made Claire stay very still, waiting, she could not have said for what.

Acercate, the old woman said now, turning her face out into the blankness of the room, and Claire felt a shiver when the gaze landed squarely on Jade's face. *Sientate aquí, conmigo.*

Jade moved forward, she knelt before the woman's bed, bowed her head. She didn't speak. The woman reached out, each movement agonizingly slow, and stroked her head with one gnarled hand, benediction.

Claire felt the little gnome behind her then, pushing her forward to sit on a little stool by the bed, next to Jade, who was clasping the old woman's hand with both of hers.

When the old woman heard Claire sit down, she smiled, a smile that creased her face into a wonderful parchment, a thousand fine, fine lines.

Muñeca, she called to the little gnome. *Un poquito de té por favor* . . .

But the gnome had already anticipated this request; she was ladling liquid from the pot into three small clay cups, not more than an inch deep. She brought them one by one, holding each cup with great ceremony, as if it contained something priceless, and Claire found herself accepting it the same way, with both hands.

When the old woman received hers, she closed her eyes, lifted it, and muttered something, one long breathless incantation. From that angle, Claire could see the shape of her skull, and she had a sudden vision of how it would look after death, the jaw's wide, ghoulish grin a grim lantern, forever still. Claire met Jade's eyes beneath her upraised arms.

What is it? she whispered.

I think, Jade whispered back, I think it's peyote.

251

The woman put the cup to her lips and sipped, one, two, three times; it was gone.

Claire's eyes never left Jade's. They lifted their cups at the same time, and swallowed.

67

THE OLD WOMAN HAD GIVEN THEM EXPLICIT DIRECTIONS about where to go — there were some Aztec ruins, apparently, just twenty miles farther up the coast — and now Jade was driving again, a familiar sight behind the wheel of the car, everything focused forward, absolutely intent.

Claire was silent, pulled all the way in; she kept tasting the tea, savage and gagging, could not rid herself of it. Now it was the center of her being, a pool at the bottom of her stomach, beginning to subvert the natural order of her body. She clutched the door handle, became aware that she was praying, the chatter of her mind coming to her as if from some vast, vast distance.

Stop, she said, it took forever to find that word, to remember how to speak it, and then it seemed ages before it registered on Jade, years before she finally twisted the car off on the shoulder of the road. Claire leaned out the door and threw up.

The ruins rose out of the shallows, a series of crumbling steps set into the incline of a cliff that culminated in a kind of pyramid at the top and, following Jade up those steep, ancient stairs, Claire found her focus was telescopic; she could see the veins that traced the backs of Jade's legs, a map of life, phenomenally intricate, her blood moving through them, rich and thick and slow. Everything sharpened and blurred at the same time and the light was like sound crashing down over her head, huge and brittle.

Time had become a physical experience, each second ripening within, individual and distinct, and she realized there was nothing else, there never had been — there was only this moment, *now,* and nothing else existed, there was no such thing as past or present, only this continuing eternity, *now,* and she saw that it was enough to just be, that she needed nothing to justify this existence, the mystery of her own energy —

Remember this, she told herself, opening and closing her eyes. *This is what's real.*

Words rode the back of her tongue, huge and clumsy, she didn't let them out. The world spoke for her, she felt ageless and ripe, sure her body would never betray her. Jade turned and looked at her, her face half shadowed by the brim of a hat, and their eyes met, pupils huge pools of dark light. Claire was aware of a deep humming at her core: the distant roar the earth made turning.

When they reached the pyramid at the top, Claire touched it and the rough texture sent shooting colors through her fingertips and into her veins. She looked around and it seemed the sky, the cliff, the sea itself were colored by her sight, as if the deep rich greens and that impossible azure were the product of the brilliant bursts of feeling overflowing in her heart.

I see faces, Jade said, she was turning around, around and around, staring at the ruins. Aztec faces in the stone . . .

They were there, like a crystal embedded deep in rock, broad-planed faces, the faces of warriors, and Claire felt their history shuddering through her, midnight sacrifices, a bloodcurdling race . . .

Jade put a hand over her heart, she let her breath out, long and shaky.

It's like a grave, she said. These ruins, all of it . . . it's a place to bury things . . .

Yes, Claire said. Here is a good place.

On the horizon, clouds approached, huge and dark, edging in toward the sun, casting sudden dark over wide swatches of beach.

Look, Jade said. The sky . . . the rocks . . . the stone . . . everything's moving, do you see it? Everything's alive . . .

Claire saw it too, how it was all vibrating, shimmering, molecules, atoms, dancing together, making things appear solid, appear dense. She spread her hand out and looked at it, saw how it radiated its own life force, pulsing, and she felt a wild current of electricity zinging through her bones, energy like a river slicing through her, swift and clean and piercing. Her teeth started chattering. Jade took her hand, pressed the knuckles with her thumb, and the chattering stopped. Their hands laced together, tightly, tightly.

I've known you for eons, Jade said, I knew when I met you that we had a past . . . people find each other, they pick up where they left off . . .

She was reaching back, Claire thought, reaching deep into some primal archive of the body to find their common history. Their gazes locked, and it was as if their eyes rode their own frequency, as if once aligned they would never see the world alone again.

Where did we leave off?

I don't know . . . maybe we were refugees somewhere, living some underground life, running from something, sleeping together . . .

Voices ascending behind them, out of nowhere. Claire peered down to see sunburned Germans with heavy cameras, and she panicked, could not think how to compose herself, how to behave. Jade slid her sunglasses over Claire's eyes, did not let her go.

Just follow me, she said.

Even with her eyes hidden behind the glasses, Claire felt exposed, inflamed, sure that everyone she passed could see right through her; she kept her eyes on the backs of Jade's sneakers, concentrated on each step, until it seemed there had never been a time when she had not been making this descent, when she had not been following Jade.

They reached the bottom, there where the stone had been turned smooth as marble by the sea, polished, beautiful.

I'm going in, Jade said. She pronounced it like some great, some final decision. She took her dress off and hung it from a ledge in the rock, where it fluttered whitely, like a flag of surrender. Claire sat with her feet in the water, and watched as Jade's body emerged, naked. The simple splendor of it struck

Claire, blinded her. She closed her eyes for a moment, and Jade
dove into the sea.

68

HOW ARE YOU, JADE ASKED MUCH LATER, THE QUESTION
low, ardent, though the peyote had faded hours ago now.

Hungry, Claire said, her eyes brilliant still.

Me too.

Walking back into their little shack, Claire had the unexpected sense a traveler has, of returning to a place once foreign,
and finding it home. Night had fallen, and wild gusts of wind
came in through the open windows, the room was alive with it.

Jade lit the oil lamps, and their dense yellow flames flickered up to cast long shadows on the ceiling, making the room
seem bigger than it was. She had a sarong tied around her hips,
and her shoulders were bare, dark-looking against a man's ribbed
white undershirt. She picked up the bag of groceries, came back
to sit on the bed next to Claire.

They took everything out of the bag, and then Jade ripped
it, laid it between them like a picnic — tomatoes, avocado,
lime, peppers, tortillas, and finally, the bottle of red wine.

She had a pocket knife, she handled it deftly, peeling the
avocado, slicing tomatoes, folding them together in the soft tortillas. She held it before Claire's lips. Try this.

It was incredible, everything so ripe, the lime juice making
it all come alive, the tortilla sweet and mealy. Claire could not
help the sound she made, how good it was, and Jade smiled at
her, a smile that came from the depths of her eyes. She pulled
the cork from the bottle of wine, Claire heard the air pop.

We're here, she said. We're in *Mexico* —

The words were magical, like an invitation, Claire thought,
to everything forbidden, everything taboo . . .

Jade stretched out sideways, watched as Claire tilted the
bottle to her mouth.

You never told me, she said when Claire gave the bottle back, what happened with your rancher.

I saw him when I was home, Claire said. She put her head back, she watched the flickering ceiling.

I slept with him, she said, for the last time.

The memory sliced through her, she had to close her eyes against it.

He told my sister I never would have stayed in New York, she said, if it weren't for you.

Jade sat up, her face was pure, serious. Her hands in her lap, she made a small gesture, as if of the inevitable.

There will always be someone to seduce you, she said, in that city.

But it was you, Claire said. For me, it was you.

You say it, Jade said, shaking her head, as if you think that's what I went around doing — that that's what I did, there —

Claire didn't say anything. They faced each other across the brief spread of mattress, their eyes met.

That trip to Paris, and then Luke . . . Jade raised her hands again, the gesture helpless now. I haven't done anything like that, it's been years . . . you don't know what I've been like, the way I've lived . . .

Claire listening, her arms around her knees.

I didn't know how much I'd lost, Jade said. You go through life, and every day beats against you — I was eroded, everything — it wasn't just an attitude anymore, being cynical . . . I just went to work, I drank too much — it was sick, you don't know . . .

All I know is you.

Jade looked at her, the deep blue of her eyes gone black, liquid.

No, she said, I had no life when I met you, no real friends. I didn't love anything, anyone — I hadn't slept with anyone for a year, and then . . .

She took Claire's hand in both her own, kissed her lifeline, and Claire felt the touch vibrating through her, a tremor she could not control.

Watching the way you live — the way you are, the way you looked at me — it changed me, I can't explain it. Jade lifted Claire's hand, she put it to her cheek. The skin of it so cool against Claire's palm, the curve of her cheekbone so sweet.

The way I feel with you, I could never have it with a man, she said, her voice so low now Claire had to hold her breath to hear the next words. It's not like anything else. I know you feel it, too.

Claire reached up then, everything translating into the same, swift impulse, and her arms came around Jade's neck, she pressed her face against her friend's, breath coming out ragged.

You make me feel brave, she said, voice as low as Jade's. You make me feel I could do anything.

They kissed, Jade's words disappearing against Claire's lips.

You make me feel the same way.

They fell back with the same motion, Claire shrugging out of her T-shirt even as Jade reached to pull it off, to lie over her, and accepting the weight of Jade's body, she felt her own yield profoundly, as though it were her spirit itself that had finally relinquished its skeletal hold.

It's only love, Jade said. It's only love.

69

CLAIRE WOKE TO THE SOUND OF THE SURF THE NEXT MORNing, the sound of someplace she had never been, and the light so bright it poured through the cracks of the shutters and filled the room, it could not be kept out.

Next to her, Jade was asleep, her face tucked into the crook of her arm, the sheet tangled around her legs. Claire moved quietly so as not to wake her, she reached for the first piece of clothing she saw, Jade's dress, discarded by the bed. She had to find a phone, today. She had to make arrangements.

But when she walked outside, she stopped still, she had to catch her breath. She was in paradise.

Palm trees grew on either side of her, soaring up skinny and brave to reach a sky of pure azure, the clouds in it piled high and dramatic, the clouds of the tropics. She followed the narrow path behind their shack and straight ahead she saw the beach, a dazzling expanse of white that curved around to make a cove, and the water was every color, aquamarine and emerald and deep, deep blue. The beauty of it burst inside her heart. She ran to the beach. There was nobody around, it was impossible to believe. Only seconds after having dressed, her clothes were off again.

The water was almost as warm as the air, the waves quiet, and she swam just past the breakers and stood waist-deep, tried to scoop up the slim silver minnows that darted in the shallows. She swam, let the ocean break over her head, imagined it washing layers of darkness away, the grit and cold of New York City, the winter. I'm young, she thought, and the truth of it was like a gift, overwhelming. I'm still young . . .

She got out. The morning sun shone down, burning gold in the sky, and she stretched beneath it like a woman enslaved, shackled, could not help thinking of it as a masculine entity, how it kept her flat on her back, how it drained her of her power.

Her eyes closed, she remembered everything from the night before, Jade's muttered phrases —

I've seen the way men watch you walking down the street — that *hair* . . . I bet they think about you later — things they make you do when they imagine you, I bet that hair is everywhere —

Jealous, Claire had said, and remembered the crush of Jade's hair in her fist, bright. Jealous of you.

She put her dress back on. She would go back, wake Jade, but she could not resist going back to the water's edge, bending down to look at the treasure the storm had washed up, broken spirals of shell like the spoils of war, their insides virginal, flesh-colored.

She had chosen one when she heard a shout, young male voices, carrying clear on the breeze. She saw them before they saw her, a group of boys approaching, slim and brown, surf-boards under their arms.

The first one hesitated, he stopped, and she heard the two behind him giggling, saw how they tweaked him from behind. They were Mexican boys, three of them, young, maybe twelve, maybe less, very dark, their chests smooth, hairless.

Buenos días, she said, her smile tentative, and instantly they smiled back. *Buenos días,* their voices gone shy, and she saw there was no danger.

She pointed at the waves, tried to ask was it very big, and they laughed, shook their heads, one of them pointing up at the sky.

No hay luna, he said. *Comprendes?*

No moon, Claire said. Yes, I noticed.

They pointed at her, asking did she surf. She shook her head, tried to tell them she'd grown up in the desert. *No hay agua,* she said, and they all laughed, as if this were the most absurd thing they had ever heard, such a contagion she had to laugh too. The first one stepped forward, lifted his surfboard, homemade, broad as a canoe, held it out.

Para ti, he said, he was gorgeous, his features straight and perfect, his dark eyes shining.

No, she said. Oh no, I can't — I couldn't —

Sí, he insisted. *Es facil!*

And in one swift, fluid motion he was throwing himself into the water, pressed long against the board, slicing out fast and clean, his knees on either side, and instantly the other two were right behind him, not to be outdone, paddling hard to get ahead.

She smiled, she lifted a hand and waved, *Adiós,* but the leader had turned around, he was leaning forward, his head to one side, gazing at her, saying, *Venga conmigo!*

He wouldn't move; every time she shook her head he said *Sí!* and he was such a boy, his face so young and sunny she could not turn away.

She sat in front of him, her dress trailing wet, and they moved over the slow swells into deep water, she could feel the smooth cold of it rising from below. He had to bend close to her to pull them out but he didn't touch her, and she watched the lean muscles of his arms as he paddled forward, steady and tireless.

I'm Claire, she said, and their eyes met quick and shied away.

Jorge, he said.

His friends were waiting for them, straddling their boards with an exaggerated carelessness, showing off, she knew, for her, *la gringa.*

Ramon, Jorge said, pointing first at the shorter boy, then at the stocky one, *y Marco.*

Mucho gusto, they said in turn, and she was surprised at the sudden solemnity of their courtesy; it gave her an image of the three of them dressed for Sunday Mass in starched white shirts, their hair combed back, those agile brown feet crowded into shoes still stiff from disuse.

Eres Americana? Ramon asked, and when she nodded asked where, both he and Marco bringing their boards closer to listen.

I'm from New York, she said, wanting to impress them, wanting to impress herself, with this fact, and found that it no longer felt like fiction; she remembered exactly the way it had looked from the ferry, a glittering island thrusting itself skyward, fearless, full of unimaginable futures. The vision was embedded in her heart, it was thick with feeling, she could not disentangle herself from it. That's where I live, and the thought was like revelation, a hard shiver.

La ciudad? They looked at her with new respect.

New York City, she said. Come visit me.

Okay! Jorge said and the other two laughed, feigned falling off their surfboards, resurfaced on the other side.

The morning was blue, it was untouchable. Claire sat with her legs in the bottomless ocean, Jorge behind her; he would not jump off, she knew that, he would not leave her, and she turned just the slightest bit to look at him, to say something, to answer him, their communication a broken mixture of language and something else; it was like love, she thought, it *was* love — they

sat there without touching, and she felt the need to speak drain-
ing from her like some long-nurtured illness finally, miraculously, gone.

He showed her how to paddle the board, and she allowed
him to place her limbs just so, his touch the touch of one who
does not yet know sex, who is poised just on the brink of that
great knowledge, so that everything is sexual, she could feel it
when he moved her ankles, when the back of his hand brushed
the hem of her dress.

They took her to a grotto, down at the end of the cove
where the rocks jutted into the sea. It was ebb tide and they
showed her how to flatten herself on the board to pass under,
she rode in on her stomach.

It was another land, light reflecting up from the white
sandy bottom to glimmer blue-green on the cool walls, and
bright fish swimming quick through the coral on the sides, their
colors outrageous, fuchsia and lime and neon yellow.

Jorge sat on Marco's surfboard while the other two dove
after the fish, trying to catch them with their hands, he stayed
close to Claire, kept hold of her board with one hand.

Tienes hambre? he asked. *Quieres comer?*

She shrugged, as if to say it didn't matter, and though her
stomach was cavernous with hunger, it was true. There was no
urgency in it, she felt sure that soon she would eat, she would
be satisfied. She would have what she wanted, she thought, and
it seemed an obvious truth, the truth she had been searching so
restlessly for her entire life, without ever realizing it had been
right there all along.

She felt herself very young, growing younger. She could
trust him to take care of her, he would revere her; his reverence
did not demean him, it was part of him, it was the way he re-
vered life itself, he did not even know it.

She took the surfboard back out, made him swim to keep
up with her, and they broke into the sun again, the other two
behind them like children, still there, forgotten.

They walked back along the beach, her dress dried in the
breeze. They stopped between the bases of two palm trees, and

she sat crosslegged, tried to comb her hair out with her fingers, it fell wild and curly on either side of her face, it was stiff with salt, there were traces of it on her arms, she could taste it on her lips. Jorge lay on the sand at her feet; he had not yet reached the age of self-consciousness and everything was expressed in his body, in his face, innocence and ardor, a certain physical grace which cannot be learned.

How long, he wanted to know, would she stay?

She shook her head, not long, and he pushed himself up on his knees saying, No, no, his face below hers, his spirit unquenchable beneath his imploring look, and she wanted to touch him, the hair that fell into his eyes, his lips. She smiled, she held her hands tightly in her lap, said, You're too young, too young — and though he didn't understand the words he laughed, he knew he was winning, knew he was invincible.

She laughed, too, her desire for him a kind of ecstasy; she knew she would not, could not, act upon it, and yet it was all she could think of, how simple it would be, to lie beneath his young, hard body, to join with him — so different from what she felt for Jade. The realization came over her slowly, in degrees, like the changing angle of the sun that passed high over her head.

When she looked at him again, he was watching her, his head on his arms, his gaze intent, unwavering. She stood, felt how his adoration conferred upon her a languid, unerring grace.

No te vayas, he whispered, words she would have understood in any language. Don't go.

My friend's waiting for me.

When she kissed him, he was right there, ready, hiding nothing, unaware of how his hands had come up to hold her arms, the strength of them, their need to keep her there, thrilling.

They turned from each other at the same time, they both looked back. He waved once, and then he was gone.

She headed back to the shack, sand still falling from the folds in her dress, but Jade saw her first, she was waiting outside.

Where've you been?

I was going to find a phone, Claire said, but then . . .

She held the conch shell out, a present. I went for a swim.

It's beautiful. Jade traced the inside, its flawless surface.

I went looking for you, Jade said, in the car.

I'm sorry, I should have —

It's okay, Jade said, her smile stunning, difficult to digest. She looked up at Claire, shaded her eyes against the sun. I found a phone.

. . . You did?

In a hotel, maybe ten miles up the road. They said there's an airport fifty miles from here, they fly to Mexico City.

Jade looked up. I made a reservation, she said.

You did? Claire said. She sat down next to Jade, neither one of them said anything after that. They sat there and the light was blinding, fell over them like something they could touch.

You can be home by tomorrow, if you want to, Jade said at last.

The reality of that departure hit Claire only then, and it seemed to carry the accumulated weight of all the other departures she'd ever made. She looked at Jade, she would not accept it.

Come with me, she said. Come back with me.

Jade's eyes meeting hers, how they knew each other.

I was, she said simply. I am.

VERY GRATEFUL ACKNOWLEDGMENT TO THE FOLLOWING,
without whom this book would not have been possible:

Jean, for being the most steadfast ally an author could ever hope
to have; Susan K., for her perfect pitch for what is true and
what is false; Peter B., who found me; Pico, who held me up
against myself and never agreed with compromise; J.S., whose
work preceded and inspired; my mother, who was never
shocked; Maggie, who made a bazillion copies; all my friends
whose ears I bent in search of ending — the Monkeys, Patrick,
Deb and Gayle; Rod N., for the glimpse into his world; New
York City; Bobby, who found the music; Maia, for the fine-tuned
depth of her analytical powers, and Eddie, die-hard fan; George,
who stayed up all night and lent me his unerring sense of character; and René, my in-house genius, who listened every time as
if it were the first.